The Castoffs

GJ FLETCHER

GDOG BOOKS

This is the paperback edition 2024

First published by GDog books 2024

Copyright GJ Fletcher

GJ Fletcher asserts the moral right to be identified
as the author of this work

ISBN 9798325749445

This is a work of fiction.
The characters and incidents are the products of
the author's imagination.

Any resemblance to actual persons, living or dead,
or actual events is purely coincidental.

The landscape described in this novel is not entirely fictitious.
It is based on a projected sea level rise of 60m
using data provided by NASA.

Visit **flood.firetree.net** for further information.

Typeset in Garamond

To Finlay and Rosie

For bringing the story to life.
Without an audience a story is just scribbles on a page.

'It is not the biggest, the brightest or the best that will survive, but those who adapt the quickest.'

Charles Darwin

Chapter 1 – Dunes

Daise stood at the top of the dune gazing out across the wide expanse of the Trent Sea. In the distance, she could just see the spire of Newark Church poking out of the water. Her friends were standing by the shoreline beckoning her down. Wrapping her grey hoodie around her waist, she enjoyed the warmth of the summer sun on her skin as she plucked up the courage to sledge down the steep sand dune.

While she would never admit it to her friends, Daise was scared of heights. She took a couple of hair grips from her pocket and fixed her floppy blonde fringe so it was out of her eyes. Playing nervously with the hem of her sun-bleached T-shirt, she repeated the wise words of a friend, 'fear is the price you pay for new experiences', before placing her sand sledge on the edge of the dune.

Her sledge was really no more than a faded piece of red plastic from an old toy box. Two rope handles had been bored into the sides to give the rider something to cling on to as they hurtled down the sheer dune face.

She let out an involuntary scream as she pushed herself off the grassy dune top. Her body stiffened in anticipation; her eyes closed as she gripped the crude

The Castoffs

rope handles on the edge of the tray. Starting slowly, she knew what was coming as her momentum built. The smooth gentle slope gave way to a sharp drop and the change in gradient made her stomach lurch. Loose, dry sand peppered her face as she picked up speed. The noise of the sand scraping the thin plastic surface of her tray became a continuous roar.

She was tempted to dig her heels into the sand to slow her progress, she had experienced the indignity of flipping the sledge before, to know that this was a bad idea. She just had to keep her body rigid and wait it out. Her eyes remained tightly scrunched until she felt herself start to slow and the sound of plastic scraping on sand gave way to the cheers of her friends.

Daise took a deep breath. It was the quickest way down to the shore but she never quite got used to it. The adrenaline buzz of the ride always left her a little queasy.

'How would you rate the descent Rey?', said Jude, the taller of her two friends.

'A solid effort Jude, I think I give it a seven. It was undeniably quick but for me, she didn't look like she was really enjoying it.'

Rey interjected, 'Let down again by the involuntary screaming.'

Daise, trying her best to look serious, said, 'Come on, that wasn't a scream. It was an enthusiastic shout.'

Rey stroked his pimply chin thoughtfully, 'You make an interesting point Daise, there's a thin line between a scream and a shout. I'll give that an eight.'

'That's more like it', said Daise smiling, 'Now let's get some foraging done while the beach is still quiet.'

Jude handed her a bucket and together they headed

towards the water's edge to forage for seaweed.

Rey took a frayed green baseball cap from the back pocket of his baggy denim board shorts and slapped it on, pulling his thick brown ponytail through the back. Kicking off tatty trainers held together with duct tape, he headed towards the waterline where sea laver hung off the rock like strips of leather.

Jude was a good two inches taller than Rey, with a warm brown complexion and his hair in a stark military buzz cut. He wore his hair short to try to make himself look tough but his infectious smile just made him appear friendly and approachable. He reached Rey just in time to be slapped around the face with a slimy belt of sea laver.

Daise laughed as the boys rolled around in the sand, play-fighting. They always had fun on a scavenge, but she made sure they also came back with full bellies. Food was scarce and it paid to get up early to forage whatever you could find. Sea laver needed to be boiled up for 10 hours to become anything near edible but it beat the pain of hunger gripe.

Daise, Rey and Jude lived on the Casthorpe Reset, a prefabricated complex of grey concrete on the edge of Greater Grantham. It was a densely packed housing estate that was built 10 years ago to house refugees when the Humber flood defence barrier failed, destroying low lying towns and cities in Yorkshire and the East Midlands. Other parts of the British Isles suffered a similar fate. The Thames Barrier could no longer defend London and that proud capital city was lost to the sea.

The political structures of England had fractured into smaller states based around the new geographies. Daise and her friends lived in the Eastern Islands, which were all that remained of the East Midlands. The South East had become the impoverished Southern Wetlands - a disease ridden marshland. To the west, the state of Mercia had become the new powerhouse based around the sprawling mega city of Oxford. The North had not suffered the dramatic loss of land felt by southern parts of England but the coastal urban cities of Manchester, Liverpool and Newcastle had all been devastated by the flood. In the south west, Dumnonia was protected from powerful Mercia by the Chard Wall — a twelve-foot-high barrier running 5 miles across the thin strip of land that attached the peninsula to the mainland.

Daise watched Rey and Jude as they splashed and wrestled in the early morning sun. She liked the early morning before the coastal city of Greater Grantham woke up. She tried to imagine the landscape as it once was, the rolling fields, punctuated by little market towns that rose no higher than their church spires. The only green land she could see now was the cornfields of Ancaster Island to the east.

'Daise, come here! We've found some barnacles. Are they any good to eat?' said Rey.

At the western edge of the beach the golden sand of Barrowby Beach turned into rugged limestone cliffs. Low tide exposed an expanse of rock. Jude was up to his neck in the water, prising shells off the rock with his pen knife — his drainpipe black jeans and faded grey T-shirt discarded on the sand.

They'd got a good system going: Jude jabbed his knife under the barnacle shells, enjoying the satisfying pop as they released their grip on the rock, before throwing them to Rey to catch in his bucket.

The Castoffs

Daise peered over Rey's shoulder into the bucket at the three shells holding slimy orange blobs. 'They're limpets, guys! - You have to chop off the guts but there's a good lump of meat on them. Get as many as you can.'

Jude scoured the exposed rock collecting all of the limpets he could reach but was now struggling to keep above water as he tried to free more.

'You're taller than me Daise, why don't you have a go? There's loads more.'

The tide must be especially low today, she thought. She had never seen this rock so far out of the water before. Judging by the contents of Rey's bucket they already had enough food for breakfast so they might be able to make a few coins selling any excess at the morning market.

Jude emerged from the water; his arms held aloft in triumph. 'Come on Rey, let's see how many we've got.'

He dried his hands by rubbing them on his prickly scalp and peered into the bucket, letting out a yelp of delight, 'Oh yes, we're going to have a proper feast today.'

Rey handed him his faded grey T-shirt and turned to Daise. 'Hey Daise, are you going in then?'

Daise untied her grey hoodie from her waist, whipped her T-shirt over her head and removed her frayed denim shorts; leaving them in a neatly folded pile on the dry sand. Her red bra top turned from pink to red as she dived gracefully into the briny sea. She kicked her legs hard, deliberately splashing water into the boys' faces. The muffled sound of their protests made her smile as she swam underwater.

It was only when she reached the rough rock that she realised she had forgotten to borrow Jude's knife.

'Jude, chuck me your knife will you,' she shouted across the water. He made to throw it by the blade and without thinking, Daise ducked under the water. She surfaced to cackles of laughter coming from the shore.

'Made you flinch,' cried Jude.

'You'll be doing more than flinching, if you don't throw me that knife properly.'

She tried to sound angry but she couldn't help smiling. Daise had known Jude and Rey since her Dad had left. They had gone to Casthorpe School together until the Greater Grantham Council had shut it down, along with all the secondary schools in the 'resets' — the resettlement zones hastily constructed to house people displaced by the floods.

Jude folded up his battered pen knife and threw it towards Daise. The trajectory was a little too high. Daise jumped out of the water to catch it but it bounced off her fingertips and plopped into the sea. A flash of light reflected off the silvery blade as it disappeared.

She dived, salty water nipping at her eyes as she searched. She swam deeper, until she saw the gravelly seabed, her eyes darting around looking for the knife, her lungs crying out for breath. If she went back up, she knew she would have little hope of retrieving the knife. She kept going until the seabed was within touching distance. Careful not to disturb any sediment she scoured the area with her eyes desperate for a glimpse of the knife.

Jude's knife was the only decent tool they owned. It looked like a normal pen knife, so it wasn't illegal to carry. But if you slipped a small section of the casing forward you could lock the main blade, making it much more useful. They used it for spearfishing — tied to the end of a pole, for making kindling for the fire and for cutting up seaweed. Without it, foraging for food would be a nightmare. Daise began to berate herself. Why had she not swum back to shore to retrieve it?

Her lungs began to burn, she felt panic in her chest. She couldn't hold her breath for much longer. Just as she was about to bolt for the surface, she saw the knife nestled in the gravel just centimetres from her face. In a single motion, she grabbed it and thrust herself off the seabed to the surface, where she took a huge lungful of air.

Jude and Rey looked worried. Daise couldn't quite work out whether their concern was for her or the pen knife.

'Are you OK?' shouted Rey. The right question, she thought.

'I'm good', she replied. But it wasn't until she held up the pen knife that their faces cracked into smiles.

Daise clutched the knife firmly in her hand, swimming a little awkwardly as the clenched fist of her left hand slapped into the water with each stroke. She reached the limpet covered rock quickly and began to prise off the limpets. When she had collected a handful, she shouted to the boys, 'Ready to catch these?'

Rey stood bucket in his arms, 'throw them in the bucket Daise, but one at a time yeah.'

'As much fun as that might be Rey, it might be a bit easier if you just caught them,' she replied.

'Right enough we don't want to lose any,' Rey walked up the beach and placed the bucket on the shore.

Holding the knife between her teeth to keep it safe,

The Castoffs

Daise threw the limpets. She alternated between the boys who scurried up the shore to place the limpets in the bucket after each throw. She returned to the rock to collect another three handfuls.

Each time her hands were full she threw them back to the shore until the rock was stripped. At the far edge of the rock, the shore rose up so much so that she could climb up the craggy surface.

When she reached the top of the rock, she opened the pen knife, held it between her thumb and forefinger and yelled 'catch!'

She didn't throw it of course, but Jude and Rey scattered. She laughed and folded the knife away. High up on the rock, she could see further up the shore. There was a small beach further up the coast. They had never explored before and it would only be a five-minute swim. She watched the waves carefully, trying to read them. Riptides could drag you out to sea in no time at all. The rolling water looked gentle and even. She was excited by the opportunity of exploring somewhere new — a private beach away from the Guardians seemed like a dream.

Turning back to the boys, eager to tell them what she'd seen, she caught sight of a strange green shape floating in the sea in the direction of Ancaster Island.

'What's that in the water?' she shouted at the boys.

Daise jumped back into the sea to investigate. Questions ricocheted through her mind — what was it? Something they could eat? Salvage? Sell?

Rey and Jude waded out into the water to meet her. As she got closer, she saw a flash of orange clothing. It was clear that it was a body of some sort.

Her stomach tightened. This was really creepy. All

three of them stopped running and started to edge slowly towards it.

Rey screamed as a cold hand bobbed up on the crest of a wave and slapped him on the thigh. Jude Daise, shocked by his scream, shouted out in fright.

They froze as they looked at the body suspended in the water, it had two arms, two legs. The face rose to the surface, like a zombie rising from a watery grave. It looked human apart from being a strange pale green.

Rey broke the silence, 'Come on, let's get it out of the water.'

Jude and Rey grabbed hold of an arm each and dragged the body out of the water and up the beach to the dry sand. The heels left two thick grooves in the sand like railway tracks.

Carrying the buckets of limpets, Daise followed the boys up. They laid the body down gently on the soft warm sand and stood around to examine it in detail.

'Man, he's tall,' exclaimed Jude 'He must be at least 6 foot 5 inches.' It looked like the body of a tall, bald man dressed in baggy orange shorts except he didn't look like any man they had ever met.

'Do you think he's an alien?' offered Jude.

'No,' said Daise tentatively. But she wasn't sure what he was. It wasn't just the skin colour. As it dried out in the sun, she noticed the body had a strange sheen which made her wonder whether he was real or synthetic.

'Could he be a robot? You know, one of those androids,' said Rey.

'No look, he's hurt, there's a big bruise behind his ear,' said Daise pointing at the man's head. She placed her hand on this bare arm. It felt smooth, almost waxy. It was

The Castoffs

cool but not as cold as the sea.

She picked up his wrist and checked for a pulse. Jude and Rey held their breath as they waited for Daise to confirm whether the strange green man was alive. Ten seconds passed. Nothing. Twenty seconds passed. Nothing. Then Daise flinched. Was that a beat? She leaned into the body and cupped her ear over his heart and listened. Sure enough, there it was again, another beat. She stared at her watch and listened for a minute. four beats. It was slow but regular.

'I think he might be alive,' said Daise hesitantly. She lifted her head from the green man's chest and turned to Jude.

'Listen for yourself, his heart is beating slowly but it's definitely beating.'

Jude leaned in to listen for himself but just as his ear touched the man's smooth chest, the body spasmed. They all leapt back from the body, stumbling back into the sand. They watched as the green man started to cough and splutter. Water was shooting out of his mouth like a drinking fountain. Then he opened his eyes.

Chapter 2 – Rowan

The tall green man wiped his face with the back of his smooth hand and sat up. His dark eyes seemed to take in his surroundings, darting across the landscape Daise, Rey and Jude kept their distance. The man, if he was one, blinked and his face became calmer. It was as if he had assessed the situation and decided that the children were not a threat to him. The kids took a tentative step closer.

'Thanks for helping me out of the sea,' he said, slowly in a local accent. His voice was calm and friendly but filled with authority. They waited for him to add more detail until the silence became uncomfortable.

'What are…' started Jude, when he was interrupted by Daise, 'Who are you?'

He paused before answering. 'My name is Rowan.'

With the silence punctured, the questions came thick and fast.

'Where do you come from? 'How did you get in the sea? 'Why are you green?'

Rowan smiled and broke into a deep warm laugh.

'Have you never met a green man before?' he said, getting his feet. 'I think some of you call us Greens. But we get called a lot worse.'

They couldn't help but look up in awe as he stood to his full height.

Daise desperately wanted to know what a green man was. Was it an alien? A robot? A mutant? But she felt too embarrassed; they were being so rude. She started to feel very self-conscious as the blood rushed to her cheeks.

She stepped forward and offered her hand, 'My name is Daisy Woods, but my friends call me Daise.'

She shook his hand firmly, looking straight up into his eyes. They were strange too: though it was a bright sunny day, his pupils were wide black dilated discs surrounded by a deep jade green rim. Unnerved, she felt like she was being sucked into his gaze.

She looked away, turning to the boys as she introduced them. 'These are my friends, Reyansh Gupta and Jude Barker.'

Rey stuck his hand out, stuttering nervously, 'uh, hi I'm uh Rey and he's uh Jude.'

Letting go of Daise's hand, Rowan leant forward and shook their hands in turn. 'Pleased to meet you uh Rey and uh Jude.' Rey was about to correct him when he looked up and saw the man chuckling to himself.

'Forgive me, I don't want to make you nervous. But I would appreciate your help. Could you tell me where I am exactly? My memory's a little bit fuzzy. I have a recollection of being hit around the head with something hard.'

'This is Barrowby Beach,' said Daise, gesturing to the expanse of sand.

Rowan rubbed the back of his head, wincing as he touched his wound. 'Perhaps if you told me a little bit more about Barrowby?'

'It's one of the old districts of Greater Grantham you know, the city capital of the Eastern Islands,' Daise

The Castoffs

replied.

Rowan muttered something inaudible under his breath about islands and stared off to the east, towards the long distant shoreline of Ancaster Island.

'Do you want something to eat?' asked Daise, pointing to their buckets of seaweed and shellfish.

Rowan's eyes followed Daise's hand and disgust flashed across his pale green face.

'No, thank you,' he said, peering into the buckets. 'Thanks for asking. I know your food is very valuable but I'm not, well, what's the word again? Hungry. All I really need is a quiet place to recuperate, somewhere warm in the sun.'

Barrowby Beach got busy in the day. The kids from the old districts of Greater Grantham were on their school holidays and they usually spent their days there, playing on the slopes and swimming in the sea. Daise wasn't sure how they would react to a giant green man in orange shorts. However they reacted, she suspected the confrontation wouldn't be quiet. Someone was bound to inform the Chief Guardian and then Rowan would be carted off to be examined by the Grantham Council. She feared if that happened, he would never find his way back home.

She didn't know why but her gut was telling her that they needed to get him off the beach and keep him safe. Then she remembered the little beach she saw from the limpet rock. Yes, that would be quiet. It would be completely cut off from the main beach once the tide came in. It would give him time to rest and they could come and check on him at low tide tomorrow. She said to Rowan, 'It gets a bit busy here. If it's quiet you want, there's a little beach over that rock.' Daise pointed to the stony outcrop, which was only just visible as the tide had started to come in as they talked. Before Rowan had time to reply, Daise set off towards the limpet rock.

'Come on, I'll show you', she said, over her shoulder. 'It's just round this rock, you can't access it from the dunes. It should be nice and quiet.'

Rowan took three large strides out into the sea and pushed himself up on the rock. He smiled as he saw the secluded bay.

Daise carried on from the shore, 'I think the beach will probably disappear at high tide, but you should be able to climb up onto the dunes and rest there. It is too steep to climb down from the top of the dunes so you shouldn't be disturbed.'

Rowan vaulted off the rock back onto the shore, his feet barely making a sound as he hit the hard, wet sand.

Rey whispered to Jude, 'Extraterrestrial powers, I told you.'

Daise shot a sharp look at Rey, worried that Rowan might have overheard.

'Is there anything else you need?', she asked.

'I couldn't trouble you for some water, could I? I can't seem to get the taste of salt water out of my mouth,' he replied a little awkwardly.

Rey did not hesitate. He stepped up to Rowan and offered his water bottle. Rowan took a sip and handed it back.

'No, you keep it', said Rey firmly. It was a generous offer. Water was rationed. The irony of the great flood was there was all this water around but you couldn't drink any of it. You never knew when the standpipe would run dry so it was good to carry around a bottle as you were never quite sure where your next drink would come from.

Rowan patted Rey on the shoulder, said 'thank you' and tucked the water bottle in the waistband of his shorts.

'Goodbye, my friends. You have shown me such kindness. I hope we meet again soon.'

'We'll come and see you tomorrow,' Daise shouted but she couldn't be sure that he had heard as he took a graceful and silent dive into the sea.

Daise didn't want him to leave. She wanted to know more about Rowan, more about green people. But he was gone. They stood in silence staring out to sea. It was as if it had never happened. Even the track marks Rowan's feet had made in the sand had been washed away.

Rey took off his cap and rubbed his temples with his palms, 'Did I just give my water bottle to a real-life alien?'

'You still think he was an alien?' said Jude, laughing at his friend.

Rey paced excitedly as he spoke, 'He might not have been little but he was definitely a green man. Did you see the way he looked at our food? It was like we were offering him a bucket of sick to eat. Oh yeah and he was green!'

Jude remained unconvinced, 'Do you really think he was from another planet? I mean his accent sounded pretty local to me.'

'Perhaps he just been here a while. I reckon he must have escaped from somewhere,' Rey suggested.

'But if aliens are here on earth, on Barrowby Beach, why haven't we seen them on The Channel?' said Jude.

The Channel was the state-sponsored information

network. It provided information, education and entertainment to the citizens of England.

Daise sighed, 'The Channel only tells us what the Council wants us to know. They're hardly likely to tell us about gigantic green men roaming around the place. It would cause panic.'

Jude laughed, 'Is this another one of your conspiracy theories? The Channel covers up aliens visiting Barrowby? Nice one Daise.'

Daise was irritated. Her dad had told her never to trust the Channel. It was their only source of information though, so she understood why people took it at face value.

Jude saw how badly his joke had landed; 'All I meant to say was that I agreed with you. As exciting as it would be to meet an alien on Barrowby Beach, that was just some tall, bald bloke with green skin.'

Rey changed the subject, 'Come on guys, it's nearly eight. We need to get cooking. The Locals are going to turn up soon. Let's get some of this food cooked up.'

Daise and Jude nodded and knuckled down to the task at hand. Rey headed across the beach towards a patch of driftwood while Daise went to find dry grass to use as tinder.

Jude sat on the sand. He used smooth black stones to create a cooking surface and drew a circle to mark a boundary for the fire. Then he carefully pulled a blackened tin out of his pocket: his fire-starting kit. The tin sat comfortably in his palm. He opened it and took out a wad of char cloth, which he unfurled to reveal a thick magnesium rod and striking blade. He was joined by Daise, who rubbed his spiky hair affectionately before

The Castoffs

chucking a bundle of dry grass at his feet and sitting down cross-legged. She grabbed the char cloth and wiped it across her eyelids.

She blinked at Jude, 'How do I look?'

'Like a skinny panda' he said, beginning to laugh. She punched him on the arm playfully. 'But pandas are extinct,' she tutted, pushing out her bottom lip in exaggerated pout.

'And we'll be extinct too', if we don't get some food down us,' said Rey returning with a stack of dry driftwood.

Jude got to work breaking up the stack of wood and arranging it into a small pyramid, open on one side. He moulded the stack of dry grass into a little bird's nest, tore off a strip of the char cloth and pressed it gently into the centre of the nest. He picked up his magnesium rod and scraped a little shower of sparks onto the small patch of cloth. As the cloth began to glow Jude picked up the nest and blew into it. With each breath, clouds of smoke bellowed out of the nest. Daise and Rey held their breath.

They had seen Jude make fire like this many times; he was a master at fire starting. There was tension in the moments before a spark caught the grass bundle, followed by the calm of his breathing as he coaxed the flame out of the bundle. Then a little whooping noise as flames erupted from the bundle and he carefully pushed it into the pyramid of wood, building it up as the flames spread. The grass burned out quickly as it set light to the wood. He pushed the stones into the centre of the fire and waited for the flames to die down and the stones to warm. Leaning towards the bucket he picked out a handful of limpets and pushed them across the surface of the stones with the tip of his knife. They let off a little hiss of steam as they started to cook.

After a few minutes, Jude passed the knife to Daise, 'Do you think they're cooked?'

She gave them a tentative prod with the knife. They seemed firm and fleshy, 'I reckon they're done,' she said as she tapped them gently to the edge of the hot stones. She cooled them down with a handful of seawater from one of the buckets. A plume of salty steam filled the air.

She got to work on a flat cold stone slicing away the gooey guts of the limpets until she had twelve little round medallions. She stabbed one with her knife and offered it to Jude. He had found the limpets and made the fire after all.

Jude put the limpet in his mouth and chewed. Then he started clutching his throat making a strange choking sound. Daise suddenly had doubts. Were they really limpets? Could they be poisonous? Then she caught a hint of a smirk on his face.

She thumped his arm, 'Jude!' He broke into laughter, cupping his mouth to stop him spitting the half-chewed limpet out of his mouth.

He took a deep breath and swallowed, 'They're gorgeous guys, try one.'

They each took turns to eat a limpet. Daise let the boys share her last one as she felt full.

They all lay back on the beach, listening to the sounds of the crackling fire and the gentle waves lapping at the shore and thinking about Rowan.

A shout from the top of the dunes startled them from their thoughts. Daise sat up and saw four boys sandboarding down the dune. She felt a ball of dread deep in her belly.

'Locals! Come on, let's get out of here!', said Rey, kicking sand over the fire.

'Locals' was the name kids from the Resets gave to the residents of the old suburbs. The boys coming down the hill were the worst kind. They wore the uniform of Guardian Cadets. The Guardians were the military arm of the Council responsible for peacekeeping and enforcing the rule of law.

The friends picked up their buckets and ran.

Chapter 3 – Cadets

There was no easy way off the beach. They had to scale the sandy face of the dune carrying their sleighs on their backs like rucksacks. Their buckets swung heavily by their sides as they punched their feet into the soft sand to get the grip they needed to ascend the slope. There was no point trying to run; the Locals would get to them before they made it up the dune.

Daise recognised one of the boys' sandboarding down the slope. His name was Gregor and she knew him from primary school, when she and her dad lived in Barrowby.

The three boys were hurtling down the slope in their direction. Gregor led the group, cutting the figure of a skilled sandboarder. His stance oozed confidence, his legs absorbing every bounce like springs. Everything about him looked relaxed, from his neck and shoulders down through his arms, which hung loosely at his side. He was a good ten metres ahead of his friends, who looked stiffer and more tentative.

It became clear that he was zig-zagging in their direction. Gregor gave no indication of slowing down until he cut in front of them at the last moment, spraying them with sand as he came to a stop. Instinctively, Jude and Rey hugged their buckets and jumped back down the dune to avoid the collision.

The Castoffs

They tumbled to the floor in a heap. Daise stood firm, staring through Gregor's sunglasses as he approached. She was taking a gamble on being able to reason with the boy she had known. It was hard to see through the black uniform and all that it symbolised. But they had been friends. Surely that would count for something.

He slid his mirrored sunglasses up his forehead and pushed his floppy brown fringe out of his eyes, flashing a look of disgust down at Rey and Jude who were scrambling around on the floor picking up stray bits of seaweed and limpets.

Turning to face Daise, he asked, 'What are you Castoffs doing on our beach?', His voice crackled with condescension.

She scraped her teeth across her bottom lip to quell the anger inside her. 'Castoffs' was the term used to dehumanise the kids who grew up in the Resets. It was meant to suggest they were a lesser form of humanity. It took all her reserves of self-control to stay calm.

'We were just on our way home, Gregor.'

She saw him raise his eyebrows as she used his name. 'How do you know my name, girl?'

Daise took a step up the dune so that Gregor was not looking down at her. She was taller than him but he had broadened out since she had last seen him. 'It's Daisy Woods, we used to play football together in year three.'

He stared at her hard, his brow furrowed and then he slapped his forehead.

'I remember, something happened to your dad. A spot of bother with the Council. Didn't you have to go and live with the Castoffs? Tough break.'

There it was, that word again. He was clearly trying to

get a reaction. Gregor was joined by two friends dressed in matching black polo shirts, swimming shorts and black daypacks on their backs. Even their sunglasses were the same. Only their hair differed. One had a bright mop of wavy ginger hair while the other had long, lank brown hair scraped back into a greasy ponytail.

She looked back at Rey and Jude making their way back up the dune again and hoped they would have the sense to let her do the talking.

'We were just making our way home. Nice to see you again.'

Daise attempted to walk past the black-clad trio but they closed ranks and blocked her path.

'What's the hurry?' Gregor asked, as he turned to his friends and continued. 'This is Daisy, would you believe she used to live in Barrowby?'

His friends laughed. Their faces were cruel and mocking. Their arrogance enraged her. Yet reacting to their provocation was exactly what they wanted. She knew it would be her, Rey and Jude who would come off second best in any confrontation. So, she remained silent.

Gregor continued, 'I'd love to make an exception for an old acquaintance Daisy but, rules are rules. No Castoffs on the beach.'

His companions grunted in agreement and stepped forward to grab the buckets from Jude and Rey. They wrinkled their faces in disgust as they peered down at the sand flecked seaweed and limpets.

Gregor took Daise's bucket, shaking his head. 'Well. This isn't going to pay your fine, is it? I don't suppose you have any coins? You don't need to answer that. If you had coins, you wouldn't be wearing those,' he said, pointing at Rey's taped-up trainers.

'You must have something of value. Damon, Tommo — shake them down.'

'Empty your pockets,' they growled in unison.

Rey and Jude looked to Daise for direction.

She nodded and they did as they were told. Rey showed them his battered baseball cap and Jude his fire lighting kit, his knife and his water bottle.

Gregor walked past Daisy and examined the items. He opened Jude's fire lighting kit and struck a shower of sparks at Rey. He closed it and put it in his pocket. He took Jude's knife, pulled out the blade and ran his finger along its edge to test its sharpness.

'I'm feeling generous today. You can keep the hat. As for these buckets, well I can't let you steal from our beach, can I? What sort of message would that send?' And with that, Damon and Tommo threw the buckets down the slope.

Daise could see Rey and Jude seething in anger as they watched the carefully collected contents of their buckets disperse down the steep slope. She beckoned them to follow her away but Gregor and his goons blocked her path.

'One thing before you go Daisy. Who was the man you were talking to on the beach?'

Daise's heart sank. How long had they been watching them? She wasn't going to tell them about Rowan. She had to keep him safe, but what could she say? Not sure, she said nothing.

Rey stepped forward to rescue her from the silence.

'You want to get yourself some new glasses if you think that shop dummy was a person. It was minging, covered in horrible green slime. We thought we could clean it up and sell it at the market but it was too heavy to carry so we threw it back in. If you want it, I'm sure it can't have drifted out too far. We lobbed it off that rock.'

He pointed at the rock, which was now just peeping out of the sea.

Gregor looked unconvinced but he tapped his sunglasses back down over his eyes, 'Go on then clear off before we call the Guardians.' He gestured to a walkie talkie hooked to his waistband as if to emphasise his point.

He placed his board on the sand and kicked off, continuing his journey to the shore.

'Come on guys', he called back to his friend. Damon and Tommo took one last opportunity to shoulder barge Jude and Rey to the ground before they sped off after Gregor.

'Charming fellas', spat Rey sarcastically as he picked himself up off the sand. He turned to face the sea and shouted, 'Are you sure you don't want my T-shirt, my shoes or maybe my underpants.'

Daise started to snigger. Gregor was too far away to hear Rey now. 'Not sure they want your pants, Rey.'

Rey flashed her a stern look but couldn't stay serious for long. It was ridiculous. He smiled and said, 'Come on let's go home.'

'But what about our stuff? We've been robbed,' Jude complained, 'We can't just let them get away with that.'

Daise sighed. She shared his frustration: 'What are we going to do Jude? Fight them? Call the Guardians? You know how it goes with the Locals. Let's get back before we get into any more trouble.'

The Castoffs

Daise looked down at the boys on the beach, kicking their buckets about like footballs.

She turned around and started to trudge up the dune, followed by Rey and Jude.

Daise, Rey and Jude shouldn't have been on the beach. The Council had passed a decree last year which banned any children from the Casthorpe Reset from being in the inner suburbs of Greater Grantham without a travel permit.

The decree had done little to stop their foraging trips and excursions to the market. But last month things had got a bit trickier: the Council had finished constructing a chain-link fence topped with barbed wire around the Reset. Two checkpoints were constructed on the road which ran through the centre of the Casthorpe Reset to enforce the system of permits. Residents were only allowed into town if they had a permit signed by their employer, which meant under 16s were not allowed out of the Resets.

The fence stopped kids scavenging on Barrowby Beach. Well, it had until Daise had worked out a way to get over it.

At the top of the dunes, a path led up to the church and the old part of Barrowby. Keen to avoid bumping into any other Locals, they headed across the dune tops. It was slow going as they took tentative steps to avoid being pricked by the jagged marram grass.

It was only five hundred metres or so before the dunes gave way to a field of oilseed rape. The bright yellow flowers were long gone and all that remained was the dried out woody mass. The dense, desiccated canopy rustled in the wind like it was alive, oilseed pods dancing about like cat claws.

Walking in silence, they followed a path around the edge of the field that led to the fence. The five grey towers of the Reset loomed in the distance.

Daise spotted a familiar plant at the base of the fence separating the Casthorpe Reset from Barrowby. She rubbed a leaf between her thumb and forefinger and inhaled a refreshing hit of mint.

'Here Jude, Rey… have a mint leaf. It will mask the smell of the dump.' She stripped the plant and handed the leaves to her friends as a peace offering.

Daise felt bad that Jude had lost his precious things. It has been her idea to sneak over the fence down to the beach, and her idea to help Rowan. They might have followed her lead but she felt responsible. Rey smiled as he took a bunch of mint leaves from her. She turned to face Jude; he shook his head at her offering. Daise put a few leaves in her mouth and got to work on scaling the fence.

The barrier was a 10-foot-high chain-link fence coated in plastic. It ran uninterrupted from the checkpoint on Casthorpe Road to the coastal cliffs.

It was simple enough to climb. All you had to do was jab your feet into the holes in the fence. The problem came when you approached the five lines of barbed wire stretched between the concrete posts at the top. The concrete posts held the barbed wire at a 45-degree angle jutting towards the Casthorpe side of the fence, which made it easier to climb back than it was to climb over.

The Casthorpe side of the fence ran alongside the edge of the Greater Grantham dump. The grass around the edge of the path was long and strewn with litter that

The Castoffs

had blown off the giant piles of refuse.

They started by taking the sand sledges from their backs and taking it in turns to throw them over the fence.

Jude got down on his knees to scrape the earth off an old piece of carpet they kept hidden behind the fence. The carpet was a sandy brown, perfectly disguised to match the colour of the earth. He held it up to Daise, who was already grasping the chain links and carefully edging up the fence. The wires rattled against the concrete posts making a noise that reminded her of wind chimes. Holding the top of the fence with one hand she leant back and used the other to stretch back and grab the carpet from Jude. In one graceful sweep she slapped the carpet over the barbed wire. She made some slight adjustments to make sure it was balanced on the arm of the concrete post, before leaning forward to grip the top rung of the fence using the carpet to protect her hands against the jagged barbs. She crawled carefully up the carpet adjusting her positioning so that she was sat on the post looking down at the litter strewn Casthorpe side of the fence.

Rey was getting restless, 'Come on Daise, we haven't got all day. Let's get back to the tower. I could murder a nice cold carton of Smart Jooce.'

She shot him a glare before launching herself off the top of the fence. Her feet slapped the ground sending a shot of pain up her legs as she rolled into the grass to break her fall. Sitting on the rough ground hugging her legs, she watched Rey follow her over the fence, landing in front of her with a heavy thump.

They both watched Jude as he climbed up the fence. He'd hardly said a word since they left the beach. His eyes looked glassy like he was going to break into tears. His knife and fire-starting kit were more than possessions, they made him feel special. They gave the group strength. He kicked the fence sulkily as he climbed, causing it to shake like a tambourine.

Daise felt guilty. It had been her idea to go to the beach. She was always pushing the boys to break the rules. There was so much more that she wanted to do, wanted to see and wanted to experience. She felt like she was living someone else's life. Things had been different when she was young, when she had a school to go to, a house with a garden, books, a computer. With every day that passed it seemed like more and more was being taken from her.

Meeting Gregor brought the loss of her dad back to her. What gave them the right to just take their things? A resentment was bubbling and burning in her guts. Perhaps she should have been stronger and stood up to them. But what good would that have done?

A rustling on the other side of the fence interrupted her. Before she could let out a warning, a mountain of a man was standing behind Jude. It was as if he had materialised from the shadows in the field. He wore the black uniform of the Greater Grantham Guardians. The bold three G logo in a white circle on a black armband left them with no doubt they were in trouble.

Jude saw the shock on his friends' faces as he reached up to the carpet covered barbed-wire summit. Instinctively he paused and looked over his shoulder.

'Oh, no you don't son,' the Guardian shouted as he leapt forward and grabbed a handful of Jude's T-shirt.

Jude grabbed out at the fence, trying not to fall

backwards. His hand caught the lowest rung of barbed wire and he shouted out in pain as the sharpened wire cut into his flesh.

The Guardian wrapped his massive arms around Jude's abdomen and started to pull him off the fence.

Daise jumped to her feet and shouted, 'Stop it you're hurting him.'

But the huge barrel-chested man ignored her and continued to pull at Jude until he lost his footing and the only things holding him on the fence were his hands clasped around the jagged metal barbs.

He let go, screaming like a wounded animal. The Guardian ignored the shouts from Daise and Rey as he threw Jude heavily over his shoulder. Jude held his wounded hands to his face. His eyes were wide and glassy. Rey and Daise stared helplessly from their side of the fence as their friend disappeared into the rape field.

Chapter 4 – Towers

Daise and Rey forlornly dragged their sand sledges down the dusty track until they reached the market at the front of the dump that sat in the shadow of the Casthorpe towers. Labyrinthine rows of market stalls packed with salvage from the dump rose up on their right. The market was teeming with activity as the residents of the Reset tried to earn some coins to feed themselves and their families. Daise felt the loss of their seaweed and limpets acutely as the salty smell of fresh seafood cooking caught her nostrils. Mrs Arkwright would have given them a coin each for the contents of their buckets.

The market was the commercial hub of the Casthorpe Reset. It was divided into four distinct zones. On the outer edge was the Artisanal Market where craftsmen from the Reset sold handmade jewellery, elaborate carvings and sculptures fashioned from recycled materials. Their customers were the merchants from the old districts of Greater Grantham who would sell them on at a massive profit. This part of the market was closest to Casthorpe Road, the main thoroughfare that ran through the Reset. The streets were paved and there was even a secure car park so that the wealthy customers did not have to worry about their cars being recycled. The stalls were protected from the heat of the morning sun by brightly coloured canopies. The stall holders were immaculate, dressed in shirts, smart trousers and bright red branded Greater Grantham Markets aprons.

Behind the Artisanal Market was the Top Market, where the cut and thrust commercial dealings of the Reset really took place. Run by the dump's employees, the stalls contained the richest pickings salvaged from the detritus of Greater Grantham — recycled, cleaned up and repaired. Bikes, scooters and pushchairs stood in neat rows alongside reconditioned tools, clockwork generators and solar cells, lined up next to repaired kettles, toasters and stoves.

If you walked deeper into the market the tidy rows gave way to the ramshackle stalls and shacks of the Flea Market. Lower value goods sat stacked on simple trestle tables; second-hand clothes reconstructed from rags and plastic bags, alongside buckets, chairs and rope. This market sold anything that could be recycled, cleaned or repaired, from simple fishing rods, catapults and spears for hunting to second-hand books, plastic toys and board games. The larger stalls were connected to outbuildings. Some were little more than storage huts while others were a patchwork of sheds, caravans and storage containers. The bigger stalls were given over to services, with everything from blacksmiths, mechanics and carpenters to spiritualists, healers and dentists.

In the centre of the Flea Market there was a large open square that housed the Food Market. Most traders sold their food from upturned boxes or buckets, as happy to barter for other goods as to take hard currency. Mrs Arkwright's was the best place to eat. She sold a delicious seafood stew for a single coin. While the food was great,

The Castoffs

Daise often just came to read. Battered books were scattered around her stall in boxes, on tables and makeshift bookcases. They were all salvaged from the dump. They were all for sale but she let her regular customers read them for free while they ate.

Books were hard to come by since the Council took over. The libraries had closed. The Council had banned so many books that even if you had the money, it was difficult to find anything decent to read.

Without any salvage to sell there seemed little point in braving the bustle of the morning market so they headed home. Daise looked up Casthorpe Road towards the Barrowby Checkpoint hoping to see Jude trotting towards them.

Daise, Jude and Rey lived in a tower block purpose-built for children in the Casthorpe Reset. Many children were orphaned during the floods and by the war that followed. Most objected to the term 'orphan' as there was so little information about what happened to the 'missing' — as the people lost during this time were called.

Daise had moved into Tower Five when her dad went missing. Jude and Rey had shown her around and became her unofficial adopted family.

The towers were set out in a five-by-five grid on former farmland. They were designed to be functional with no care given to how they looked. Dreary prefabricated concrete shells stacked up twenty-five stories high, all the towers were identical. Each ground floor housed a canteen, launderette and exercise room while the remaining twenty-four floors contained rows of male and female sleeping quarters separated by bathroom

The Castoffs

blocks.

The sleeping quarters were made up of what their residents called 'bread bins' — small sleeping pods stacked five high. Too small to be called bedrooms, each pod was little more than a single bed with a small cupboard for clothes at the head and, at the foot, a screen giving access to The Channel.

Daise and Rey walked up to their lockers at the side of Tower Five and pushed in their sand sleighs. Rey had been half tempted to chuck his sleigh in the bin, certain as he was, they would never see the slopes of Barrowby Beach again.

They swiped their hands against the identscanners on the turnstile and they were let into Tower Five. They headed into the canteen to pick up their ration of Smart Jooce.

The breakfast rush was over and most of the children had returned to their bread bins to watch the Channel or to the dump to see what they could scavenge off the Pile. Daise and Rey walked up to the bank of ten vending machines lining the back wall of the canteen. The machines were known as 'nannies' as they provided sustenance to the children. All of the machines were filled with cartons of Smart Jooce — a viscous green multivitamin shake. Residents were allowed three cartons of Smart Jooce a day, which was, if you believed the adverts that ran on hard rotation on the Channel, enough to provide 'every nutrient needed for a healthy body and mind'.

In practice, a diet of three cartons a day left the children feeling tired, sluggish and permanently hungry. Rey had suggested an alternative slogan which had a more truthful ring to it: 'Smart Jooce — it tastes like crap but it keeps you alive!'.

Daise held her hand up to one of the nannies so it could read her implant. The machine made a clicking noise as the lock was released, allowing her to pull the lever on the side of the machine, which dropped a 330ml green carton of Smart Jooce into a collection bay at the bottom. Daise picked up her carton and joined Rey, who was already sitting at one of the tables next to the windows that looked out towards Casthorpe Road. Rey was glugging his Smart Jooce down greedily. He was gasping for a drink having given his water carton to Rowan.

'What are we going to do Daise? How are we going to get Jude back?' he asked.

With the passing of the decree and the new restrictions on travel, Daise was worried about Jude but she didn't want to scare Rey. She knew he was looking for reassurance.

'He'll be OK. The Guardians normally just take your stuff and he's got nothing they can take, thanks to Gregor and his mates,' she replied.

'What if they fine him for travelling without a valid permit?' asked Rey.

'They'll know he hasn't got any money.'

'But won't they lock him up if he can't pay the fine?'

'I don't think so. Their prisoners get fed better than us. I reckon they just want to give him a scare. He'll be back by the end of the day.

Rey still looked unsure, 'But did you see the size of that Guardian?'

'Jude did the right thing; he didn't put up a fight. He

The Castoffs

won't get hurt if he does as he's told.'

Rey fell silent. His brow furrowed. He looked unconvinced.

Daise opened her carton of Smart Jooce and took a sip. She had never liked it; thick and gloopy like milkshake but with a nasty metallic aftertaste. She pushed it away from her and stared out of the window. She could just make out the sea in the distance through the gaps between the towers.

She started thinking about how they were going to see Rowan again now that the Guardians were patrolling the fence. Would he still be there? Something about Rowan that was nagging at her: he was so strange but at the same time so familiar. Had she heard about green people before? She rubbed her head.

A memory flashed to the surface of her mind. Her dad sat on the edge of her bed. She could see his shiny black acrylic spectacles, his unkempt beard and warm smile. He was reading her a story. Something that he had written. She closed her eyes for a second and she could see the book. It was a small leather-bound hardback book. It was cracked down the spine and small flecks of leather were missing from the edges.

The story was about a green mouse. It was one of those picture books for children, with a few sentences on each page. The sort of story that had a moral to teach. Like how 'the boy who cried wolf' was really telling you not to lie. She could see the cover in her mind: light brown leather with gold lettering. She squeezed her eyes shut and she saw the title: '*The Green Mouse.*' She couldn't remember the story but she felt it was connected somehow to these green people.

Noise from the large flat screen TV fitted above the nannies broke into her thoughts. It was the Channel NewsHour.

'Greater Grantham is on high alert today. A dangerous criminal has escaped from the high security prison on Ancaster Island. The prisoner is infected with a highly contagious virus and so should not be approached. He is a tall, bald male in his forties. We repeat, he should not be approached. If you see him call the Greater Grantham Guardians.'

A phone number appeared on the screen alongside a photo of the prisoner. The prisoner was clearly Rowan, except his skin colour had been changed to pale pink. He had thin eyebrows and a shadow of stubble on his head, as if it had been shaved. Despite the changes, there could be no doubt that this was Rowan.

Daise and Rey spoke in whispers as they looked about the dining hall, where other kids began to chatter about what they had seen.

Rey spoke first, 'That was Rowan, wasn't it? But he looked well, normal in the photo. They said he had a disease, Daise… do you think we're infected? What are we going to do?'

Daise took a deep breath. 'Something doesn't add up here Rey. They said he was dangerous. The guy we met on the beach had to be one of the gentlest people I've met.'

Rey's voice started to crack with worry. 'Shouldn't we tell someone? I mean we might get sick. I don't want to turn green and have all my hair fall out. Should we be quarantined?' He swept his hands through his shoulder length hair as if to highlight his concerns.

Daise leaned across the stained wooden canteen table, 'Calm down Rey, we don't want to attract attention to ourselves.'

She touched him gently on the forearm and nodded towards a portly man in grease-stained brown Greater Grantham Council worker's uniform who was tapping the glass on the nannies with his baton to see if he could get a carton of Smart Jooce to drop.

Rey slurped on the last dregs of his carton and let out a deep sigh.

'They're lying to us, Rey. There must be a reason they've changed his skin colour. There's something they don't want us to know. It might sound silly but my dad used to tell me bedtime stories about the old days — you know before the flood? When we were a United Kingdom.

'I can remember there was a little green mouse. It was an allegory; you know one of those stories with a hidden meaning. I think it might have been really talking about green people.

'What did it say about them?' said Rey.

'Well that's just it. I can't remember the details exactly. It was a long time ago, but there is something about it that makes me sure that we can trust Rowan.'

Rey rubbed his head thoughtfully, 'I'm sorry Daise, I don't get it. What's an old book…'

But before he could finish, a boy barged him along the bench. It was Jude.

Chapter 5 – Alone

Daise grinned up at Jude. His brow was prickling with beads of sweat and his closely cropped hair was wet. Breathing heavily, he leaned forward using the table for support. Both of his barbed wire shredded hands were wrapped in rags encrusted with blood.

'What happened? What did they do to you? Are you OK?', asked Daise.

He rolled his eyes, 'Give me a minute to catch my breath and I'll tell you.'

Daise pushed her carton of Smart Jooce towards him. He grabbed it with his injured hands and drank it down in a series of noisy slurps, before letting out a gasp. Daise was not one for public displays of affection, but he looked so sad she had to get off the bench and hug him. Up close, she noticed a tear stain smeared across his face.

Rey got up too and joined them for a group hug, 'Sorry mate. We were worried, you know — that Guardian was massive and it looked pretty painful being dragged off that fence.'

Daise felt a pang of guilt for leaving poor Jude on the other side of the fence. But what could she have done?

'Let's have a look at those hands,' she said, gently unwrapping the makeshift bandages and discarding the rags on the floor.

'Hey don't chuck them. They're my socks', Jude

The Castoffs

protested.

Rey screwed up his face, 'That's pretty rank Jude.'

'I didn't exactly have access to a first aid kit. I did think about going to Greenacres Hospital, but then I remembered I was just a stupid Castoff. Do you want to know what happened to me or what?'

'I was only joking,' mumbled Rey, a little taken aback by his friend's vitriol.

'Don't be like that Jude, of course we want to hear what happened,' said Daise.

They all sat down on the bench and Jude told his story.

'Well, I thought I was in big trouble when that Guardian pulled me off the fence and carried me off like a bag of spuds. I asked him what he was going to do to me but he ignored me. He cut through the fields past the church and up the road to the Guardian station. I thought I was going to get locked up but we didn't go inside. He took me round the back to the car park. There was this big black van parked behind the station.

'Prisoner transport' was written in white letters above the Greater Grantham Guardians' GGG logo. The Guardian dropped me to the floor, put some handcuffs on me and threw me in the back of the van. That's when I started to freak out. I thought I was going to be taken to a detention centre. I was scared I'd never see you guys again.'

'Where did he take you?' asked Rey.

'Well that's it, they didn't take me anywhere. He made a call on his walkie talkie and then waited until this other guy turned up'

'What, another Guardian? You must have been

wetting yourself', said Rey.

'Yeah, I think it was the Chief. He was tall, thin and mean looking. The big Guardian called him sir. They started talking about an escaped prisoner. I didn't twig to start with but the boss guy handed him a picture and I caught a glimpse — it was definitely Rowan.'

He continued, 'Well, they walked out of earshot for a good few minutes. I thought they'd forgotten all about me. I was going to make a run for it but the boss guy approached me. I thought he was going to hit me at first but he dragged me out of the van and told the big fella to unlock my handcuffs.

'The boss guy showed me the picture of Rowan and asked me if I'd seen him.'

Daise couldn't help but interrupt, 'You didn't tell him, did you Jude?'

Jude looked offended, 'Of course not! I'm not a snitch. He mumbled something about Gregor I think, signed a checkpoint pass and handed it to me.'

'They just let you go?' asked Daise, sounding more incredulous than she'd intended.

'Yes, I know, it kind of freaked me out too. They didn't exactly wish me well though. The big Guardian said if he saw me trespassing in Barrowby again I might not make it to the Guardian station in such good condition. I didn't hang about after that; I ran up the road to the checkpoint. They took the pass off me and I sprinted home. I think they were so focused on finding Rowan they didn't have time to deal with a trespassing kid from the Resets. He must be dangerous if the Guardians are so rattled.'

'You didn't think he was dangerous when you met

him? Did you?' Daise asked.

'No, but if the Guardians are worried then he must be able to handle himself. And what do we really know about him?'

'We know he needs our help. We've got to warn him before the Guardians get him,' insisted Daise.

Rey blurted out, 'They said he was sick with some sort of virus, perhaps that's what made him so weird looking. I don't want to get sick, Daise. Perhaps we should just stay out of this. We've got ourselves into enough trouble.'

Daise feared she was losing the argument, 'If he was so contagious, how come they just let Jude go? If it was some sort of outbreak, they'd have put him in quarantine. Gregor must have told them about the green man he thought he saw on the beach. It doesn't make sense.'

'Are you calling me a liar Daise?' barked Jude, his voice a little bit loud. Other kids in the hall were starting to look at them.

Daise started, 'Come on Jude!' Then checked herself and whispered, 'I didn't mean it like that. It's just that this all sounds like the usual Council nonsense. We just need to talk to Rowan and…'

Jude snapped at her in anger, silencing Daise. 'You want to go back to the beach! No way Daise. I've just got home. If the Guardians catch me again I'll get locked up for sure. I thought we were friends.'

Daise grabbed his arm as he started to walk away.

'Jude, don't be like that. I'm sorry but, I just can't shake this feeling that we should help him.'

Jude tugged his arm out of her grasp and stomped off, not looking back when Rey called out after him.

'I'm sorry Daise but I think he's right. It's too risky

The Castoffs

going back. I'm sorry.'

Daise sat alone on the rough wooden bench as Rey hurried after his friend. The two of them walked out of the canteen. She wanted to follow but her body felt too heavy.

Daise felt a crushing weight of guilt on her chest. Rey and Jude looked up to her. She had been born in Barrowby with an education. She should be helping them, not getting them into trouble.

But she couldn't get rid of the image of Rowan lying helpless on the beach. He only had enough water to get him through a couple of days. What chance did he have of escaping now that the Guardians were looking for him? She had to warn him.

She needed a plan. It was too risky to scale the fence now it was being patrolled. But if she could find some rope it might be possible to lower herself down to the secluded bay where Rowan was hiding. Finding rope wasn't going to be easy, but she might be able to salvage something from the piles.

The rubbish heaps that lay behind the market were known as the piles. Before any refuse reached the piles, it had been searched for anything at the recycling plant. Anything that could be repaired or repurposed was removed. The leftover mulch of low-grade refuse was stacked in large heaps and for a coin Reset residents could get a pass to scavenge for an hour. It could be time well spent; if you were lucky you could find something to sell on for two or three coins. Equally you could come up empty handed and be left one coin lighter and with a foul smell clinging to you for days.

Daise had a small stash of coins that she kept for

emergencies. She made up her mind. She would spend an hour salvaging material to make rope and use it to reach Rowan. She strode across the canteen, passed the security desk to the staircase and tugged open the steel fire doors that led to the stairwells.

Out of breath, she presented her implant on the identscanner that opened her Breadbin, a small sleeping pod that was little more than a single bed and some storage cupboards.

What few clothes she had, were folded neatly next to a small collection of books she had bought from the market. Behind her clothes were her most valued possessions: a small notebook; a tin that contained an assortment of coloured pencils; and a small leather purse which contained twelve metal discs on which was written 'One Eastern Island Credit'. She took a couple of coins, replaced the purse and headed back down the stairwell.

When she reached the canteen entrance she looked around for Rey and Jude. It was starting to get a bit busier as hungry children sat patiently waiting for the lunch credit to be activated. Her friends weren't there. They didn't want to help. She would have to do this on her own.

Walking out of the tower past the row of lockers, she saw a man flyposting the wall above them. There were rows and rows of white posters with 'Wanted' written in bold capital letters above a roughly sketched picture of Rowan. It was clear that the Council was desperate to find him. She walked up to the wall and read the smaller print below the picture.

A 100 coin reward will be given for any information

that helps lead to the capture of this individual. Please do not approach him as he is infected with a highly contagious virus that makes him unpredictable and dangerous. Contact your nearest Guardians' office.

She ripped one of the posters off the wall in frustration.

'Hey missy, I just put that up.' The flyposting man was waving at her with his brush. Globs of glue splattered on the floor in front of him. She folded the poster and stuck it in the back pocket of her shorts and ran off towards Casthorpe Road ignoring his protests.

Chapter 6 – Dump

Casthorpe Road was gridlocked all the way from the market exit to the Barrowby Checkpoint. The Artisanal market was closing and all the traders from Grantham were leaving. The road would normally be busy at this time of day but she had never seen the traffic jammed up like this. Daise carefully edged her way through the stationary cars, vans and pick-ups, looking out for bikes and scooters whizzing through the gaps.

Some drivers were hitting their horns in frustration, while others were leaning out of their windows shaking their fists in fury at the road ahead. She peeked into the back of a flatbed pickup truck and saw a couple of kids from the Reset hiding among some elaborately carved lamp stands. They put their fingers to their lips in a silent plea to Daise not to give them up.

For a moment she thought about changing her plan and sneaking on to the back of a pickup but she figured that the tailback was being caused by the heightened levels of security at the checkpoint. They were bound to be searching vehicles. No, her plan was better. She reached the other side of the road, following the pavement past the car park until it opened out into the wide dirt track that veered off to the right.

It was a relief to be away from the noise of the road.

The Castoffs

There was a steady stream of people walking towards her. She saw a couple of kids from Tower Five carrying assorted junk. One had a collection of rusty tin cans crammed into string bags, another a bag of old plastic bottles.

'How are the pickings at the dump today?' she asked the small ginger haired lad clutching his collection of cans like trophies.

'Pretty good. Five rubbish trucks turned up this morning, so I got all this in an hour,' he said, wiggling his shoulders proudly to rattle the tin cans. She smiled back at him and walked with a bit more purpose. She wanted to get to the dump entrance before everything of value had been stripped from the Pile.

Up ahead, the dirt track met a tarmacked road that led to the recycling plant. A couple of rubbish trucks thundered along it as Daise continued down the dirt track. She began to taste the rotten smell of decomposition in the back of her mouth as the path narrowed, still more than two hundred metres from the dump entrance.

Casthorpe Dump took all the rubbish from the Greater Grantham district. The rubbish trucks backed into the plant and dumped their contents into the centre of an oval track. Around the outside of the track were cages for different materials, from metals to plastics to household appliances. The staff then stripped the pile of all items of value, running around the oval putting items into the right recycling cages. What was left was a stinky mulch of decomposing vegetable matter and dirty nappies, mingled with soiled rags, small pieces of plastic, and assorted junk of little value. This mulch was scooped up by a digger and thrown on the Pile.

The process was notoriously haphazard and it was not uncommon for high value items to be scooped up with the mulch and dropped in the Pile.

The towers were full of florid tales of Castoff kids striking it rich by scavenging. Daise had heard of a kid who had found a ring with a diamond as large as an acorn. Apparently, he had bought an apartment in a gated community in Barrowby. But Daise thought it was more likely that he was robbed by the Guardians and detained.

Daise was going to search the Pile for rope. She knew she would be lucky to find a good length of intact rope but she figured she could construct something by piecing scraps together.

The dump was spread out over a square kilometre. They kept it as spread out as possible to make it easier for kids to sort through. She couldn't see many kids on the pile. Most did their salvage runs in the early morning before it got too hot and stinky.

The stench became more overpowering. It seeped into her nostrils and her mouth. It was a foul mix of rotten cabbage and ammonia. She pulled a bunch of mint leaves from her pocket and put them in her mouth to mask the acrid taste.

There was a small shack up ahead: mismatched off-cuts of wood nailed over an old caravan. A roughly hewn wooden service counter was cut into the side of the caravan and a blackboard was mounted on the side. It read:

Welcome to Greater Grantham Council municipal dump

The Castoffs

Scavenging passes
1 coin - hourly pass
5 coins - daily pass
10 coins - weekly pass

Glove hire included in the price of admission.

This site is monitored by CCTV. Failure to declare high value salvage or contraband will result in detention.

In purchasing a scavenging pass you agree to abide by the rules set out in GCC Municipal dump operating policy section 25.

A couple of years ago there had been an outbreak of fleshrot that had been traced back to a scavenger. The gloves were more about reassuring the wealthy patrons on the Artisanal market than protecting the kids who worked on the pile. Nevertheless, Daise was grateful for the protection.

A boy, not much older than her, sat behind the counter next to a row of coin operated turnstiles. He sat on a tall wooden stool leaning back precariously with his arms stretched behind his head and through lank greasy hair that seemed plastered to his face. He was oblivious to Daise as he was absorbed by a screen perched on the counter. Daise coughed to get his attention but his gaze remained focussed firmly on the screen. It was the local news; Rowan was the main story again.

She was relieved — this meant they hadn't caught him

The Castoffs

yet. Suddenly the boy spoke.

'Name?', he barked urgently in a thick Yorkshire Island accent.

Daise looked around to see if there was a queue behind her. But she was the only person standing there.

'Daise,' she said.

He wrote her name down on a piece of card and stuck it in a slot on the wall marked with the time.

He slapped a receipt down on the rough wooden countertop and stamped it with her exit time.

'Can I have some gloves' she asked. Tutting, the boy hopped off his stool and pushed a pair of muddy red gardening gloves across the counter.

'Don't lose the gloves or you won't get your salvage.' He waved in the direction of the coin operated turnstiles and returned his attention to the news. Daise took a coin from her pocket, dropped it into the slot and pushed her hip against the cold metal barrier.

Gloves on, she walked round the dump to look for a space to forage. She could see a few kids scavenging in the distance. Some of them could be fiercely territorial so she kept walking until she found a quiet spot. It was easy to get into a fight over some worthless piece of junk when you had been rummaging through filth all morning.

Daise's first task was to find a makeshift scoop. She scanned the pile and soon spotted an old pot nestled in among some decomposing nappies. Glad of her gloves, she picked the pot out of the pile. One of the nappies stuck to the pot and, as she pulled, it fell apart releasing its fetid odour. Daise retched, suddenly so keen to get away that she almost lost her footing, which was a really dangerous thing to do on the Pile. It was easy to fall on

The Castoffs

something sharp and injure yourself.

Some of the older kids on the Reset loved to tell gruesome tales of children falling on spikes and being finished off by rats. The real danger wasn't the rats or the injuries but the infections that followed. If you had a stash of coins the Patcher might have something that could fight the infection or try an amputation before blood poisoning set in. Daise shook her head, keen to get the image of the Patcher in his thick rubber butcher's apron out of her mind.

Focusing on her task, Daise started to look for a cutting tool. Normally she would have borrowed Jude's knife but it was pretty easy to find a piece of broken glass on the Pile. Carefully, she tapped it on a nearby stone to create a sharp cutting edge.

She knew that finding a good length of rope was a long shot. But she figured that any length of old string, discarded clothing or electrical cable could be bound together to create a crude rope. Jude had taught her a bunch of knots so with a bit of patience she could create something that could hold her weight.

She sorted through the rubbish methodically, collecting lengths of ribbon, string and any old clothing, bundling her pickings into an old potato sack that she had found sticking up out of the pile.

The trick to salvaging was to have a purpose. It was easy to get distracted with an object, thinking about what it was, how it could be fixed, what you could use it for. Daise had been digging for half an hour when she uncovered a book.

The list of books that the Greater Grantham Council had banned grew every year, which meant people often threw away perfectly good books. Most of them would be fished out in the recycling plant, bound for Mrs Arkwright's book stall on the flea market. But given the speed of the recycling operation, it was inevitable some books were missed and ended on the pile.

She looked up at the nearest camera mounted on a large wooden pole ten metres away. She wasn't clear whether the camera worked but it certainly made her feel like she was being watched. Turning her back to the camera, Daise examined the book. It was a thin paperback. She rubbed the dirt off the front and saw the title was ***Human Evolution for Beginners***. All that Daise knew about evolution she had learned from the Channel. It was a dangerous political ideology that said we were no different from the animals.

She could just about make out the blurb on the back of the book. It made evolution sound more about science than politics. She pushed it to the bottom of her potato sack, determined to read it later when she was sure she wasn't being watched. Anyway, she was going to have to work hard to salvage enough material to create enough rope to climb down the exposed cliff that towered above the secluded beach where they had left Rowan. She hopped around like a bird picking out materials to build a nest, collecting pieces of string, wire and cloth until the potato sack was full.

She had been studying knots and she figured that she could tie all the stuff together into strings that she could twist and bind into a makeshift rope. She looked at her watch, time was running out. She started to make her way back when she spotted a thick blue cord poking out of the pile like a juicy worm.

The Castoffs

She grabbed it with both hands and pulled, the thick cord was wound up in mushy cardboard and funky smelling gunk but as she pulled she the rope kept coming. She wound it around her forearm, counting the coils as she went. When the frayed end finally emerged from the pile it must have been at least 15 meters of rope.

As she pushed it in her sack, the dull monotone of the boy at the counter called out over the tannoy system.

'Scavenger Daise — Time's Up! You have 5 minutes to return to the gates or you will forfeit your salvage.'

Then came a squeal of feedback that made her head hurt. She took a couple of rags from the sack and used them to tie it onto her back.

She walked back to the gates, had the camera seen her find the book? Was it worth risking detention? Then she thought of the greasy haired boy. He didn't imagine he was paying that much attention to the CCTV feeds. Besides, the book looked interesting and she felt sure Mrs Arkwright would give her a few coins for it.

Daise pushed through the turnstile and threw the soiled gloves on the counter. The boy flicked his eyes up and removed a card from the time ladder.

'Did you find aught on the pile?'

Was he accusing her of something? Would he search her bag and find the contraband book buried underneath her scraps?

She pulled out an assorted handful of string, rags and wires and waved them at the boy.

'That would be a "no" then,' he muttered.

'See ya then,' replied Daise. She slung the potato sack on her back and walked off.

'Hold on, not so fast there.'

Had he spotted the shape of the book at the bottom of the sack? Should she just run? She turned her head slowly and took a step back to the counter.

'You have to sign this.' He passed her a timecard with her name on and a pen attached to a string. She scrawled her name and pushed the card back across the countertop. The boy placed the card in a small metal box and returned to watch his screen.

Daise let out a deep breath and headed off to find Rowan. She walked for ten minutes through a small, wooded area that ran around the edge of the dump until the trees thinned out to a small clearing next to a cliff that overlooked the Trent Sea.

She picked up the rope in loops and threaded it through her legs, across her body and over her shoulder. Imitating the action of rappelling. She felt a burn around her neck. It was clear that this was going to hurt unless she could find something to protect herself. Sorting through the fabric she had collected from the Pile, she found a section of a grubby red T-shirt that was long enough to fashion a short scarf.

She was about to discard the potato sack when the spine of the book she had found knocked against her shin. It was a bit of a squeeze but she managed to shove it into her back pocket.

She looked west up the coast towards the sweeping crescent of Barrowby Beach.

The secluded beach must be close. She continued up the coastal path for a few minutes and tentatively walked to the edge of the cliff. Looking down made her belly flip but she could just make out a small sliver of sand at the shoreline. This was definitely the spot.

The Castoffs

She needed to find something secure to attach the rope to so she could safely lower herself down. Daise smiled, of course, the fence that they had scaled that morning. She could use that monstrous construction to her advantage.

The fence curled round the cliff edge in a barrel of barbed wire to stop people climbing round. She got the rope out of her bag and looped it around the metal post at the bottom of the fence. Giving the rope a good tug to reassure herself that the post was solid she tied the two ends of the rope together and threw the mass of rope over the edge.

The cliff was a series of vertical drops punctuated with a series of ledges. If she lost her grip on the rope there was no way she would be able to stop tumbling to the ground. The rope seemed to have had enough momentum to unravel, but there was no way of knowing whether it was long enough as she couldn't quite see if it had reached the beach.

She wrapped the rope around her leg, brought it up across her body and pulled it over her shoulder and behind her head. The small knots in the ropes made it difficult to slide but with a bit of effort she managed to back out to the edge of the cliff.

Jude and Rey would have bounded down the slope by now, shouting up words of encouragement but she was all alone and perched on the edge of a cliff. For the first time since she had left Tower five, she started to doubt herself.

She called out, 'No!', there was no way she was giving up now. Closing her eyes tightly, she focused on all she had achieved today; thinking about all the effort that had

The Castoffs

gone into finding the rope, the knots she had tied. Biting her top lip, she stepped off the edge of the cliff.

Chapter 7 – Gregor

Gregor walked with purpose towards the Guardian station. 'Come on!', he barked at Tommo and Damon who were dawdling along ten paces behind.

He was unsettled by their encounter with the Castoffs. Seeing Daisy after all those years had distracted him. He knew he would be in trouble for not detaining them. Since the fence went up, they were meant to be cracking down on trespassers.

Gregor, Tommo and Damon were Guardian cadets entrusted with patrolling the streets of Barrowby and reporting any suspicious behaviour back to the station. They had the power to stop and search anyone under the age of seventeen. Since the fence went up, they were given the additional powers to confiscate belongings and detain any child they believed to be acting in a suspicious manner. As a senior cadet, Gregor outranked Tommo and Damon and got to make all the decisions. It also meant that he would be the one that got into trouble if they screwed up.

The Guardian station was a small single-story building at a corner of an intersection that marked the centre of Barrowby. Gregor barged open the shiny black door with his shoulder and waited for Damon and Tommo to catch up. The waiting room was stark; bare white walls on three

The Castoffs

sides lined with wooden benches. On the far wall there was a glass fronted counter next to a solid steel door.

As they walked in, they folded their sandboards and propped them up against the wall. Gregor walked up to the counter and rang the bell. His companions were already slumped on the bench playing slaps.

Gregor drummed his fingers against the counter nervously waiting for one of the Guardians to appear, when a bellow from the back office made him jump. He couldn't quite make out what the voice was saying but he knew it belonged to his father — Cillian Whitmore, the Chief Guardian of Greater Grantham.

Damon took advantage of the distraction to swing his hand in a huge arc.

'Slap,' the sound of Damon's hand connecting with the back of Tommo's hand, echoed around the bare walls of the waiting room.

'Not fair! I wasn't ready,' screeched Tommo, waving his bright red hand. Damon's laughter was brief as Tommo pushed him off the bench. Gregor turned around to find them wrestling on the floor. He bit his tongue in frustration as he tried to separate them.

The heavy clunk of a mortice lock opening stopped the wrestling. Chief Guardian Cillian Whitmore walked in. He was a tall gaunt man with hollow cheeks and sharp features. His salt and pepper goatee beard gave him the look of a wolf. His face was flushed in anger. Gregor took a step back away from his companions.

'What the hell is going on here?' Chief Guardian Whitmore screeched at the boys. Damon and Tommo sprang to their feet and stood to attention.

The Chief reached the boys in two quick strides, 'This

is no way for cadets to behave. I ought to take your badges from you right now.'

He turned to his son, 'And you… you're meant to be responsible for these reprobates!'

Gregor looked down at his shoes.

'What's wrong boy? Has the cat got your tongue?'

Gregor hated it when his dad spoke in clichés but knew better than to argue, 'Sorry dad,' he mumbled.

'What was that?', his dad barked back.

'I said, I'm sorry,' a little more loudly than he had meant to.

Chief Whitmore's eyes were tired and bloodshot as he glared at his son. He looked more disappointed than angry.

'Gregor, I really haven't got time for nonsense. We had a prisoner escape from Ancaster Island and Guardian Fogg found a Castoff boy climbing the fence. I thought you were meant to be patrolling Barrowby.

Gregor felt the blood rush to his ears, as if he had been struck by his father's words. That had to be one of Daisy's friends that he'd let go. He would have to tell his dad everything. The Chief was an experienced interrogator. He would extract the truth from his son. He always did.

'We saw some Castoffs on the beach this morning. I took their stuff off them,' he said waving the bag containing Jude's pen knife and the fire-starting kit.

'You know the protocol. Why didn't you detain them or at least walk them back to the checkpoint?'

The question was left hanging in the air as the Chief grabbed the bag. He had a look inside and pulled out the knife and stuck it in his pocket.

The Castoffs

'Gregor, get yourself back home and stay there! I'll deal with you this evening. And you two, consider yourself lucky to still be wearing the black shirt!'

Noticing the sandboards propped up against the wall, the Chief booted them across the floor.

'Well, what are you waiting for? Pick them up and get out!'

They didn't need to be told twice. The boys scrambled to collect their sandboards and hurried out of the station, the Chief barging past them. They watched the tails of his black jacket bob about in the breeze as he walked towards his car. They waited for the gentle electric hum as he turned the ignition and the soft crunch of wheels on gravel as Chief Whitmore sped off towards the Casthorpe Reset checkpoint.

Damon and Tommo hoisted their sandboards onto their backs and drifted off towards their homes. They grunted, 'laters' at Gregor who had already started wandering up to the Old Rectory, the Chief Guardian's official Barrowby residence. He lived in one of the nicest houses in the village because his dad was one of the most senior officials in town. The house came with the job as the Council had banned private house ownership, redistributing the housing stock to senior politicians and public servants.

Too lazy to remove the key from his pocket, he knocked on the door. It was opened quickly to reveal a young woman dressed in a long, shapeless smock dress. It was their housekeeper, Jessie. She smiled, 'Good afternoon, Master Whitmore how was your morning?'

Gregor dismissed her with a wave of his hand, kicked his shoes off and threw his sandboard up against the wall.

As he headed up to his room, she called up after him, 'Is there anything I can get you?'

'For pity's sake Jessie, can you just leave me alone?', he shouted.

Jessie sighed and muttered, 'I'll just finish the ironing then. if you need...'

Her voice was cut short by the angry slam of Gregor's bedroom door. He sat upright in his bed bouncing a ball against his bedroom wall. He'd been doing this for the last half hour hoping the thud, thud, thud was annoying Jessie. He wanted to be out there searching for the escaped prisoner, not stuck inside.

There was a knock on the door. He threw his ball hard in response. The wooden panel made a sharp bang and Gregor smiled to himself at the sound of Jessie scuttling away like a startled rabbit. When he was sure that she was gone, he opened the door and picked up a lunch tray from the floor. She had left him a plate of cheese and pickle sandwiches and a tall glass of milk.

He bolted down the neatly cut, triangular quarters and gulped the milk down in one swig. He had to hand it to Jessie; she sometimes knew what he wanted before he did.

Putting the tray to one side, he continued bouncing his ball, thinking through the events of the morning. There was something nagging at him.

When they had spotted the Castoffs from the top of the dunes, he had felt there had been more of them.

He'd believed Daisy's story about the mannequin. The ocean was awash with plastic debris; it was a hangover from the consumerist era. Plastic washing up was common enough but a full mannequin, now he thought about it, seemed very unlikely. Even if such a thing fell into the water, it would surely be broken to pieces by the waves.

He tried to remember what he had seen at the top of the dunes as he had tied the Velcro straps on his sandboard.

Could it have been a man diving into the sea? And if it had been a man, could it be the prisoner? Gregor let the ball drop to the floor. He got up off his bed and turned on his GG terminal. An arc of five silver stars appeared on the screen above the GG logo, followed by a pop-up message, 'Access to GG net is limited to essential information workers. Please try again later.'

It looked like the net was locked down while the Council focused resources on finding the escaped prisoner.

He swiped the message away and the terminal began to load up the Channel. His hand hovered over the power button but he paused as he heard the broadcast. It was about the prisoner. There was a reward:

A 100-coin reward will be given for any information that helps lead to the capture of this individual. Please do not approach him as he is infected with a highly contagious virus that makes him unpredictable and dangerous. Contact your local Guardian's office.

The thought of a 100-coin reward strengthened his determination to return to the beach. He reached up to his shelf and pulled down his map of Greater Grantham. If you swam out to sea from Barrowby Beach where

The Castoffs

would you go to be out of sight of prying eyes?

He scanned the Trent Sea on his map. The prisoner had escaped from Ancaster Island... It was around 7 miles. If you were a strong swimmer and caught the tide coming in, it was possible you could wash up on Barrowby Beach.

But if the prisoner swam out to sea after meeting the Castoffs he would have been too tired to go far. He looked at Allington Island, but that would be a tough swim. No it was much more likely that the prisoner had swum a little way up the coast. He peered at the map. There was a tiny little cove just round the head of Barrowby Beach. It was on the other side of the fence but if you were a fugitive that would make sense. That must be where he was hiding.

Gregor looked at his watch. It was 5pm. His dad wouldn't be home until 6pm. There was time to check out the little cove. Could he risk defying him? He had been pretty clear that he was to stay home. But surely even his dad would forgive him if he found the prisoner. This was his chance to prove he wasn't useless.

It was time to decide. Gregor rifled through his wardrobe and changed into his swimming shorts. He packed his waterproof bag with a towel and some fresh clothes and ran down the stairs, taking three steps at a time.

His shoes had been neatly stowed in the rack under the stairs along with his sandboard. Above the shoe rack was his dad's gun cupboard.

The cupboard was locked but knowing his dad, the combination would be something obvious. It couldn't hurt to try.

The Castoffs

He slid the combination lock to 12082052, his dad's birthday. He suppressed a little whoop as the door clicked open, first time, displaying his father's selection of guns. He ignored the shotgun and hunting rifles. They would be too difficult to conceal. On the bottom shelf was an antique Beretta Px4 Storm semi-automatic pistol. He took it off the stand. It felt reassuringly heavy in his hand.

He did the safety check like his dad had taught him. First, eject the magazine. It was empty. He pulled back the slide to check the chamber. The sight of a live round tumbling out of the ejection port took him by surprise. He felt his stomach turn. The gun felt alive in his hands. For a moment, he considered whether he needed ammunition. But if the prisoner was as dangerous as they were saying he might actually need it.

He picked up the live round from the floor, inserted it into the magazine and clicked it firmly back in place. The gun felt different now, as if he had given it life. He took a deep breath and clicked the safety decocker, before placing it in his waterproof rucksack as if he was handling delicate porcelain. Having a gun in his bag made him nervous. A noise startled him. It was just Jessie in the kitchen. He closed the door of the gun cupboard and mixed up the combination lock. When he was happy that everything looked as if he had found it, he slipped on his black mesh waterproof shoes and pushed the cupboard door open.

He heard the thud of wood followed by glass smashing. He pushed the kitchen door open.

'For god's sake Jessie, you clumsy Castoff! Watch what you're doing!'

The Castoffs

Apologising, she dropped to her knees to pick up the tiny shards of glass.

As helpful and compliant as Jessie was, Gregor just didn't trust her. She wasn't Nanny that's for sure. He didn't like to think about the kind lady who had brought him up. She had died of a lung infection two summers ago.

Jessie was only a few years older than Gregor and was a Castoff too, so he certainly wasn't going to listen to anything she had to say. He suspected his dad had employed her to spy on him.

Kicking the tray angrily towards her, he blustered out of the house with as much drama as he could muster. He made sure he gave the door a good slam to be sure she was left in no doubt that he was annoyed at her clumsiness.

The dunes of Barrowby Beach were only a few minutes' walk from the Old Rectory. The sun was low in the sky above Allington Island. He could just see the surface of the rock at the western edge of the beach where he had seen the large figure with the Castoffs.

He tried to put himself in their shoes. If they had found a body, they would have been too scared to call for the Guardians. They wouldn't want to be caught with him either. So of course, they would have encouraged him to swim down the coast. It all made sense.

Gregor snapped his sandboard together, attached the Velcro straps to his shoes and careened down the slope. At the shoreline, he stowed his board and T-shirt into his backpack and dived into the sea. The buoyancy of the backpack made it difficult to swim so he took it off and tucked it under his dominant arm.

Slapping his left arm against the water and kicking his legs furiously he headed up the coast only to discover that his route was blocked by rocks protruding up from the seabed. Gregor swam further out to sea until his legs started to burn. He stopped for a moment, holding on to his backpack to stay afloat. Looking back to shore, he saw the small, sheltered cove that he spotted on the map in his bedroom.

That was it, he felt sure he would find something there. He swam with renewed intensity towards the little beach. He approached the shore tentatively. The idea of an encounter with the prisoner was becoming very real. The beach was only five metres wide and the sand rose sharply to a cave. He opened his bag, towelled himself dry and put on his shoes, T-shirt and hooded top. He was shivering a little but wasn't certain if it was due to the cold or to fear. Pulling the Berretta out of the bag, Gregor slung his backpack over his shoulder and edged up the shore.

Chapter 8 – Cliffhanger

This was not her first experience of rappelling. Last year, one of the porters had rigged up some ropes from the 10th floor of Tower 5 and charged the older kids a coin to abseil down the building.

The setup was basic, essentially a rope hanging out the window of a storage room. What the porter lacked in equipment he made up for in enthusiasm. He spent a good 10 minutes with each kid teaching them the Dülfersitz emergency rappelling technique. He even offered refunds to the kids who became overwhelmed by fear when they stepped out onto the ledge.

Jude, Rey and Daise had spent a coin each getting the hang of it pretty quickly. Rey had then managed to 'borrow' the key to the storage room. While Jude distracted the porter with a complicated question about knots, Rey snuck into the Lodge to lift it off the peg. They had returned in the night by bribing a couple of blackshirt prefects to let them out of the dorm.

It had been a fantastic night. Bouncing off the side of the building made Daise feel like she was a superhero defying gravity. They took turns all night until they were exhausted from running up all the stairs.

They returned the key just before sunrise by sliding it under the Lodge door. Rey, Jude and Daise stayed away on the second day just in case the porter worked out how the key ended up on the floor of the Lodge.

Abseiling became the latest craze. Word got around to the family tower, the queues got longer and the prices went up. It was an accident that put a stop to it. An 11-year-old kid from the family block had fallen; luckily, he had got most of the way down and he only busted his leg. The news wasn't so good for the porter who was taken by the guardians and never returned.

Daise looked down the cliff at her salvaged rope untidily strewn across the steep slope of sharp drops punctuated by grassy ledges. It looked nothing like the sturdy rope they had used to descend the tower. Still she was in no rush. There would be no points for style or speed. Her priority would be just making it down in one piece.

Daise wiped a film of sweat from her forehead and carefully leaned back to take her first step down the cliff edge.

The rope burned as it slipped through her hands. She cursed herself for forgetting gloves. This was going to be a cautious descent if she was going to avoid messing up her hands. She looked up at the rope rubbing at the lip of the cliff. A clod of earth broke off and hit her on the forehead, spraying sand into her eyes. The rope was digging into the soil as she moved down the slope. There's a reason that people wear helmets to do this sort of thing, she thought to herself.

She blinked hard, trying to force the grit out of her eyes. She desperately wanted to wipe her face but she was too scared to take a hand off the ropes. Slowly her vision cleared and she kicked out at the cliff face to try and shift the loose debris. Her stomach turned as clumps of earth smashed apart on the ledge below. She stared up at the deep blue sky for a moment to distract herself from the fear and when she felt her breathing settle, she slowly inched downwards towards the first ledge.

The sheer terrain changed and she was able to stand up straight again on the narrow strip of grass. She gave the rope a good tug to make sure it remained firmly secured to the fence above. It was reassuringly solid.

Looking down at the next section of rope looked a little worn. Pulling it up she saw little bite marks. The rats on the pile must have been gnawing at it.

But there was now turning back now. She took a deep breath and let the damaged rope take her weight. It stretched out as she stepped off the ledge. She gripped it tightly but she could see sections of twisted cords breaking. The remaining fibres stretched out to hold her weight.

She tried to find some footholds on the sandy cliff face to take some of the pressure off the rope but the more she kicked the more she lost control. The rope began to spin. She felt like it was unwinding. It was at least a 15-metre drop. Would she survive the fall? Perhaps? But how badly injured would she be? She would be sure to break some bones or worse, be knocked unconscious. Would she have internal bleeding? Her arms began to shake as white-hot fear spilled into her veins. Beads of sweat prickled on her brow and her heart thumped hard in her chest.

Jude and Rey were right. What was she doing? Why was she risking her life to warn a strange man they had met on the beach? A man who, if the posters were to be believed, was a dangerous criminal. Why hadn't she listened? She was gripping the rope so tightly that she could feel her fingernails cutting into her hands. She was paralysed by fear.

But the rope stopped stretching and the spinning slowed. It seemed as if it was holding her weight. Slowly she opened her eyes and tried not to look down. There was only one way she was going to get down safely, and that was to get control of herself.

She focused on the wall of sandstone directly in front of her. It looked like someone had taken a big bite out of the top of the cliff face, which explained why she couldn't get a foothold. Slowly she began to thread the rope through her hands until she got her footing. Her hands were fully extended, grasping the knot that marked the end of this section of the fabric rope. As she moved her hands down, she felt the disconcerting stretch of the rope dropping her half a metre down, but again it held. The rope felt alive in her hands, expanding as she edged down.

With each movement, she held her breath, waiting for the rope to snap. But she moved down the rope, she began to get more confident, building up a rhythm, albeit a very slow one. When she looked down through her legs, she could see the grassy tufts of some sand dunes that fringed the small beach.

There was one small problem. Daise had overestimated the length of the rope. She could see the frayed end flapping in the breeze, three or four metres short of the ground. Frantically, she tried to think of a solution but there was no way she had the strength to climb back up the rope. The futility of her plan was clear, even if she made it down safely and Rowan was there. How was she going to get home? Fixated as she had become on seeing him again, she hadn't thought through the consequences. The only way back now would be to swim out of the bay to Barrowby Beach. With the high state of alert there were bound to be Guardians patrolling the beach.

Daise's eyes welled up. With both her hands firmly clamped to the rope, she felt the tears spill out and trickle down her face. She wept silently, re-playing the hopelessness of her situation. But her only option was clear; she was going to have to jump. The sand dunes should be relatively soft so perhaps they would cushion the fall. Maybe, just maybe, she wouldn't break anything.

She moved down the rope until it slipped out of her left hand. Reaching up she held the rope in both hands and moved down it rope hand-over-hand until she reached the last section. Her arms ached as she dangled at the end of the rope waiting for the courage to let go.

Closing her eyes, she began a countdown… five, four, three, two…

But before she got to one, a familiar friendly voice said: 'It's OK, I've got you. You can let go.'

She looked down. It was Rowan. He was taller than she remembered and his skin was a darker bottle green rather than pale pistachio. It had a waxy sheen. Despite the strangeness of his appearance, it was clear he was doing much better. His face was beaming in a broad emerald smile.

She returned the smile, exhaled and let herself drop into his arms. He caught her under the arms but her momentum caught him off balance and they tumbled to the ground. Daise felt a little embarrassed to be wrapped in the arms of a stranger and as if sensing her awkwardness, Rowan let her go.

They sat on a broad grassy hill that led down to the small beach. It felt great to be free of the rope and have her legs on solid ground.

'Hello Daise. Nice to see you again.' Rowan offered her his hand. She reached out to shake it. It felt much warmer than this morning and despite the unusual colour it felt very human.

Daise didn't know where to start. She wanted to know so much about him. Where had he come from? Was he sick like they were saying on the posters? But she needed to warn him first.

'The Council there are posters up all over town I had to come to tell you.' said Daise in one breath.

'Slow down Daisy. I didn't catch a word of what you said.'

Daise took a moment to collect herself and then explained all about the wanted poster, the reward, and that the Council were saying he was meant to be sick and dangerous what was going on. This time he understood.

Rowan stroked his chin. He didn't look surprised, just thoughtful. 'What are they saying I have done?'

Daise was a little confused by the question. After all the posters hadn't said anything about his crimes.

'They just said you are an escaped prisoner. That you are sick and dangerous.'

'Yet, you have taken a big risk to warn me,' he replied.

Daise felt a little worried. Had she made the right choice in coming to find him?

He paused for a moment and continued, 'It is just, I

didn't expect people to be so friendly. I've been on Ancaster Island a long time.'

Rowan looked pensive. 'I don't want to put you to any trouble, Daise, I really don't, but I need to find Mrs Arkwright. I was told she would be able to help me.'

'How do you know Mrs Arkwright?' Daise demanded, surprised that he knew the nice woman from the food market. He could hardly have sauntered up to her stall without getting noticed.

'I mean, I'm just surprised,' she said more softly. 'Have you been to Greater Grantham before?'

'It's been a long time Daisy but yes, I've been here before. Although it all looks very different. If you can imagine, this vast expanse of water was fields of rapeseed and wheat.'

There was something deeply mournful in his emerald eyes as he recalled the time before the flood. He turned his back to the sea and changed the subject, 'I've not met Alice Arkwright in person but we've been in correspondence.'

Daise realised that Rowan seemed much more focussed. 'You've got your memory back.'

'Oh yes, an afternoon in the sunshine has done me a world of good. I know what I am here to do.'

There was an intensity in the way he was speaking. His eyes were determined, unblinking. Daise tried to wait for him to finish but impatience got the better of her.

'What's that then?'

'I need to set the green people free from the Ancaster Gulag.'

Ancaster was a small village to the east. It was the gateway to a chain of islands that were once the old

The Castoffs

English counties of Lincolnshire and East Yorkshire.

You could see Ancaster Island from the beach. As far as she knew it was an agricultural island. It was also home to Cranwell Airport. Daise had never heard of a gulag.

She felt a bit stupid asking but she wanted to know all about Rowan and his people. They sat on a sandy part of the dune while Rowan explained that there were 10,000 green people being held as prisoners on the farms of Ancaster Island. They were forced to work the fields for the Council.

It sounded horrible. But before she could find out more, she looked up to see a figure pointing a gun at them.

Daise's body stiffened. It was Gregor. How had he found them?

Rowan leapt up and took a step towards him.

Gregor responded with a screech, 'Don't come any closer or I'll shoot!'

The Beretta shook in his hands as he aimed it at Rowan.

Daise opened her mouth to speak, but her words wouldn't come out.

'Put your hands up, both of you', shouted Gregor, trying his best to sound authoritative.

Daise threw her hands in the air and swallowed hard. Her initial rush of fear was replaced with anger. 'For God's sake Gregor, what is your problem?'

Gregor swung the gun around to point at Daise, 'You. You are the problem Daise. You are in so much trouble. You had a chance to tell me about the prisoner this morning but you lied. It could have been so much simpler if you had only told me the truth.'

The Castoffs

He continued, 'I thought we were friends, it's why I let you off this morning.' He edged closer, keeping his pistol firmly pointed in her direction.

Daise was really cross now. She knew she shouldn't antagonise him, but she couldn't help herself. 'I am sorry, did you say let us off?,' she said sarcastically. 'You assaulted my friends, destroyed our buckets and stole our stuff!'

Gregor was getting closer and closer to Daisy. His expression was strange and vacant and she could tell that he wasn't really listening.

His monologue continued, 'I thought you were different but I can see now that I was wrong. I can see why they closed down your schools, no point wasting taxpayer's money if they're all as stupid as you. Do you not see what I am holding in my hand?' he said, waving the gun around recklessly. His voice had become high pitched and squeaky.

Rowan edged towards Daise, until Gregor swung the gun back in his direction. Rowan's voice was slow, calm and deliberate. 'Look son, take it easy, nobody is going to hurt you.'

Gregor laughed. 'Oh, that's funny! You think you can hurt me.' He took the safety catch off the gun. 'Do you even know what this is, you freak?'

'Yes, it's a gun, but you're not going to use it.' Rowan said as he took another step towards Gregor.

Gregor took a step back. He screamed at Rowan, 'If you don't back off now, I will shoot you. Don't think that I won't. You're wanted by the police. No one is going to care if I shoot out your leg or something.' He took aim at Rowan's leg.

The Castoffs

'Gregor, you have no idea what's going on here. Why don't you just go home,' said Daise.

But before anyone could say anything else, the gun went off. A vicious crack echoed against the cliff face. There was a silent pause and then the soft thud of a body hitting dry sand.

Chapter 9 – Alice

The Rec was located in the basement of Tower 5. It was a large grey cavern of a room, with breeze block walls. The space was broken up by the nine pillars that held the tower up. A large chalkboard covered the wall at the foot of the stairs to log reservations for different sections of the Rec. Jude picked up a piece of chalk and scrawled their names in a box. Each slot was thirty minutes.

Rey had been forced to choose between his friends. Like Jude, he didn't want to get into any more trouble but at the same time he agreed with Daise that Rowan was a decent guy. He didn't believe all the stuff the Council was saying on the wanted poster. And he was curious about Rowan. Who — or what — was he and what did he want?. Rey knew that if Jude hadn't got so upset, he would have helped Daise.

They normally started with fifty push-ups but Jude could only manage five before he was overcome by the pain in his hands. He moved on to do fifty sit ups. They both lay flat on their backs exhausted by the end of the session.

Rey hoped that the workout had given Jude a bit of time to calm down. Perhaps he might reconsider helping Daise.

'Jude?', he left a pause, trying to judge his friend's

The Castoffs

mood.

'Yes Rey'. Jude sighed in anticipation of an awkward conversation.

'You're still friends with Daise, aren't you?'

Jude let out another deep breath. 'Of course, I am. I just could do without getting into more trouble today.'

He held up his injured hands to reinforce his point.

'Don't you want to know more about Rowan? Daise was talking about a book her dad used to read to her when she was little. It was about green mice, I think, but she was convinced it had some sort of hidden meaning. That it was really about green people, like Rowan.'

'There are plenty of made-up stories about little green men. It's a bit of a leap to think some old story is connected to what we saw on the beach. And it's not exactly convincing enough to risk getting detained.'

'I get it Jude, I really do. You've had enough drama for one day. It's just well, I feel bad for leaving Daise on her own. What if we took a trip to the market? That wouldn't be dangerous. We could talk to Mrs Arkwright. She's got loads of books and she might know about the green mice story. It would be a good way to make peace with Daise. It wouldn't hurt to ask.'

'I don't know,' said Jude, rubbing his cropped hair.

Rey removed his battered left shoe and pulled back a piece of duct tape to reveal a shiny silver coin. He hopped around waving the coin in front of his friend's face.

'I'll treat you to a bowl of Mrs A's seafood soup,' he continued. His face plastered with a broad grin.

'I guess that would be OK,' replied Jude, a little begrudgingly, before he began to laugh again, 'If you can just stop it with the hopping. You're bringing shame to the floor 5 boys.'

'Whatever you say boss.'

Rey led the way to the exit, but Jude stopped in the hallway. 'What's up?' asked Rey.

'Are you not going to have a wash?

'We're going to ask her about a book, not ask her out on a date.'

'Fair point,' replied Jude and they left the tower laughing.

They walked past the row of wanted posters slapped over the side of the tower. And like Daise had done earlier, Rey ripped one off the wall and stuffed it in his pocket.

Most of the market was starting to clear out, but the central area of stalls stayed open later as many of the traders came to eat after packing up.

Mrs Arkwright ran a bookshop and cafe. Her stall was a ramshackle assortment of uneven trestle tables packed around a rusty old van. The tables were full of small wooden bookcases which were protected from the sun by two large sun-bleached grey awnings.

Inside the van, Mrs Arkwright made a huge vat of seafood soup every morning. She sold it for a coin a bowl, which meant even the kids from the towers could afford to treat themselves from time to time. She would also take books as payment for soup, which allowed some of the children who worked the Pile an easy way to feed themselves. It also meant that Mrs Arkwright got a steady stream of salvage.

Mostly the stall sold escapist fiction. Stories set in different worlds or different times. There was a small section of non-fiction housed in a woodworm riddled oak shelf. Over the years, her selection of non-fiction books had been whittled away as the list of banned books grew bigger. Most of the history and science books were forbidden as they did not fit with the Council's narrative. It was mainly books about space and physics that remained. It would seem that their control didn't quite stretch to the working of the universe, just the activity of human beings within it. Concepts such as evolution or climate change were erased, along with any sense of human history. Old maps that held hidden secrets of what the world looked like before the flood were also banned. The Council called this purge the Fresh Start. Their idea was that the sum knowledge of human beings had led them to destruction, discord and death. They argued that human beings needed to be reborn to forge a new world. The idea of a 'Fresh Start' seemed very appealing to the many people suffering in the aftermath of the flood and the civil unrest that followed.

Despite the market closing it was busy with children hoping to get leftovers from the food stalls. When they were younger, Jude and Rey used to come here to beg for scraps, which stallholders would always give to the younger children. The generosity ended when you reached about eight. Some older kids still came along to steal food from the younger children. Some teenagers even organised the kids into gangs of beggars, offering them protection from the thieves, for a price off course.

Arkwright's was bustling with market traders looking to get a bowl of hot soup before they headed home and there was a small group of young kids hoping to get some leftover soup.

The Castoffs

Mrs Arkwright was a tall woman in her late fifties. Her hair was long and wavy; a choppy mixture of auburn with bright white streaks.

She was busy dishing out bowls of piping hot soup to her customers. The boys joined the queue, and Jude ordered two bowls. A warm smile stretched across Mrs Arkwright's freckled face as she served them. The heat from the soup made her skin glow and made her translucent plastic-framed glasses slide down her small delicate nose.

Mrs Arkwright took the coins and looked at the crowd of young children who had formed a long queue a few meters back from the serving hatch.

'It looks like you're my last paying customers,' said Mrs Arkwright as she beckoned to the line of ravenous kids.

Rey and Jude sat down on a picnic bench and noisily slurped down their soup. The soup warmed their bellies and fat grains of barley melted in their mouths.

It was going to be a little while before she had finished serving the leftover soup so the boys returned their bowls and began to browse the books as they waited to talk to Mrs Arkwright.

Rey wasn't a great reader. With over a hundred kids in each class, it was easy to fall behind if you were a little slower to pick things up. Ironically, his reading had come on more in the past year, since the Casthorpe School was closed. Daise, who had been top of all the classes, had been giving him and Jude lessons.

Rey traced his index finger down the spines of the books, mouthing the titles softly to himself. Occasionally he picked up something that sounded interesting and

The Castoffs

read the description on the back. He picked up the 'Immorality Engine' by George Mann thinking it would be about trains but it turned out to be a Victorian detective story.

'Is there a particular book you are looking for,' said Mrs Arkwright as she stepped out of her trailer to pull down the shutter to close the serving hatch.

Her thin black polo neck sweater, soft blue jeans and thick heeled cowboy boots made her look tall, authoritative yet approachable.

'Yes, we want to know about a book that our friend recommended', said Jude.

'I tell you what boys, you help me clear up the books and perhaps we could have a little chat over tea. I think I have a nice piece of carrot cake that needs to be eaten today.

'That sounds great', replied Rey, his eyes lighting up at the word 'cake'. 'But if we pack away all the books, how will we find what we are after?'

'I assume the book you are after is an important book?'

Rey and Jude both nodded.

'Well then, it's not likely to be on my stall,' she said, winking at the boys.

The boys helped her collect up all the books, section by section into packing boxes. They stacked the boxes and bookcases in a small storage shed built onto the side of the van.

It wasn't long before Jude began to struggle; his injured hands began to bleed again as the weight of the boxes cut into them.

Mrs Arkwright appeared with a bowl of water and a

The Castoffs

first aid kit.

'You really, need to keep these clean. Do they not teach you about the dangers of infection?' she chided before stopping for a second, 'though, of course, you can't learn since they closed all the Reset schools.'

She continued, 'When I was a girl, we used to have antibiotics that would clear up an infection in a few days. But you need to be more careful nowadays.'

She beckoned him to an empty picnic table. He winced as Mrs Arkwright gently washed his hands in the warm water and patted them dry with a cloth. She removed a bottle of iodine and some cotton wool from her first aid kit.

'I'm afraid this is going to hurt a little,' she warned Jude as she dabbed the bright yellow liquid into his lacerated palms. Jude gritted his teeth and tried to hide the pain but was betrayed by a single tear that rolled down his face. Mrs Arkwright gently wiped it away and wrapped his hands in clean bandage.

'Now, I think I've got a little bit of the Patcher's Phage Broth somewhere. That should help fight off any nasties lurking in those wounds.'

She rummaged around in her first aid bag and pulled out a clear thick glass bottle. Labelled 'Patcher's Phage Broth #3' in spidery handwriting, the bottle contained 100 ml of clear straw-coloured liquid. She squeezed the red rubber balloon pipette and removed it from the bottle.

'Open wide,' she said, smiling at Jude.

There was something about the way Mrs Arkwright smiled that put Jude at ease. He did as she asked and she squirted the pipette of broth into his mouth.

The Castoffs

'All done,' she said, giving his arm an affectionate pat.

Jude fought back the urge to cry. He felt silly but her kindness made him think for a moment that this must be what it's like to have a mother.

'Where do you want these trestles?' Rey butted in.

'Just stack them on top of the book crates,' Mrs Arkwright replied.

Rey did as he was asked and Mrs Arkwright locked the shed. A silence had fallen over the flea market, the customers made the way to the exits and traders had all packed up for the day.

'Now then boys, come with me and we'll find that cake, shall we?'

She opened the door to the van and disappeared inside.

Rey and Jude stood outside, unsure whether to follow. Jude asked Rey, 'Do you think this is a good idea. This seems a little weird.'

Rey looked serious for a second and then grinned. 'Jude, did you not hear her — she offered us cake?

Jude smiled, muttering, 'Fair point Rey, fair point', as they followed Mrs Arkwright into her van.

It seemed much bigger on the inside than it appeared on the outside. The van was her kitchen. It was decked out with shiny metal work tops and was immaculately clean. To the left was a cooker with a single large gas hob, which she used to make her soup. Along the back wall was a row of cupboards and a boiler with a single tap for dispensing boiled water.

Mrs Arkwright was at the worktop, putting a couple of pieces of cake on to two small plates. 'Would you like a cup of tea boys?'

The boys nodded in unison. She put three cups of tea on a tray with the cake, walked through a door and down a couple of stairs. The boys followed her.

It felt as though they had stepped into a forest. They stepped into a room that was roughly square in shape. It was built out of a shipping container but the harsh metallic box was disguised with soft furnishings and it actually seemed quite homely. The floor was lined with rich oak floorboards and an intricately woven Turkish rug in a lush crimson. The walls were draped in exquisitely patterned fabrics. Deep lush greens, blended into vivid sky blues patterned with intricate Celtic rope designs.

Mrs Arkwright placed the tray on to a small coffee table and invited the boys to sit down on a battered brown leather sofa.

Sinking into the sofa, the boys started on the cake. It was a rich carrot and courgette creation, with thick frosting. The boys savoured the powerful blast of sweetness.

Mrs Arkwright settled into her armchair with a cup of tea, 'you're Daise's friends, aren't you?', she said.

Jude started to cough as a bit of cake caught in his windpipe.

'I'm sorry, take a sip of tea.'

Rey felt a little jolt of fear run through him. He was normally really cautious around grown-ups. Remember Hansel and Gretel. Was Mrs Arkwright just a kind lady or did she want something from them? What did they really know about her after all? He felt a long way from the towers. Part of him wanted to run but the cake was good, the sofa was comfy and most importantly he wanted to find out more about this book.

In that moment, with Jude coughing crumbs of cake on the table, he decided to take a chance and trust her.

'Yes, we're Daise's friends.' He replied trying his best to sound confident. He reached into his pocket and unfolded the poster of Rowan.

'See this man, well we've met him in real life except he's got green skin you know like the Incredible Hulk but without all the muscles. He's not angry or anything. He's just like this tall chilled out guy but his skin is green. Anyway, Daise told me that her dad read her a book about green mice. She said it was an allegory. You know, like a story with a deeper meaning. She couldn't remember the details. But I thought, well, you might know something about it, what with you being a book expert.'

Mrs Arkwright picked up the poster, copies of which had been posted up around the market.

'So, am I to understand that you are not after the reward money.'

'No!' said Rey indignantly, 'That's not why we're here.'

Jude looked alarmed. He leaned forward and whispered in Rey's ear, 'How do we know we can trust her?'

Mrs Arkwright stood up, 'You're right, but if you want to know more, you'll have to take a leap of faith. But before you make your decision. I'll tell you one thing, your friend Daise is no ordinary girl. If she is important to you, you're going to want to know what I have to say.'

'But take a minute, finish your tea and cake.' With that she stood up and disappeared behind an emerald velvet curtain that was drawn across the back of the room.

Chapter 10 – Blood

Gregor dropped the gun as if it was contaminated. He began to shake. What had he done? He couldn't hear what the green thing was saying, deafened by the reverberating crack of the gunshot.

Daisy lay flat on her back clutching her left arm. He could see blood seeping from her upper arm into the fine white sand. Gregor wanted to go to her but he couldn't move. It was as if he was watching the scene unfold from outside his body.

Slowly the noise in his head sharpened in pitch as if he was surfacing from a deep pool of water.

It took him a moment to recognise the screaming noise. He couldn't quite tell if it was inside his head or coming from the outside. He fell to his knees and watched as the green man went to Daise.

She was bleeding from her left arm, that was good, Gregor thought. He hadn't killed her. You didn't die from an arm wound. But what if he'd clipped an artery? She could bleed to death. He started to rock backwards and forwards, clutching his head to drive out the dark thoughts.

'Boy! Listen to me. This is important.'

He became aware of somebody shouting at him and then a hand on his shoulder. The emerald green monster

The Castoffs

was touching him. He opened his eyes and recoiled in disgust.

'Get your filthy hands off me', Gregor spat as he scrambled backwards on the sand like a demented crab. What if he had been infected? He looked at the tall bare-chested figure whose deep green torso shone in the late summer sun.

Then he looked at Daisy. The green man had ripped a strip of orange material from his shorts to make a tourniquet. She was sitting up, her face looked pale. Gregor wanted to go to her and apologise. He hadn't meant to shoot her. He was adjusting his aim when it just went off.

The green man looked angry as he hurled the gun into the ocean.

There was no way round this. The Chief was going to find out that he had stolen his gun and shot someone. He could be kicked out of the Cadets; worse, he could be sent to live in one of the Resets. He thought for a moment what it would be like to live in one of those ugly towers. His dad wouldn't let that happen? Or would he?

Gregor couldn't be sure, and emotions began to boil, threatening to overwhelm him. Get your shit together he said to himself.

The green man was now standing in front of him. He was big, at least 6 ft 5 inches. He lowered himself on to one knee, so he could look Gregor in the eye.

'My name is Rowan. I am going to assume that you did not mean to shoot Daisy, is that right?'

Gregor didn't know what to say. He didn't want to speak to this creature. He didn't want him so close.

'Look, I don't know you, but we are going to have to

work together to resolve this situation. This is how I see it. Daisy's been shot and she has lost a lot of blood. She needs to see a doctor. I need your help to get her to a hospital.'

Gregor ran to Daisy, across sand that was starting to turn scarlet. He tried to apologise but she stared right through him as if he was made of cellophane.

'She's in shock.' said Rowan. 'I need your help if you want her to be OK. Do you hear me?'

If Gregor had heard him, he did nothing to acknowledge it. Rowan slapped him hard around the face.

He looked away from Daisy and focussed on the green man. His face burned with a mix of pain and anger. That filthy thing had touched him. He clutched his cheek and pulled it away quickly at the thought of being infected. He rubbed his hands against his shorts and looked into Rowan's dark green eyes.

'There's a hospital on Low Road in Barrowby. It's not far but how are we going to get her off the beach.'

'You leave that to me…' replied Rowan 'What's your name?'.

Gregor was conflicted. This Rowan person, if indeed he was a person, had just hit him. But he was right, they were going to have to work together if he was going to get Daisy to safety. He didn't want to be accused of murder. He also wanted to be seen by a doctor to make sure he wasn't infected.

A plan started to form in his head. Rowan was a criminal. The truth didn't have to come out. There was another version of events. What if he said that Rowan overpowered him, took his gun and shot Daisy. That seemed like a plausible story. He was a Guardian cadet after all. His dad was Chief Guardian. Who were they going to believe? He would still be in trouble for taking his dad's gun but if he captured the prisoner surely his dad would be pleased.

'Gregor, my name is Gregor,' he said as calmly as he could manage.

'Ok Gregor, we're going back into the sea. I want you in front of me where I can see you.'

Gregor struggled to take off his clothes as they stuck to his sticky salty skin. He packed them back into his waterproof bag and hurled it into the sea. The water was colder than he remembered. He swam out to his bag and hung onto it waiting for Rowan to follow him.

Rowan scooped up Daise in his long green arms and carried her to the shoreline. There was something really graceful about the way he moved. He walked out into the ocean holding Daise tightly across his chest. Gregor heard her murmur as a small wave splashed up at her. She looked to be drifting out of consciousness.

'Throw me your bag,' instructed Rowan over the gently rolling waves. Gregor was indignant. What right did this criminal have to order him around? He was the only son of the Chief Guardian of Greater Grantham. Using his bag as a float he swam out deeper towards the rocky outcrop, looking back over his shoulder at Rowan.

Rowan repeated himself, his volume increased but his tone still calm and measured, 'Throw me your bag. Now. I need it to keep Daise safe. Do you want to have this girl's death on your hands?'

Gregor felt a sharp pain in his stomach. He guessed that was what guilt felt like. He was responsible for hurting Daisy but the green man was exaggerating, wasn't he? You didn't die from being shot in the arm, did you? He looked across the beach. The large patch of bloodstained sand filled him with dread. What if she was losing too much blood? You could die from that. He threw the orange waterproof bag at the green man, trying not to hit Daisy.

The bag landed with a gentle splash. Rowan tucked it under his arm helping him cradle Daise's head out of the water and keep her injured arm draped across her chest. Lying back in the water he was able to propel himself backwards out past the rocky outcrop and round onto Barrowby Beach.

Gregor continued swimming to the shore and when the water was shallow enough for him to stand up, he walked up through the surf to the beach where he waited for the green man to propel Daisy to the shore.

Gregor watched as Rowan carried her through the surf. Her hair clip had washed out in the sea leaving her fringe plastered across her face. He could see a trail of blood drifting out from her left arm like a bloody oil slick.

Rowan walked up the beach a little and lay Daisy on the warm soft sand in roughly the same spot he had lain that morning. She was shaking with cold.

'Give me your clothes,' he said.

Gregor fished his bag out of the shallow water and pulled a faded blue hoodie and towel out his bag. Rowan patted Daise gently with the towel and wrapped her in the hoodie. Gregor retrieved his sandy, blood-stained towel and stuffed it in his bag.

It was getting late. The sun was starting to fall behind the Casthorpe Hill, releasing a broad palette of warm orange to deep scarlet. The air was cooler too. Gregor rubbed the goose bumps on his arms and put on his dry T-shirt. The steep face of the sand dunes looked intimidating in the fading light.

While gathering up his things, Gregor spotted a piece of driftwood long enough for him to use as a walking pole. The ocean had stripped the bark from the birch branch, leaving it smooth sandy colour.

A thicker section at one end formed a natural handle. Gregor bounced it into his palm. It felt reassuringly solid.

'Come on, let's get going,' said Gregor.

Rowan nodded solemnly, picked up Daise and followed him up the steep face of Barrowby Dune. Climbing the slope was tough going even with the wooden stick for support, and it wasn't long before Gregor was lagging behind.

There was something effortless about the way the green man bounded up to the top.

Gregor was thinking hard. While his priority was to get Daisy to a doctor, he also was plotting how he was going to capture the prisoner. Could he just walk them to the Guardians office? Would the green man sacrifice his freedom to ensure that Daisy lived? Gregor started to wonder if people might actually believe his version of events. There was something very reasonable about him. The way he spoke was confident, authoritative and measured.

Letting him speak would be a risk. But how was he going to stop him? Without the gun there was no way he could overpower him. He was almost a foot taller than him. He looked up to the brow of the dune and saw Rowan waiting. He took a deep breath, ignored his

The Castoffs

burning leg muscles and made his way to the summit.

Gregor stared up the street. There didn't seem to be anyone about. He approached Rowan. 'The quickest way to get Daisy to a doctor is going to be to take her to the Guardian station.'

Rowan frowned. 'I've spent the day avoiding Guardians. I thought you said there was a hospital nearby.'

Gregor tried to create a sense of urgency, 'But look at her, she needs to see a doctor as soon as possible. The Guardians will put her in a car and take her straight to the hospital.'

Rowan adjusted his grip on Daise. She murmured weakly.

'Your plan is flawed. If we turn up to a police station with a girl with a gunshot wound, we will both be detained. If we take her to a hospital, we will both be able to escape.'

Gregor had underestimated the green man. He clearly knew he was in danger. Daisy must have warned him that he was a wanted man. But it was also clear that he didn't know Gregor was a Guardian cadet.

'OK, we can go straight to the hospital,' said Gregor.

Gregor looked into Rowan's eyes, desperate to appear trustworthy. He had no intention of walking into the hospital and letting him get away.

'It's left at the end of Church Street.' He added, waiting nervously for Rowan to make his next move.

'Up there!' he continued, waving his arms up the road past Barrowby Church. Rowan stared at Gregor for what seemed like an age. It felt like he was trying to look into his soul. Gregor stood in silence waiting for Rowan to turn his back and make his way up the road.

Rowan turned his head and took a step toward the sandy tarmac. But before he could take a second step Gregor threw his makeshift walking stick in the air, caught it at the base and swung the wooden pole at the back of Rowan's skull.

Rowan fell to the ground like a felled tree. Daisy screamed as she tumbled out of his arms onto the unforgiving tarmac. Rowan lay in silence as a pool of thick green liquid pooled around his head.

Gregor wasted no time. He got on his hands and knees and started to roll Rowan's body away from the road. It was difficult at first but as he shoved Rowan over the edge of the dunes, he started to roll, slowly at first. Then Gregor watched as the limp body of the green man tumbled down the hill. The body gained momentum quickly. Each rotation became rougher, limbs bouncing higher and crashing down harder. The thudding noises made him feel queasy.

Just a few steps away, Daisy was beginning to groan. Was she returning to consciousness? For his plan to work he needed Daisy to be silent. If she started saying that she had been shot by Gregor his plan could fall apart. He considered hitting her with his stick. But he was worried that he might kill her.

He walked across to her; her eyes were still closing and her groaning had turned into a low whimpering. Gregor struggled to pick her up. She was much heavier than she looked. He balanced for a moment with Daisy resting on his thighs before using all his energy to stand up.

He made slow progress carrying Daisy towards the

The Castoffs

hospital, needing to stop and rest every few steps. At one point he had to lay her flat on the stone wall to catch his breath. The 10-storey Greenacres Hospital served the wealthy inhabitants of Barrowby and the western edge of Greater Grantham. Gregor wasn't entirely sure they would treat Daisy, but he hoped that as son of the Chief, he could convince them to admit her.

As he approached the ambulance bay he began to shout, 'Help me, help me.'

Two women dressed in black scrubs ran towards him. 'My friend, she's been shot by the escaped prisoner, please help her.'

'It's Gregor isn't it' said the larger of the two women as she took Daisy from his arms and placed her on a wheeled stretcher.

'Yes,' replied Gregor, overjoyed that the doctor had recognised him. 'You'll look after her, won't you?'

The doctor held his hand reassuringly, 'Of course we will, Gregor. What's her name?

'Her name is Daisy, Daisy Woods,' and with that he turned to leave.

'You can wait over there,' said the doctor pointing towards a row of comfortable armchairs.

'I've got to get my dad. I won't be long,' said Gregor and with that he ran off in the direction of the Guardians office, smiling to himself all the way. This was going to work out perfectly.

Chapter 11 – Dread

The operating theatre was busy with the crashing, metallic symphony of drawers slamming; instruments clanged into shiny sterile bowls as the medical team prepared to remove the bullet from Daise's arm. It was the disinfectant that brought her back to consciousness. The noxious chemical smell nipped at her nostrils. She opened her eyes to the further assault of the theatre lights burning her eyes.

She blinked away a thick and greasy film of tears, frantically trying to get her vision to adjust to the brightness of the room; desperate to get an understanding of what was happening to her. Masked figures loomed over her. Dressed in black scrubs, they all wore matching hats covering their hair. Their eyes were obscured by bulbous goggles. They looked like giant fly-people poised to devour her.

'Let's give her one unit of O Negative, before we start', said the largest of the fly-people. He had slug-like grey eyebrows peeking over the top of his goggles. His baritone burr buzzed in her brain making her temples throb.

Shuffling noises came from the back of the room, then a man appeared holding a blood bag that he hung on a stand next to Daise.

The Castoffs

She felt a pin prick in her arm and was overcome with the feeling that something bad was going to happen. This was the end; she was going to die. She tried to speak but her throat was too dry. All that came out was a croak.

Another fly-person came into view. He was standing behind her; a tall skinny man with hollow cheeks. He hovered over her with a black rubber mask. He was poised to put her to sleep. She tried to push it away with her good arm but she was so weak she could barely raise it off the bed. The cold rubber pushed up against her face forming a seal. She felt these were her final moments. Her eyes began to feel heavy.

But before she lost consciousness, the slug-browed man leaned in and said, 'Wait, she looks like she is trying to say something.'

The mask was taken from her face and the fly-people leaned in waiting for her to speak.

'Something bad is happening, really bad,' she whispered.

The hollow-cheeked man drummed his fingers impatiently, 'Let's get on with this operation. I've got a dinner reservation at the new seafood place that's opened up on the pier.'

A third fly-person spoke. Female. A warm Scottish accent. 'Her blood pressure is dropping, something's not right here.'

Slug-brow held his hand up, 'Wait,' he said with absolute authority. He focused on a machine behind her head. All the fly-people stopped and gazed at the green flashing numbers on the screen. The room was silent except for a steady beeping. They waited for his instruction.

The silence was broken by an alarm. 'Shit,' he growled, 'She's having an incompatibility reaction! Give her oxygen.'

The blood bag was quickly replaced with a clear bag of liquid. The black rubber mask was pressed up against her face again. A blood sample was taken. The footsteps and buzz of activity compounded her sense of impending doom. What had they done to her?

Daise found it difficult to breathe. Air from the oxygen seemed thin and insubstantial. Her skin felt hot and her mouth dry.

'She's still bleeding from this bullet wound. Give a unit of FFP and let's get this bullet out,' said Slugbrow before crouching down to Daise. 'This is going to really hurt.'

Daise felt a pair of hands pinning her to the bed. She tried to struggle but they held her firm. She could see beady little grey eyes behind the glasses of the tall hollow-cheeked man. He seemed to be enjoying this. For a moment everything was still, then Slugbrow barked, 'Ten blade'. Daise felt a piercing flash of pain as he sliced into her arm and then it went dark.

**

Daise stared up at the ceiling. It seemed too far away. It gave her a sick feeling deep within her belly like she was going to fall. It took her a moment to realise that she was in a hospital bed, not safely enclosed in her own sleeping pod.

The room was so bright it seemed to go on forever. It was pristine; white walls, white floor, white ceiling. It hurt her eyes to look. It didn't seem real. Where was this place? She began to wonder if she had survived the operation.

As her eyes began to adjust, Daise decided she was lying in a private room in a hospital. Her left arm was bandaged up. She seemed to be attached to a drip and a big monitor that kept beeping. That was good, she thought to herself. Beeping means I'm still alive.

With some difficulty, she managed to push herself up the bed with her good arm and sit up. Everything looked so clean. Even the cushions on the armchair sat in the corner of the room were shiny and white. There were no windows, just a white door with small glass panels, which would have been indistinguishable from the walls if not for a faint glossy sheen. She tried to push herself up a little higher to see out. But she couldn't make out anything beyond the expanse of white ceiling tiles that continued on the other side of the door. To her left there was a door to a small bathroom. She opened the door to reveal a toilet, sink and compact shower cubicle.

The last thing she remembered was the operating theatre and her belief that she was about to die. But here she was, lying in a swanky hospital bed. There was no hospital in Casthorpe, so she figured she must be in Greenacres or Grantham General. She scanned the room for clues. Her pillowcase had a small green farm printed on the bottom left — Greenacres it was then, which meant she was still in Barrowby.

She glanced at her arm and the painful memory of Gregor appearing on the beach returned. That stupid boy had shot her. She remembered the searing pain as the bullet ripped through her flesh and the warm blood as it trickled down her arm before dripping off her fingertips onto the sand. Then nothing until the operating room. She took a deep breath to counter the panic that rose up from the pit of her stomach. She had been so sure she was going to die.

A small bean-shaped patch of blood was seeping through the heavy bandaging just below her left shoulder. Her right hand was attached to a thin tube dispensing a clear liquid into her blood. A sensor attached to her chest hooked her up to some machine that was measuring her vital signs.

She began connecting the dots. If Rowan had brought her in, he must have been detained. Why hadn't they taken her back to the reset and left her with the Patcher? Why were they giving her top-notch health care? She was a Castoff, she wouldn't be able to pay for this.

Taking care not to get herself tangled up in the cables, Daise swung her legs off the side of the bed and tried to stand. The movement triggered a biting pain in her arm and dull throbbing in her temple. She had to reach out for the mattress with her good hand as she became lightheaded. A punch of nausea hit her in her guts. She clenched her fists to keep herself from slipping out of consciousness, she leaned into the mattress for support and slowly the dizziness began to pass.

It took a minute for her body to adjust to standing. She waited calmly for the nausea to subside. When she was ready to move, she took it slowly; transferring her weight from the mattress to the drip stand. She was attached to a drip bag by a thin tube which had been inserted into a vein on the back of her good hand.

Moving in shuffling steps she was able to push the

drip stand with her away from the bed. But after only a couple of steps, the wire that was taped to her began to tug at her chest. She peeled the sticker off but as the contact with her skin was broken a persistent loud beeping alarm sounded followed by the slapping of footsteps on lino outside the door. Her chest tightened with fear as she stuck the sensor back on her skin and scrambled into the bed. She clamped her eyes shut in a desperate attempt to feign sleep; listening to every sound as the door brushed opened and two people entered.

'The bloody machine's on the blink again', said one of the hospital workers, a man with a deep nasal monotone.

The second hospital worker approached the machine by her bedside. She heard the clicking of buttons as the machine was reset.

'The sensor connection has been broken', said the second hospital worker. Daise recognised the woman's Scottish accent from the operating theatre.

She had spoken up for Daise, perhaps even saved her life. But just as Daise started to relax, a hand reached into her gown. She couldn't help but flinch but she managed to keep her eyes firmly shut. The fingers were cold but soft. They gently smoothed down the sticker sensor on her chest. Daise let out a sleepy groan and rolled over in an attempt to convince them she was asleep.

She heard a rasping scratch along the metal bed frame as the man approached the end of the bed and picked up a clipboard.

'A gunshot wound, we don't see many of those in the Barrowby,' said the nasal man. He paused a little longer as he read her notes, 'and a blood compatibility reaction. She has been in the wars.'

The Castoffs

Daise didn't know what that meant but it sounded bad.

'It was the strangest thing. I was convinced there had been a screw up and someone had given her the wrong type. But the bag said O Negative,' explained the Scottish woman. Daise heard footsteps as she walked across the room to join her colleague.

'But no one should react to that,' said the man.

'That's just it. We've no idea why she reacted. We're doing some tests with the blood bag to see if it had been tampered with.

'That's frightening. Do you really think someone has been messing with the blood bags then? I guess all you would need to do is swap the stickers over.'

'Well, it's either that or there is something really strange about this girl's blood.'

Daise listened intently. She didn't feel safe. If someone was messing with blood bags, were they trying to kill her? Was it Gregor, trying to finish what he'd started?

'She seems stable now, we'll know more in an hour when we get the results of the blood tests back from the lab,' said the Scottish woman.

And with that, the clipboard was replaced on the bed stand and they left the room. It wasn't until she heard the gentle click of the door closing that Daise dared to open her eyes. She took a deep breath and started to formulate a plan.

At first, it seemed impossible. But she did what she always did in difficult times; she thought of her dad. He would always tell her that planning was like cooking. Bits of information were your ingredients. Once you had collected all the information it was just a question of deciding how you were going to put them together to make your plan.

She could stand, and if she could walk a few steps then it was at least possible to get out of this room. But running was out of the question. She needed to blend in. It wasn't like she could just shuffle out of there in a green hospital robe with the Greenacres farm embossed across her chest.

Her eyes swept the room, there was no sign of her clothes. Had they thrown them away? To the eyes of the locals, her favourite T-shirt probably looked like a rag.

OK, so that was a problem. But perhaps the most pressing issue was how she was going to detach herself from the machine and drip without tripping the alarm. It felt weird to be plugged into machines like she was some sort of inhuman cyborg.

She hovered over the control panel, a dizzying array of switches, buttons and dials. She couldn't risk hitting the buttons in case they made some sort of noise that alerted the staff outside. But then she spotted a thick cable spilling out of the machine. Shuffling round to the back of the monitor she located the power socket. Careful not to tangle up the line from the drip, she bent down and gave the plug a firm tug with her good arm. The lights on the machine slowly faded and a faint whirring noise faded away.

Daise waited a moment until she was sure it had powered the machine down before she slowly peeled the sensor from her chest, poised to roll back into bed if it triggered an alarm. But there was no sound. The next step was to unplug herself from the drip. This was going to be

The Castoffs

a much trickier task with only one hand.

By scraping her front teeth down the edge of the surgical tape Daise managed to reveal the plastic cannula that was inserted into her vein. It had to come out. She gripped the cannula and gave it a sharp tug. It was a strange scratchy sensation but hurt much less than she had expected.

Now she was free of wires and tubes, finding her clothes became her number one priority. Hunching to ensure she couldn't be seen; Daise shimmied around the bed. The bedside table turned out to be a small cupboard. She swung the door open and her clothes were neatly folded in a small pile. Getting dressed proved to be a lot trickier than finding her clothes as she had to remove her sling and put on her T-shirt and shorts one-handed. Her T-shirt was badly stained and there was a bullet hole in the arm. It was particularly tricky to get into her shorts as they seemed tighter than she remembered. It took her a while to realise it was because she'd shoved a book in the back pocket; the book on human evolution she had found on the dump. Finally, she managed to replace the sling to support her injured arm.

The next step of her plan was to find out what was on the other side of the door. She ducked down to hide from view and approached the door by sliding along the wall until she could see out of the edge of the glass panel. The corridor contained a series of identical doors running down its length. She took a risk and looked through the centre of the window. There was no one around. Perhaps this was her chance.

She turned the handle of the door gently and pulled it open. The corridor was quiet. She edged along it, ducking

The Castoffs

under the doors of other rooms till she arrived at a big pair of double doors with windows. Like a meerkat surveying its territory, she popped her head up to peek through.

It seemed to be some sort of reception area. She recognised the woman sitting at the front desk — it was the Scottish woman from the operating theatre. She was talking to a tall mean-looking Guardian. It was impossible to hear what he was saying but by the way, he was waving his arms around like he was conducting the room — this was clearly a man who was used to getting what he wanted. He turned around and beckoned to a boy from across the room, who approached the desk reluctantly, his shoulders hung in a petulant slouch. It was Gregor. Daise felt a surge of anger rise within her.

After a brief exchange of words, the Guardian pushed his hand up to the Scottish woman's face dismissively and began to walk towards the double doors.

Chapter 12 – Identity

Daise ducked quickly, jarring her injured arm and swallowing the yelp of pain. They were coming for her. There was no time to think. 'Storage cupboard 003' was written on a door across the corridor and she made a dash for it.

Her heart beating hard, she grabbed the handle and pulled open the door. A light was triggered to reveal a room full of shelves stuffed full of assorted linen, blankets, scrubs and gowns. There was a small space between the shelves and the back wall. She winced as she squeezed herself into the gap and waited.

The corridor outside boomed with a chorus of shouting and banging. Daise waited for the door to burst open. An alarm sounded three short beeps, followed by the patter of footsteps outside the door but no one came in. For a moment it was silent and all she could hear was the hum of the overhead strip lighting before the corridor again erupted with shouting. It was difficult to hear what was being said, so she shuffled around in the gap to push a stack of blankets away from her ear.

'Gregor, you wait here in case she comes back.'

There was a pause before Gregor responded. But, Dad…' But he didn't get to finish his sentence.

'How many times have I told you, Gregor? You call

me Chief when I'm at work. And for once in your life can you just do as you are told!'

So, Gregor's dad was the Chief. This surely meant Rowan was captured. He must have sacrificed his freedom to get her to the hospital. Tears welled up in her eyes. But no, it wasn't her fault. It was that nasty, stuck up, scumbag Gregor. She had a good mind to confront him. The thought of punching his smug face lifted her spirits, but she knew it was just fantasy. Even if her arm weren't in a sling, the odds of her beating him in a fight were pretty low.

The footsteps came closer until she was sure they were next to the storage cupboard door. Then the booming voice of Gregor's dad barked, 'Get this hospital locked down. I want that girl found.'

It seemed Daise had little choice but to wait it out. By pulling a couple of fleece blankets from the shelves, she was able to build a nest in the gap to make herself a bit more comfortable. Every now and then the lights went out but she found by waving her hand in the air she could trigger the light sensor.

As she twisted her body trying to trigger the sensor for the third time, she was jabbed in the back by the corner of the paperback book in her pocket.

It occurred to her that the book might have some information on blood groups. Perhaps she could find out more about what happened to her in the operating theatre.

Flicking through the index she looked up blood types. There was a paragraph about how different blood groups were susceptible to different sorts of diseases but nothing about blood reactions. She was about to put the book away when she noticed the next chapter was titled 'Enhanced Humans'. She started to read...

'Anatomically modern humans are believed to have emerged in East Africa around 200,000 years ago. During this time human beings have continued to evolve, becoming resistant to diseases and developing new abilities such as the ability for adults to digest lactose. Evolutionary changes in humans are slow, happening over tens of thousands of years.

Many scientists have suggested that human beings should take control of their own evolution if they are to adapt to the new environments created by the systematic depletion of carbon energy reserves.

The science of enhancing humans is called transhumanology. Using technology to enhance humans began with correcting faults in vision and hearing but the challenges of the climate extinction event (CEE) has led to the development of new genetic therapies to make people resistant to drought and famine.

If these genetic changes were passed on to the next generation, they would give human beings the capacity to direct their own evolutionary destiny.'

Daise was scared; the information in this book was dangerous. The only reason she knew about the CEE was her father. He had told her exciting bedtime stories about exotic animals like tigers, elephants, wolves, bears and giraffes that had evolved to live in environments that had then been destroyed by the CEE.

This sort of talk was considered heresy by the

The Castoffs

Council, which classified tigers and bears as mythical beasts in the same way as dragons and unicorns. You had to be careful challenging these views in public places. The previous year, after the school closed, some of the older kids started teaching classes in the canteen of Tower Five. Daise remembered one of the younger kids had a thing for cats and asked, 'what's the biggest cat in the world?' This innocent question prompted a discussion on lions and tigers and extinction, which turned into an angry debate.

Challenging Council views on how the world worked was a detainable offence. The next day the classes were stopped and the kids who ran them were gone.

This stuff about enhanced humans in the book really made her think. What would you do to enhance humans? Would you make them bigger, stronger or give them new abilities? And then a thought occurred to her — was Rowan an enhanced human? He was big and strong and perhaps his green skin was an enhancement too.

It made a lot more sense than him being sick or an alien. Daise felt elated. It was like finding the last piece of a puzzle. It would explain why the Council were so keen to get hold of Rowan. If he was an enhanced human, his existence threatened their version of the world. Instead, they had cast Rowan as sick and dangerous. It all made sense.

Of course, none of this helped her with her current problem of being trapped in a linen cupboard in Greenacres Hospital, Barrowby. But perhaps there was no way out of here. The Guardians had the hospital on lockdown and were looking for her. But what did they want her for? She was the victim. Gregor had shot her

The Castoffs

and, strictly speaking, the bay was on the Casthorpe side of the fence so they couldn't even charge her with breaking the curfew.

She made her decision; she was fed up with hiding. It was time to take control of the situation. Stepping out of the gap in the shelves, she put the blankets back and tucked the book underneath them. If they found her with a heretical book she would be detained without question.

Using as much confidence as she could muster, she stood straight with her shoulders back and took a deep breath. She turned the handle and walked into the corridor.

Gregor was standing guard right outside. Startled by the opening door, he jumped in shock. He hurried towards Daise.

'I'm so sorry I didn't mean to hurt you are you OK?', he garbled in one long sentence. Daise was confused. The last thing she had expected was an apology.

'And so you should be. You bloody shot me! What the hell did I do to you?' She prodded him in the chest with her good arm to press her point home.

'My Dad wants to speak to you about the green man.' So, they wanted to interrogate her. That made sense. Perhaps she could talk her way out of this. But what could she say about Rowan? She couldn't remember anything between collapsing on the beach and waking up in the hospital. Gregor would know more about that. So, what did he want from her? How much had Gregor told his dad? Whatever he had said, it was bound to be a lie.

'Gregor, what happened to Rowan?', she asked, keen to get his version of events.

For a moment he looked wild eyed like a startled

animal. Collecting himself quickly, he said, 'He made a run for it. When I needed his help to get you to hospital, he showed his true colours.'

'A patrol is out searching for him this morning. I know you think he was some sort of friend but he deserted you Daise. I know I made a terrible mistake shooting you. I was afraid. He came at me when you were unconscious. I thought he was going to kill me.'

Daise didn't believe a word of it but she thought she would probe deeper into his web of lies to see if they started to unravel.

'Where did he go?', she asked.

Gregor stroked his chin nervously, 'I don't know Daise. The last time I saw him he was swimming out to sea. Maybe he's gone back to wherever he came from?'

Daise recalled her conversation on the beach with Rowan. He was looking for Mrs Arkwright. There was no way he would swim back to Ancaster Island. No, if he had deserted her — and she doubted that — he would have climbed up the rope and headed towards Casthorpe.

Gregor spluttered, 'I'm really sorry Daise but it was me who saved you. I swam you up the shore to Barrowby Beach and brought you here.'

'You're forgetting one small thing Gregor; if it wasn't for you, I wouldn't have this bloody hole in my arm. You owe me, Gregor. I just want to go home. Let me go.'

She started walking past him and he didn't stop her. There must be a way out.

'Which way can I get out?', she demanded.

But before Gregor could answer, his father burst through the double doors.

'Good job Gregor, you've found the little Castoff

urchin. Finally, you managed to do something right.'

Gregor's cheeks flushed crimson and he started to say something, but before any words came out, his dad cut him short, 'Go now Gregor and try not to get into any trouble on the way home.'

Shoulders slumped; he sloped off through the double doors.

Chief Whitmore patted Daise on the head like a dog, 'Right missy, follow me. I want to have a word with you.'

He pushed her forward towards an office door along the corridor. The sign said 'Clinical Director's Office' but it seemed to have been commandeered by the Chief. He sat down behind the solid oak desk and gestured to her to sit on a wobbly looking wooden stool.

'Ok Daisy Dawkins. Tell me what the resistance is planning!'

Daise swallowed hard. She had no idea what he was talking about. She started to stutter.

'B… b… but, my name is Daisy Woods.'

The Chief took an upturned glass from the desk and a glass of water from a tall green ceramic jug. He passed it to her and waited as she gulped it down.

'Better?' he asked. She nodded.

'I know who you are Daisy, I knew your dad. I'm the reason you're still alive. If I hadn't sent you to the Casthorpe Reset you'd have died alongside your fool of a father.'

Her father, what did the Chief know about her father? Daise suddenly found it hard to breathe. Her clothes felt too tight. She wanted to scream but she had no words. The bright white walls faded to grey and then black.

Chapter 13 – Mouse

Mrs Arkwright walked out from behind the green velvet curtain clutching something to her chest. It was a book wrapped in a yellow crocheted baby blanket. She sat down across from Rey and Jude and placed it on the table.

'Have you made your decision?', she asked.

The question lingered in the air like dry ice. Rey looked to Jude and whispered, 'What do you think?'

The gravity of the decision weighed heavily on Rey; the idea of trusting Mrs Arkwright went against his instincts. He had learned not to trust people. The towers were teeming with snitches and informants. The Guardians happily paid for information and with most of the people living in the Resets in a state a perpetual hunger, the offer of a coin to buy a hot meal was enough to breed a culture of fear and mistrust.

Rey had seen kids get detained for an idle comment such as criticising the taste of Smart Jooce. The information Mrs Arkwright wanted would be worth much more than a coin. It could also see them detained or maybe something worse. She wanted to know all about Rowan.

He looked up at her face and stared at the lines around her warm brown eyes, desperately trying to detect

The Castoffs

her motivation. In his experience grown-ups were the worst; they always had an angle. He couldn't think of a grown-up who hadn't left him disappointed.

But Mrs Arkwright had been kind to them and they needed help. He wanted to help Daise too. He still felt bad about letting her go off on her own. And meeting Rowan was the most exciting thing that had ever happened to Rey. He felt part of something bigger than himself, something important. He didn't want to walk away from that.

But before he could speak, Jude stood up, 'I think we should go', he said firmly.

'No,' replied Rey.

He was surprised to hear his voice louder and more forceful than usual. Daise normally made the difficult decisions; now it was time for him to step up.

'I need to know more about this book, Jude. We owe it to Daise. We shouldn't have let her go off on her own. We're family. We have to look after each other.'

Jude looked for a moment like he was going to leave. But much to Rey's relief he sighed loudly, sat back down again and said, 'I just want to find her. It will be getting dark soon.'

Mrs Arkwright smiled, 'Let's have a little chat and we'll all go looking for Daise.'

Rey returned the smile and told their story to Mrs Arkwright. Explaining how their morning foraging expedition had turned into an encounter with the strange man everybody now seemed to be looking for.

Mrs Arkwright smiled, 'Thanks for your trust boys, I know that couldn't have been easy for you.

'Now it is my turn to trust you. I think you're right

about Daise having a connection with Rowan.'

Rey was surprised; it was like she already knew him. But he didn't say anything.

'What do you know about Daise's father?' Mrs Arkwright continued.

'Not much. He looked after Daise when her mum got ill. He sounded kind. Daise tried looking for him but there was nothing in the library on Dennis Woods. We even got on a terminal once and she did a search. When she arrived at the towers, she was always talking about "finding dad and going back to live in Barrowby". But that sort of talk doesn't win you any friends in the Resets. She didn't really talk about him much anymore. In fact, the story she told about the book was the first time she had mentioned him in ages.

'Daise took her mother's name, Woods. She was a strong, independent woman too by all accounts.'

Both boys smiled. Mrs Arkwright paused for a moment, looking puzzled.

Jude spoke, 'It's something Daise says to herself when she needs a boost of confidence.'

Mrs Arkwright smiled, 'From what I understand, her mother was a remarkable woman. Both of her parents were brilliant research scientists working for the government. Back when the country was united, before the great flood and the war that followed. We knew it was coming, the famine, the war — it was inevitable. It took over 350 million years to create the earth's reserves of fossil fuels. We managed to burn through it all in 300.

'We couldn't fix the climate but Daise's father thought he could fix people. His idea was a simple one. Our response to the energy crisis had focused on getting energy from the sun. In his early career he worked on making solar panels more efficient. He helped develop biological solar cells, harnessing the same chemical process that plants use to make energy from sunlight.'

The boys were impressed. Daise's dad was a hero. Green cells were the only source of power on the Resets. The roof of each tower was coated in a green cell mat which powered the whole block.

Mrs Arkwright continued, 'Green cells revolutionised the energy business. But as the sea levels began to rise there was less land available to build solar farms and less fertile land to grow food. Wars began to break out as countries became unable to feed their populations. The focus of the global crisis moved from energy to hunger.

'Daise's dad changed his field of research. He figured that the answer to the hunger problem couldn't be solved by making more food because the oceans were advancing, leaving less farmland.'

Mrs Arkwright removed her glasses and rubbed her eyes.

'What happened next?' asked Jude impatiently.
Rey could see Mrs Arkwright was struggling to tell her story and wished Jude would be patient. She cleared her throat and continued.

'Well, our lives all changed when the flood defence barrier failed and the war broke out. It was chaos in the weeks that followed the great flood. But a few years ago, one of the kids from the tower brought me this book. He had salvaged it from the dump.'

'On the surface, it's just a kids' story about prejudice but I think it tells us more about his research.'

She peeled the blanket off the book to reveal a black

The Castoffs

A5 notebook. The faux leather cover was deeply lined. The title was written in bold golden lettering along the spine.

Green Mouse: An Allegorical Tail
By Dennis Dawkins

Mrs Arkwright moved round the table and sat herself between Rey and Jude. The aged spine crackled as she gently opened the book.

The first page was written in beautiful cursive script.

This book is dedicated to my beautiful wife and daughter. May we all find our way back to each other one day.

Mrs Arkwright turned each page. It was a simple picture book for under-fives.

It told the story of a little mouse who was green. All the other mice were scared of him because he was different. He tried to play with the other mice but they didn't want to be his friend. The other mice were mean. When he asked for food, they told him that the food was for mice. When he pointed at his mousy nose and his mousey tail and his mousey whiskers, they told him that he couldn't be a mouse because mice weren't green.

The poor green mouse's tummy hurt with hunger. Every day he would ask the other mice if he could have some of their food. But they told him that he couldn't have any food because he wasn't a mouse.

The little mouse got used to being hungry and soon found that he didn't really need to eat. So, he stopped

The Castoffs

going to ask for food. Instead, he lay in the sun relaxing.

Then one day there was a terrible flood that washed away the grain store, leaving all the mice hungry. Slowly, one by one, all the mice began to starve.

Finally, the little green mouse was visited by one of the starving mice; he was so frail you could see his little ribs poking out of his chest. He asked the little green mouse if he could have some of his food. The little green mouse replied, 'But I don't have any food. All the grain was washed away in the flood.'

The hungry mouse looked confused, 'But all the mice are starving how come you look so well.'

'Oh, that's simple', the green mouse replied, 'I'm not a mouse.'

Rey and Jude looked at each other confused for a moment. Then Jude said, 'So the green mouse is like Rowan then?'

Mrs Arkwright nodded and smiled. 'Yes, I think that Rowan is a green human. I think he can make food like plants do. Trapping energy from the sun and making it into food like the mouse in the story.'

'I'm sorry. It's complicated,' she said. 'You see, I think that this book tells us that Daise's father had managed to create green mice that could survive with little or no food. Of course, if he had done this work in mice, it raises the possibility that he had done human trials.

'The work was all top secret of course but my friend Jon — you might know him as the Patcher — well, he worked for Dennis and he confirmed they had made people green. But we had assumed that the programme had been shut down after Dennis disappeared.'

The Castoffs

'Disappeared?' Rey repeated.

'Yes, that's when Daise had to move to the towers. We don't know what happened to him. The best guess was that he was detained. He didn't want to work for the committee you see. But his wife was sick and if he didn't work for them, she wouldn't get the treatment she needed. Jon told me it had all been shut down but we took a boat trip out to Ancaster Island and, well, it looked more like a prison than a farm.

'Is that where Rowan came from? See Rey, I told you he wasn't an alien!'

Jude started to giggle a little nervously at first. Then Mrs Arkwright joined in. Rey felt silly. He opened his mouth to defend himself but instead found himself laughing along with them.

Mrs Arkwright stood up abruptly and clapped her hands, 'OK, are you boys going to help me find Daise and Rowan? I imagine they could do with our help.'

Chapter 14 – Checkpoint

Mrs Arkwright walked over to a coat rack and picked out a red trench coat and an olive-green wool hat, embroidered with yellow flowers. She grabbed a metal flask and tucked it into the side pocket of her battered black rucksack. Hoisting it onto her back, she clapped her hands again, startling the boys. 'Chop-chop, let's get on our way then. It's getting late.'

The boys followed Mrs Arkwright outside and she began the laborious task of locking up. 'Be a darling Jude and pass me the end of that chain,' she asked.

A length of thick chain was coiled up near a post at the front of the stall.

Jude passed one end to Mrs Arkwright who began threading it through a series of steel loops that were attached to the outside of her van.

The chain made a melodic clattering as she dragged it through the loops. Finally, she pulled out three large padlocks which she used to secure the chain to the front of a shack.

The market felt unfamiliar without the usual bustle of customers. Most of the stalls had been packed away. Some of the larger shacks were boarded up and wrapped in thick chains like Mrs Arkwright's. Others looked occupied but were no longer welcoming. Signs that

The Castoffs

advertised great deals spun round to reveal warnings to deter thieves: 'Dangerous dog lives here'. 'Trespassers will be shot'.

A stocky obsidian rottweiler snarled at the boys as they walked past the shack where he stood guard. Unperturbed Mrs Arkwright walked up to the dog and said affectionately 'Hello Bertie,' holding the back of her hand out for Bertie to sniff. The boys froze, fearful the dog would snap at her. But instead, he stopped snarling, rolled over and let Mrs Arkwright rub his tummy.

They heard a noise from inside the shack. A short man with a shaved head and a grey beard stuck his head out of the window.

'Bloody hell Alice! How many times have I told you not to pet Bert? He's a guard dog for goodness sake.'

'But he is just so cute, aren't you boy' said Mrs Arkwright, in a high-pitched voice.

The man sighed as he spotted Rey and Jude.

'Alice! Really.' His voice was filled with exasperation. 'Why don't you just write a sign saying — get your free stuff here.'

'Oh Jon, don't be so serious. You don't have to worry about Jude and Rey here, they're good lads.'

Mrs Arkwright walked away from Bertie and approached Jon at the window to his shack. She whispered something to him and handed him a scrap of paper.

Jon read the paper, smiled, folded it up and put it in the top pocket of his shirt.

'Well, make sure you don't get into too much trouble and let me know how you get on,' he said, before slamming his window closed.

The Castoffs

Before the boys could ask any questions, Mrs Arkwright headed off along the dusty deserted path towards Casthorpe Road.

She walked briskly and with purpose, the long tails of her trench coat flapping against her calves. The boys hurried behind, unsure where she was headed.

At the market's main entrance, she waved at the security officer who was sitting in a booth next to the gate at the perimeter fence.

The security officer waved back and pressed a button which raised the barrier arm.

They turned left down Casthorpe Road towards the Barrowby Checkpoint. Mrs Arkwright paced off ahead. But Rey stopped.

'Wait!' he said. 'Where are we going?'

Mrs Arkwright walked back towards Rey. 'I thought I made myself clear. We are going to find Daise.'

'But she could be anywhere,' said Rey, a little forlornly.

'I suppose that's true. But what we have to ask ourselves is, where is she likely to be? Given that you said she went to find Rowan and that he was on the beach at Barrowby, it strikes me that that would be a good place to start looking.'

Mrs Arkwright set off again towards the checkpoint. Rey started to follow her but Jude grabbed him by the arm.

'What's wrong now?' said Mrs Arkwright with a hint of frustration in her voice.

Jude explained, 'I can't go back to Barrowby. I almost got arrested this morning for trespassing. I don't want to be detained so perhaps it would be best if I just went

The Castoffs

home.' Turning to his friend, he added, 'Rey, do you really want to risk being detained?'

Rey stood still for a moment. 'It's a fair point, Mrs Arkwright. How are we going to get through the checkpoint?'

'Oh, don't you worry about those border Guardians, they're not so scary — especially if you give them a little present.' She tapped the flask in the side pocket of her rucksack.

'I know I'm asking a lot but if you want my help, you're going to have to trust me. Look if we have any trouble at the checkpoint you can just run home. The Guardians don't care what you do on this side of the fence. Do you really want to abandon your friend so easily?'

Her words were cutting. Rey already felt guilty enough for letting Daise go off on her own.

Rey walked forward to Mrs Arkwright, leaving Jude standing alone. As she continued up Casthorpe Road, Rey paused and looked into his friend's eyes. 'Are you coming then?'

Jude nodded and they both hurried after Mrs Arkwright.

By the time they reached the checkpoint, daylight was starting to fade. The sun sank into the horizon behind them, casting long shadows up the road.

The road was devoid of cars and there was a foreboding stillness in the air. The checkpoint was a wooden shed painted navy blue, with a tiled pitched roof. A large blue sign stretched above the window, stating *BARROWBY CHECKPOINT* in unambiguous white capitals.

The Castoffs

It stood in the middle of the road. Red and white striped metal barrier poles reached out on either side to block the road. Inside the checkpoint, two men sat back-to-back. The Guardian facing them sat back in his chair, arms stretched behind his head and his feet perched on a desk. His eyes were hidden behind aviator sunglasses.

Jude tapped Mrs Arkwright on the shoulder, 'Is that Guardian sleeping? He hasn't moved.' Mrs Arkwright stopped walking. 'I'm not sure whether he's having a nap or is just blinded by the sun. Let's take things slowly, we don't want to startle him.'

They slipped into single file and approached the checkpoint with slow and steady steps. As they edged closer still, the Guardian remained frozen.

'I think you must be right Jude; he must be asleep. But there's another Guardian behind him so keep your wits about you,' said Mrs Arkwright.

They moved to the edge of the road so they could peer in the hatch at the side of the booth. Rey began to speak. But before he could get a word out, Mrs Arkwright clamped her hand over his mouth. She paused until she was sure that Rey understood she wanted silence. 'Shush,' she whispered in his ear.

She gestured to the boys to crouch down and they all edged up to the barrier. Mrs Arkwright kept her eyes fixed on the Guardian as they crept forward. They were ready to sneak under the barrier when there was a yelp from the booth.

The Guardian jolted forward and shouted, 'What did you do that for!' He turned around to confront his colleague when he caught sight of Mrs Arkwright.

He pulled his gun from its holster and aimed it at her,

The Castoffs

'Take a step away from the booth and show me your papers.'

Rey and Jude stood up. The Guardian responded by adjusting his aim as if to demonstrate that he could shoot them all before they had a chance to rush him.

Mrs Arkwright spoke calmly, 'I'm just going to reach into my bag to get my papers.'

The Guardian was not much older than Rey and Jude. His patchy beard was clearly an attempt to look like an adult but it simply served to advertise his adolescence.

He looked edgy and unpredictable. It was a relief when the other much older Guardian stepped out of the booth — a man-mountain with arms like tree trunks. In a deep soothing tone, he said, 'Put the gun down Charlie, it's just Mrs A'. Charlie did as he was told and put the gun back in his holster.'

The older Guardian stood and greeted Mrs Arkwright with a perfunctory kiss on her left cheek, 'Have you got any of your tasty soup for us?'

'As a matter of fact, I have' said Mrs Arkwright. She stopped rummaging for her papers and pulled out the flask.

'Charlie, make yourself useful and fetch our mugs. You've got to try this soup. It's incredible.'

The tension faded away as the Guardians slurped down the soup. Even Charlie smiled.

Rey and Jude watched as Mrs Arkwright charmed the Guardians with small talk and flattery. After a few minutes the older Guardian was waving them all off without any further discussion.

'How did you do that? I thought we were going to be shot.' asked Jude.

The Castoffs

Mrs Arkwright smiled, 'A little bit of old-fashioned friendliness goes a long way.'

'But I thought there was a curfew? They didn't even scan us.'

'Old George knows me well. But I must admit I was a bit nervous when young Charlie started waving his gun around.'

'But let's not hang about, I told them I was just dropping off some books to the Guardians for incineration.'

She started to jog along the track that ran off Casthorpe Road down to Barrowby Beach, the tail of her red coat flapping in her wake. The boys set off after her, surprised at her pace.

They ran for a kilometre until they reached the Barrowby Beach dune. The sun had fallen below the horizon leaving a pale orange stain and what light there was fading fast. Mrs Arkwright came to a stop where the earth gave way to sand. Shrugging off her rucksack, she took out a large black torch. She started to systematically search the beach with a long narrow beam that extended to the shoreline.

Rey and Jude arrived a few seconds later trying their utmost not to appear out of breath. They stood still watching carefully as Mrs Arkwright scanned the beach with a focused beam of light.

'Look! Do you see that?', she shouted.

It was a dark shape half-way down the dune. Even with the torch pointed straight at it they couldn't quite make it out. Then it moved and it became clear that it was someone lying on the sand. At once all three of them ran down the dune.

Though the torch jiggled around as she ran, Mrs Arkwright tried her best to keep the light focused on the figure on the sand.

'It's Rowan', cried Mrs Arkwright, striving to keep her footing in the soft sand. Blood was streaming down the left side of his face. The boys knelt in the sand, panting as they tried to get their words out.

'Rowan are you OK?' asked Rey.

'I'm not feeling so good, young Reyansh. I seemed to have developed a propensity for getting knocked out.'

Rey wasn't sure what 'propensity' meant but smiled at Rowan anyway.

'Boys, I could really do with some help getting to my feet.' But before they could help him, Mrs Arkwright butted in, 'You'll do nothing of the sort, old friend. You'll sit still while I tend your wounds.'

Chapter 15 – Escape

'Daisy… Daisy… Daisy!' Daise looked in the direction of the voice but couldn't locate where it was coming from. Cold hands grabbed her arm, there was a sharp sting and then she was back in the room facing the Chief.

'We lost you for a moment there, but we're not finished. I want to hear your story.' His voice was slow and deliberate.

Daise took a moment to get her bearings. She was sitting in an office with the Chief Guardian — Gregor's dad. The Scottish doctor was putting a small circular plaster on the inside of her forearm.

The woman stepped away from Daise and addressed the Chief, 'It's not right you know, what you're doing here. She's only a wee girl and she's sick. She should be in bed, not running around the hospital.'

The Chief waved his hand dismissively, directing her out of the room. She gave Daise a gentle rub on the arm and a half smile before she left.

'Now back to business. What do you know about the resistance?' said the Chief.

The Chief made Daise feel guilty before she'd even tried to say anything.

'Err nothing, I don't know anything,' she mumbled.

'Come on Daisy don't take me for a fool. You made

contact with Rowan Lightowler and you want me to believe you are not part of the resistance. And with your history. What are you plotting?'

'Nothing,' she repeated.

The Chief hit his desk in anger, took a deep breath and continued. 'OK Daisy, how about you just tell me what you were doing on the beach this evening before you were shot. I've already spoken to Gregor and let's just say there are a few inconsistencies in his version of events.'

Daise told her story, leaving out details of their morning encounter with Rowan. She explained how she had spent the afternoon abseiling and was unable to climb back when she saw the green man. She made a conscious effort not to use Rowan's name. But apart from that she told the truth about how Gregor had stormed up and shot her.

The Chief looked frustrated. He really wanted to know what had happened to Rowan as the patrols had been unable to locate him on Barrowby Beach.

'Are you sure you don't remember anything after you were shot? Gregor says Lightowler came at him but he managed to knock him out with a stick.'

Daise shook her head and shrugged. The Chief slumped back in his chair unsure of how to proceed with his interrogation.

'I don't like this; I don't like this one little bit. I don't know what happened on that beach but I will get to the bottom of it. He got up from his chair and walked around to sit on the edge of the desk. Daise could feel his warm breath in her face.

'You're going back to that hospital bed and don't even

The Castoffs

think about escaping. There will be a Guardian stationed outside your door. Dr McInnes wants to run some tests. I'm not finished with you. Let's see if you change your story when I've got hold of Lightowler.'

The Chief stood up, opened the door and shouted down the corridor. 'You! Get a wheelchair and get this girl back to her room.'

Another Guardian dressed in black walked into the office pushing a wheelchair. He parked it next to Daise, grabbed her roughly by the arms, shoved her in the chair and wheeled her back to her room.

Daise fell back into the mattress in the sterile white room and kicked her shoes off. She felt exhausted and was starting to close her eyes when Dr McInnes — the Scottish woman — walked in with a colleague who didn't look much older than Daise.

The older woman was carrying a blanket, which she placed on the end of the bed and unfolded to reveal some green hospital scrubs, a stethoscope and a surgical cap.

'We're getting you out of here Daisy. Quick, put on these clothes. Mrs Arkwright and your friends are waiting in reception.'

'Mrs Arkwright? From the market?' she asked.

What was Alice Arkwright doing here? Then she remembered Rowan had been trying to find her.

'There's more to Mrs Arkwright than you might think,' said Dr McInnes, smiling at Daise.

'Is she working with the resistance?' asked Daise in a whisper.

'All in good time Daise, let's just say, she's a friend and she can get you back home. But first things first. We need to get you out of this room and past that Guardian,' she said nodding towards the door.

'But what about her, won't she get into trouble?' said Daise pointing at the young doctor.

'She'll be fine. I'll walk out with you, then come back later to pick up Carrie. It will take them ages to work out what's happened and by that time, you'll be long gone.'

Daise picked up the bundle of clothes and got dressed in the bathroom. She came back into the room and wrapped the stethoscope around her neck.

'So how do I look?' she said looking to Doctor McInnes for approval.

'You look bonny love, but before we go, I need to tell you something. We did some tests on your blood and, well...'

She paused for a moment then continued, 'None of the guys in the lab has seen anything like it. Some of your cells have been infected by…'

Daise butted in, 'Infected by what?'

Dr McInnes tucked her hair behind her ears nervously, 'That's it really. We don't know.'

Daise took a sharp breath, trying her utmost to keep her composure.

'Am I going to die?'

Dr McInnes smiled, 'I didnae mean to scare you love. Your vital signs look really good. You're a strong lass. I'd like to keep you here to be on the safe side. But with the Guardians on your case, I think you'd be better getting yourself off home. Mrs A will see you right.'

Daise felt relieved but not quite reassured. Mrs Arkwright was a nice lady. She'd always been kind to Daise; giving her a free bowl of soup or refusing to take money for a book. But how did she know Rey and Jude?

It felt like so much had happened in such a short space of time. She sat back down on the bed. Her eyes started to pool with tears.

Dr McInnes sat down and gave her a hug. The kindness broke her. The tears fell like water from a leaking tap as the events of the day caught up with her. She felt fractured. Like falling apart was the only choice she had left.

The younger doctor moved back towards the door to give Daise some privacy. But the squeak of her shoes on the linoleum floor brought Daise back into herself. She wiped the tears from her face, shrugged off the doctor's embrace and stood up.

Dr McInnes passed Daise the surgical cap, 'Are you OK?'

She took a deep breath before answering, 'Yes, can you get me out of here? I just want to go home.'

The doctor smiled, 'Stay on my left side as we walk out and you'll be fine.'

She passed Daise a clipboard and added, 'Hold this, nobody questions you when you're holding one of them.'

She tucked in a few loose strands of Daise's golden hair into the surgical cap and opened the door. A tall Guardian stood to the right. He looked startled by the door opening. Daise looked down at the clipboard, as if trying to make sense of a chart. The Guardian tried to regain his composure by standing upright; his hand placed on the grip of his gun.

Dr McInnes turned to face the Guardian. She put her hands on her hips, to further block Daise from his view, 'Tough job you've got there soldier boy; guarding a twelve-year-old girl. Is she dangerous?'

The Castoffs

The Guardian's eyes narrowed and his lips contorted into a snarl. But before he could respond, Dr McInnes had spun around to face Daise. They both set off towards the double doors that led to the hospital reception. The Guardian stuttered something guttural in their wake but he did not follow.

In reception, a dozen people sat waiting patiently to be seen. Three young women sat behind a large glass-fronted desk, processing patients. They scanned idents, took bank details and directed people to the benches. Unless of course you worked for the Council. Council workers did not have to wait on the benches. They were directed to the luxurious west wing of Greenacres Hospital.

Daise waited until the double doors closed before whispering, 'Why did you tease that Guardian? I thought my heart was going to jump out of my chest.'

Dr McInnes replied, 'I didn't do that for fun. Although I can't deny I might have enjoyed it, just a wee bit. I wanted to make sure he was entirely focused on me. I bet he was so worked up, he barely noticed there were two of us leaving.'

There were two more Guardians stationed at the main exit. Both were big burly men with machine guns. Daise looked down at her clipboard again to avoid their gaze as Dr McInnes guided her towards the waiting area.

'Daise, look up,' someone whispered.

On the rows of benches, Daise saw Mrs Arkwright, wearing a bright red coat. Sitting next to her was Rey and her hand was firmly clasped around his wrist to stop him running to his friend and attracting the attention of the Guardians. But where was Jude? Had he abandoned her.

Perhaps she shouldn't be surprised. They were risking big trouble coming to Barrowby after curfew.

Doctor McInnes placed her index finger to her lips and ushered them all towards a door.

Mrs Arkwright, Daise and Rey followed her in silence until she closed the door of the consulting room and drew the blind.

Rey threw his arms around Daise and hugged her hard. She let out a little yelp as he squeezed her wounded arm. Everyone started to speak at once. Rey blurted out questions at Daise. Daise wanted to know if they knew anything about Rowan. Dr McInnes fired off questions at Mrs Arkwright. The small room was filled with a cacophony of voices but no one could hear anything until Mrs Arkwright took control with a single clap of her hands.

'Come on people, we're not out of here yet. We have to get Daise past the two Guardians at the door and then back to Casthorpe. There'll be time to catch up later.'

'Meg, thanks so much for helping. I hope you don't get into too much trouble. I think we all need to meet. Can you round up the academy?'

Dr McInnes nodded, 'Noon tomorrow should give me enough time to get everyone together. If you can get yourselves to the bunker, you should be safe.'

'That's the plan. Right Daise, give me your arm.' Mrs Arkwright grabbed Daise by the arm and pulled a small pair of nail scissors from her inside pocket.

Rey reacted instinctively, barging in front of Daise, knocking Daise's arm out of her grasp in the process. He puffed his chest defensively. Mrs Arkwright shook her head and let out a disappointed sigh.

The Castoffs

'Rey, what did I say about trust earlier?'

'But you've just pulled a blade on my friend.' he replied defiantly.

Mrs Arkwright pointed at Daise's arm, 'Do you see that wristband?'

'Yeah,' he grunted back at her.

'Well, if we don't remove that from Daisy's arm before she walks out that door it will set off an alarm that will attract the interest of all the Guardians in Barrowby.'

Rey shuffled back awkwardly to one side and let Mrs Arkwright remove the wristband.

'We need to get out of here quickly before they discover Daise is missing,' urged the doctor with a real sense of urgency.

She knelt down in front of Daise. 'How are you feeling love, are you strong enough to walk out of here on your own?

Daise nodded.

'Great, you don't look much younger than some of the junior doctors. If anyone challenges you, tell them they're short-staffed in maternity.'

Mrs Arkwright continued, 'If you turn to the right and head up past the ambulance bay there's a small outbuilding with the sign 'Sterilisation Clinic'. Rowan and Jude are waiting for us there.'

Daise was excited to hear about Rowan, 'Is Rowan OK?'

'Yes, he took a nasty bash on the head but he seems OK considering,' replied Mrs Arkwright.

'Come on, we have to go now. Daise, you go first. We'll follow you out in a moment. Ready?'

Daise tried to ask another question but Mrs Arkwright

The Castoffs

interrupted, 'I know you have lots of unanswered questions but we are all in danger. We all need to get out of here safely.'

Dr McInnes embraced Mrs Arkwright, 'I better get back to work. I don't want to arouse suspicion.'

'Thanks Meg, I'll make sure the academy knows what you've done for the resistance.'

Dr McInnes turned to Mrs Arkwright, 'If Daise needs any medical attention, take her to the Patcher.' She stroked Daise's cheek and left the room.

Mrs Arkwright nodded at Daise, 'Time to go.'

Daise walked out of the door. The chatter of the other patients in the waiting area seemed too loud. She glanced at the security Guardians stood on either side of the door, casually talking.

She gripped the clipboard so tightly she could feel the coarse grain of the wood. The Guardians opened the doors as she approached. She lifted her head and smiled.

'Excuse me, Doc,'

Daise didn't react until the Guardian tapped her on the shoulder.

'Yes?' she replied, trying to sound confident.

'Do you know what's going on? We've all been called out to do overtime. Have they caught the green man? Is he here in the hospital?'

Thinking on her feet, Daise snapped, 'I can't discuss confidential information like that with you.'

It had the desired effect. The Guardian stood back and let her leave.

The cool night air was a contrast to the stuffy hospital. She turned right as she had been told and saw

The Castoffs

the outbuilding. Before she got there, Jude rushed out and gave her a big hug. She was so pleased to see him she almost forgot to ask about Rowan. But as Jude let her go, she saw a tall figure step out from the shadow of the building. Rowan had a bandage wrapped around his head, his eyelids drooped and his shoulders looked rounded and heavy. His gentle face looked so sad.

Mrs Arkwright and Rey arrived a moment later but before anyone could say anything, she led them down a small tarmac path heading away from the hospital.

Jude broke into a half run to catch up with her. They seemed to be travelling away from the Casthorpe Reset. 'Where are we going?' he asked.

Suddenly, an alarm cut through the night air. They all looked back at the hospital, which was lit up with security lights.

'Come on, we haven't got long,' instructed Mrs Arkwright. Her voice cracked nervously. It was the first time they had heard her sound anything less than confident. In the distance they could hear the sound of voices, a door slam and the hum of a battery-operated car in among the sound of the security siren.

Mrs Arkwright shouted, 'Run!'

The tarmac road gave way to sand as they hit a bank of dunes. The headlamps of the car drenched them in light. A warning shot echoed across the darkness. The chase was on.

Rey dropped back to Daise and Rowan who were struggling to keep up. Daise was wincing with each stride, desperately trying to keep her sling as still as possible.

The bandage wrapped around Rowan's head was a deep crimson. He had clearly lost a lot of blood. His eyes had a vacant hollow blackness about them. Rey was worried he might collapse.

Jude reached Mrs Arkwright first. She was on her hands and knees desperately scraping around in the sand.

'What are you doing?', he cried.

'Jude, help me.'

Jude couldn't figure out what she wanted him to do until he got down on his knees. There was a shiny silver circle underneath the sand. Mrs Arkwright had pulled a crowbar from her rucksack and was trying to prize the metal disc out of the ground. Jude grabbed her hands and together they pulled down on the crowbar. The metal cover popped up but the tip of the crowbar slipped out and the cover clicked closed.

Rey, Rowan and Daise were breathing heavily watching Jude and Mrs Arkwright as they tried again to flip the manhole open. They all ducked instinctively as they were picked out by the beams of the approaching car.

Rowan knelt next to Mrs Arkwright and Jude. 'I can do this.' he said.

They handed the crowbar to Rowan, who flipped the disc off in a single action revealing a deep shaft. Mrs Arkwright ushered the kids down first.

They heard voices from the car and the double slam of two car doors. It had come to a stop where the tarmac gave way to sand — 20 metres away. Mrs Arkwright pointed to Rowan to go down. But he shook his head.

'We know you're out there!' came the voice of the Chief. 'Give yourselves up and you won't get hurt.'

Mrs Arkwright made for the shaft looking upwards as she stepped down the rungs of a ladder built into the wall. As she hurried down, her foot slipped and she stepped on Jude's hand. Her feet flapped in the air for a moment as she held on desperately. Then it went completely black as the metal lid clunked down on the entrance, sealing them underground.

Chapter 16 – Underground

Daise tried opening her eyes and closing them. It made no difference. She could see nothing. Climbing down the ladder was hard work with one of her arms out of action. She quickly worked out that it was much safer to slide her good hand down the side of the ladder rather than try and grab out at each rung. Not only did it mean that she always had a hand on the ladder but she also avoided being stepped on from above.

She waved her hand in front of her face. It was so close that she could feel it gently brush her nose but she still couldn't see even the faintest outline of her fingers.

Mrs Arkwright called out from above, 'Rowan, did you make it?'

The gentle tapping of shoes on the metal rungs had stopped as they all clung to the ladder in the still darkness, waiting for Rowan to speak.

The seconds stretched out as they waited for him to respond, 'Yes, I made it. I've secured the cover with the crowbar, so we should all be OK.'

The lift shaft seemed to warm as the whole group breathed out in a collective sigh of relief.

'Is everybody OK?' Mrs Arkwright called out softly.

'Yes,' they all replied in whispers.

'Does anyone have a torch?', asked Daise. As the first

person to enter the shaft, she was worried about what was lurking below.

A light emerged from up above. For a moment Daise thought that the manhole cover had been removed and they had been caught, but she was relieved to see a flash of Mrs Arkwright's red jacket and the shiny metallic underside of the manhole cover.

They passed the torch down to Daise who held it in her mouth as she made her way down the shaft. By the time she reached the bottom rung, her jaw was aching. Using her good arm, she grabbed the rung and helped guide her companions down. One by one they jumped off the ladder and huddled together on a concrete ledge.

Mrs Arkwright took the torch from Daise and walked a few paces along the ledge. She shone the light at the wall, picking out a large metal handle. Holding the torch in her mouth for a moment, she pulled down on the handle with both hands. There was a clank of metal on metal and a series of lights flickered on one-by-one illuminating what appeared to be a long service tunnel in a cool blue light.

Daise had assumed they were descending into a sewer and so was relieved to be standing in a tunnel that looked more like an underground transport network. The ledge they were on looked like a platform. She ran her fingertips along the rough tunnel wall, glad to be out of the shiny white hospital. They seemed to be in a wide section of tunnel that spanned around twenty metres before breaking into a much smaller section that faded into darkness in both directions.

Mrs Arkwright turned off her torch and walked back towards the group. 'There were grand plans for the

The Castoffs

Greater Grantham area before the flood,' she said. 'The government chose ten expansion towns that were at least fifty metres above sea level. The idea was to create new cities to house the refugees when the floods came. There were plans for an underground railway network, a university, a new hospital. They got as far as creating a short stretch of tunnels and a model station. Of course, the barrier defences broke years before the construction work could be completed. The government fell and the local Council seized power. The rest is history. But these tunnels show what could have been.'

Mrs Arkwright rubbed her eyes with the back of a hand and continued, 'They sealed up the main entry points in the old town and Barrowby and that was that. At the time I remember talk of some test drilling but we didn't realise exactly what was down here until we discovered the first access shaft near Barrowby Church last summer. When we discovered it, it was like no one had been down here since they abandoned the project.

'We've been using the Barrowby Central Station as a base. I've not used the hospital shaft before, so I wasn't exactly sure where the access point was. According to the plans Greenacres Hospital was going to be a huge regional centre of medical excellence, replacing the teaching hospitals in Nottingham and Lincoln. Where we are standing now is the platform for Hospital Station,' she explained.

'The tunnel runs for two and a half miles to the centre of the old town,' she said pointing to their left. 'But if we walk for five minutes in this direction, we'll reach what would have been Barrowby Central Station. We'll be able to rest when we get there.'

The Castoffs

Mrs Arkwright ushered them all down to the flattened base of the tunnel where the train tracks would have been laid. She removed her rucksack from her bag and pulled out a wooden stave. She foraged around again and pulled out a collar which she slotted round one end of the stave. Next, she wrapped a hessian rag coated in a waxy substance and pushed it into the collar.

With the torch prepared she walked back to the light switch and plunged them back into darkness. They waited in the black, listening to the sound of metal on flint as sparks danced through the air and then a whoosh as the torch caught a light.

'Time for a bit of old school lighting. You never know when you're going to need those batteries,' announced Mrs Arkwright.

Daise smiled; there was something about the drama with which Mrs Arkwright had lit the torch that lifted her spirits. They walked in line out of the station area into the smaller tunnel, Daise keeping as close to Mrs Arkwright as she could. Rowan brought up the rear, his head flicking back from time to time to check there was no one following.

As they entered the smaller tunnel, Rey and Jude began chattering, 'Are you sure it is safe?

It feels like a train could be coming down the track at any moment,' whispered Rey.

'Come on Rey don't be daft. There aren't even any tracks, are there,' replied Jude.

Daise didn't say anything. But she understood Rey's fears. As the tunnel curved round to the left Daise caught a glimpse of the flickering torch light bounced off a reflective patch of wall and imagined it was the lights of a train. Even the rhythm of their footsteps started to sound like the clickety clack of distant carriages. She reached out in the dark and grabbed Jude's hand. She looked round and saw his teeth and his broad grin illuminated in the faint torchlight.

After they had been walking for ten minutes, Daise caught sight of flashes of Barrowby Central Station. They walked up a slope that led from the tunnel to the platform and once again Mrs Arkwright pulled the light switch and illuminated the station.

'Wow!', said Daise. The tunnel above them was lined with a skin of grey stone tiles. There were platforms on both sides of the tunnel, surfaced in polished concrete slabs. A little way from the edge ran a line of bumpy tiles and a bright painted yellow line.

Rey ran up ahead, 'Hey look, the tunnel just stops here.' He threw a couple of rocks at the roughly drilled tunnel wall to illustrate his point.

Daise climbed up onto the platform, stopping at a poster which mapped out the proposed underground railway network. She traced her fingers along the blue line which ran from Great Gonerby, south through Barrowby, Casthorpe and Harlaxton before looping off to the east through Denton before terminating at Belvoir Castle station. There was another green line that started at Barrowby and looped around the old town and up the coast past Londonthorpe, Syston, Honington terminating at Ancaster.

Mrs Arkwright walked up to Daise, 'They had big plans for Greater Grantham alright.' She said almost wistfully, 'Now let's get off the platform and up to the concourse.'

The Castoffs

She turned off the platform lights, picked up her fiery torch and headed through a small tunnel at the end of the platform. They stopped halfway along and headed up a flight of metal stairs. Daise pulled herself up the stairs gripping the weird black plastic handrail. They were the strangest stairs she'd ever seen. They started with a set of flat steps and built up in height like a wave frozen in time.

The steps rang out as they climbed; the rhythmic clanging was almost musical. At the top of the stairs Mrs Arkwright slotted her torch in a leather loop attached to the wall and turned on the lights. Daise had never seen so many books in one place. It was a huge high room built to be a ticket hall that was being used as a library. An elaborate chandelier hung above dozens of bookshelves.

She ran her fingers along the book spines as they walked to a large oval table that sat in the centre of the room. It was a wooden table that could probably seat twenty, surrounded by fancy chairs upholstered with soft red leather and with shiny chrome bases.

Mrs Arkwright and Rowan sat at the head of the table. Daise, Jude and Rey took the seats down the left-hand side of the table.

Only when Daise sat down did she realise how tired she was. Her injured arm felt stiff. Both of her bare arms looked ice white in the blue light of the concourse.

Rowan took in a deep breath and began to speak, 'I want to thank you all again for helping me. It has not gone to plan, but with your help, I think we will be in a position to free my people.'

Daise started to interrupt, but Mrs Arkwright shook her head, 'Let him tell his story.'

'I left my home on Ancaster Island yesterday. I had

arranged to meet Mrs Arkwright at Casthorpe Bay but my boat hit a rock and I washed up on Barrowby Beach. I have been in correspondence with The Academy for the last six months devising a plan to overthrow the Greater Grantham Council. I believe that if we join forces, we can tear down these walls that separate our communities and once again taste freedom.'

'Ancaster Island is a labour camp. The green people are forced to work in the fields to produce foods to fill the bellies of the rich. Those who raise concerns go missing. We suspect they are put to work at the Port Fulbeck industrial complex in the north of the island but no one has ever returned to confirm our suspicions.'

'Mrs Arkwright has told me about your struggles in the Casthorpe Reset; the introduction of the barrier, checkpoints and the restrictions on travel. This is how it started with us. I believe we have a unified cause. The Council must be stopped before you too are forced into bonded labour.

'We may look different to you but we share a common bond.'

'Our plan is to break into the Channel offices and broadcast a television programme we have created called 'the truth'. It shows the oppressive nature of the regime; people enslaved and beaten if they don't work hard enough. We hope it will encourage people to rise up against the Council.'

'It reminds people of our real history. Not the Council's version. It tells of how England was broken up in the aftermath of the flood and how our proud democratic ideals have been discarded by the Council's regime.'

The Castoffs

'Most of the adults know this history but they are too frightened to speak out. Your children are being brainwashed by the lies broadcast by the Channel. They are not just enslaving us they are erasing us from history.' Rowan's hands shook and became fists as he spoke.

Mrs Arkwright said, 'I know this is a lot to take in. I have been trying to unite the factions of resistance in the communities that lie outside of the fence. The Academy has the knowledge — we just need the people to rise up. I have been working with my colleagues to identify like-minded resistance groups and then Jon, the Patcher, put me in touch with the Ancaster Island community.'

'Jon thought that's where the green people were being kept. He said it was where Professor Dawkins worked before he disappeared.'

Daise blurted out, 'You mean, my dad worked on Ancaster Island? Was he involved in enslaving Rowan and his people?'

Mrs Arkwright shook her head, 'No Daisy, Dennis Dawkins was a great man. He's not just your father. He's the father of the green people. He wanted them to be free.'

She paused for a moment, looking a little confused, 'But I thought your father's real name had been kept from you?'

Daise told her story from the start, about how she had met Rowan on the beach, how she had been shot. Rowan chipped in with a few details and explained how Gregor had hit the back of his head. She also told them about her time in the hospital, her brush with death on the operating table and her conversation with the Chief Whitmore, ending with the revelation that she was Daisy

Dawkins — daughter of Dennis Dawkins, a resistance fighter.

She could see the grave concern in the eyes of Rowan and Mrs Arkwright. Jude and Rey sat with their elbows on the tables and hands under their chins trying to take in the twists and turns of her tale.

She shivered as she recalled her conversation with the Chief. Her injured arm felt cold and limp by her side. She rubbed it vigorously to try and warm it up. When she looked up at Mrs Arkwright, Rowan, Jude and Rey, they were all staring at her.

Rey spoke first. 'Daise look, there's something wrong with your arm.'

Chapter 17 – Patcher

The Patcher sat in a big, battered leather armchair in the corner of his shack. Bert, his Doberman pinscher, lay sound asleep beside him. A small puddle of Bert's drool collected in a deep crack in the arm of the chair. In his prime, he'd been an excellent guard dog. But in his advancing years, like the Patcher, he had lost his edge. He was more likely to lick the hand of a stranger than bite it and he spent a lot more time sleeping than barking.

The Patcher watched as Bert's rib cage rose and sank on his lap. The Patcher had been a professor at a state-of-the-art hospital in Nottingham. That seemed like a different life now. He'd made some terrible choices and all he had to show for his hard work was a beat-up shack in Casthorpe market. But he wasn't bitter; he deserved to be here.

It had been a busy day — all the posters of the green man had brought the hypochondriacs in. He was cleared out of stocks of echinacea and his multivitamin broth.

The shack was a rough mishmash of prefabricated storage units, static caravans and sheds.

The walls were clad with an assortment of wooden shelves constructed from offcuts on which sat row upon row of glass Kilner jars. At first glance it looked ramshackle but each jar was carefully labelled with a

The Castoffs

white square on which the Patcher had written a description of the contents in his spidery handwriting.

Some jars contained pills he had procured from an old pharmacist colleague. But most were filled with concoctions of his own making; a cornucopia of powders, dried herbs, tree barks and brothy liquids of every conceivable colour. Each had an identifying number that corresponded to a ledger the Patcher kept, which described the treatment, dose, side effects and expiry date.

The Patcher winced as a sharp pain shot down his leg. His sciatica was playing up. He stretched his leg out, startling Bert from his slumber.

'It OK Bert, you go back to sleep', he mumbled as he stroked the back of his dog's head affectionately.

He gazed through his window across to the open dusty square of the food market. In the dim moonlight, he could see it was still chained up. She must still be out with those boys. He pulled the piece of paper from his shirt pocket. It wasn't unusual for Alice to pass him a note. Usually it was a list of books he might be interested in. He had smiled when he had seen the note as he had assumed it was a joke. The note had simply said. 'Gone to find Rowan. If I don't return, convene the Academy.'

He picked Bert from his lap, stood up and placed him gently in the armchair. The dog let out a whimper and settled back down to sleep. Two doors opened from the back wall of his shop into separate storage containers; the first was his living quarters and the second his procedures room. This is where the Patcher performed surgery. The walls were lined with ceramic tiles and in the centre of the room was his operating bench. The bench was a salvaged aluminium kitchen worktop he'd been given by the market manager after he removed a tongue tie from her baby. The poor child had been wasting away unable to feed until the Patcher had performed a simple procedure in his back room. Word got around and before long he had a selection of surgical tools from scalpels and scissors to retractors and clamps. He even had an assistant, a young girl from the towers. She was great with the customers and he trusted her to sell remedies using his ledgers but, while she was a useful assistant in the operating room, he knew she lacked the dexterity and precision to master the art of surgery.

He did his best to keep his equipment clean and sterile using a countertop dishwasher and electric pressure cooker. But it was a world away from the sterile operating theatres in which he had trained. Post-operative infections were a huge problem. He longed for the days in his youth when a simple course of antibiotics could keep an infection at bay. They'd known about antibiotic resistance for years but, as with climate change, they'd argued about what to do until it was too late.

He was tired but he had to clean the surgery before he could relax for the night. He hated this job but he knew if he let his standards drop his patients would suffer. Normally his assistant would do this but he let her go early on Thursdays.

He spent the next half hour spraying down all the surfaces with vinegar and polishing them dry with a cloth fresh from the pressure cooker. He knew the place wasn't sterile but it was the best he could do with the materials he had available to him. As he was mopping the floor, he heard a banging at the door. Thump, thump, thump. Bert

The Castoffs

woke up and started growling.

It was not unusual to get a late-night visit from some desperate family. But it was not the custom of the Patcher to open his clinic out of hours. If he stayed up all night working, he wouldn't be fit to help in the morning. There were only so many hours in the day. He continued with his mopping and left Bert to bark. The hammering continued, thump, thump, thump. If they banged any harder, they were going to knock his treatment jars off the shelves.

The Patcher started to sing to himself to drown out the thumping and the barking.

But still the thumping and the barking continued. He sang louder. They were not normally this persistent, he thought to himself. Then he heard the knuckles wrapping on glass and a woman calling him by his name, 'Jon, let us in! Jon, we need your help.'

The voice was muffled but there was only one person that called him by his real name. It was Alice Arkwright. He sighed, pushed the mop and bucket into the corner of the room and went to investigate. He liked Alice but he did not do out-of-hours work. He guessed he could, at least, tell her that to her face.

He propped the mop against the wall and opened his surgery door, almost toppling to the floor as Bert jumped up at him. 'Calm down, Bert. It's just Alice,' he said.

But when he opened the door, it wasn't just Mrs Arkwright, it was a crowd of people. A huge man pushed himself to the front. He was carrying a teenage girl. As his eyes ran across his face, he took a step back. He knew this man. A memory flashed in his mind and he felt a rush of guilt.

The Castoffs

Mrs Arkwright, 'I'm sorry to call after hours Jon. But we need your help. This girl's sick and Dr McInnes at Greenacres Hospital said you could help.'

Before the Patcher could protest, the tall man was striding towards his surgery. He was haunted by the memory of this man. It felt like he had been punched in the guts. The Patcher remained at his door staring into the black night sky as two boys followed Alice into his shack. A cool breeze danced across his face, chilling the beads of sweat that had formed on his forehead. Memories he had long-suppressed danced to the surface. He had been Jon Greaves, Chief Medical Officer at the Ancaster research facility. He had taken over from Professor Dawkins when he had disappeared. But Dawkins had destroyed his own research and the green mice.

With the help of the Council, Jon had rounded up the last of the Green people. They had been set to work farming. They liked being out in the sun and didn't need food. It made food production so much cheaper. The operation was so successful that the Council demanded more people were transformed and put to work. But with the research destroyed, he had no choice but to run tests on green people.

He didn't know the name of the man carrying the girl. He had just called him 'Test Subject Three'. He had become the Patcher's lab mouse.

The focus of his research was rediscovering Dawkins' method for transforming humans. He shuddered to think of all of the human test subjects who had died as part of that programme. But the research that filled him with the most shame was the work he had done on Test Subject

The Castoffs

Three.

The Council were very keen to find a way of reversing the transformation process. They wanted to be able to transform the prison population. It would save on the cost of feeding the huge number of people incarcerated following the civil war, while reducing the costs of feeding the rest of the population. But the transformed were impressive specimens; they grew taller and stronger and their ability to make their own food made them resilient to famine. The Council feared that if they released transformed prisoners, they would represent a threat to their authority.

The Patcher had begun a programme to see if he could reverse the transformation. With all the mice dead, he had no choice but to use green people as his test subjects.

This man was the third subject of his experiments. The trial involved attempting to destroy the chloroplasts by keeping subjects in the dark and injecting them with clomazone, a potent weed killer.

Jon Greaves had set up a hospital room in the basement of the lab. There were no windows and the only light was a dim red bulb that was only turned on when he carried out the procedures. He drew blood from a cannula on the back of Test Subject Three's hand on the hour, every hour for six weeks.

Exposure to prolonged darkness was a distressing experience for green people. After two days, they became violent and had to be strapped to their beds. When they stopped drinking fluids, the Patcher sedated them and attached a drip to their arms. When they stopped eating, the Patcher fed them through a tube directly into their

The Castoffs

stomachs.

The Patcher took meticulous notes, documenting their vital signs, carefully running lab tests on every aspect of their blood chemistry he could think of.

After 14 days, the test subjects' skin turned white, and their irises faded from bright green to grey. The dark treatment bleached the chloroplasts in the blood and skin. The second phase involved injecting a dilute solution of the weed killer, clomazone.

The first subject had taught him that spinal injections of clomazone caused instant paralysis and death. Intravenous injections in Test Subject Two had been similarly unsuccessful, triggering violent convulsions followed by a cardiac arrest.

Checking his careful notes, the Patcher was certain that he had reduced the concentration of the herbicide sufficiently to destroy the patient's chloroplasts without killing them.

Within 15 minutes of administering the first dose to Test Subject Three, he had started to scream. He begged the Patcher to stop. Within 30 minutes the patient was pulling at his restraints so hard his wrists and ankles were bleeding. After 45 minutes, he began to beat his head against the wall to knock himself unconscious,

Only then did the Patcher stop the treatment. But he was still hopeful the experiment had been a success. Over the next week, he slowly increased the light levels in the room. For the first three days the chloroplast load was zero. He thought he was on the brink of a scientific breakthrough. If the transformation was reversible, perhaps ordinary citizens could use it to get through a hard winter without the stigma of becoming a Green. But as the light levels increased the chloroplast reappeared and, day by day, he watched the patient's skin change. Green patches appeared, just on his arms at first, then slowly his whole body turned green as his photosynthetic machinery repaired itself. After a week, Jon abandoned the experiment. The patient was shipped out to work on the farm on the north of the island. The Council were unimpressed with his research and he was fired six months later.

He heard Alice Arkwright calling, 'Jon, we need you.'

The girl was laid flat on the table in his procedures room. The two boys that he saw earlier stood on each side of the girl holding her hands. The green man — Test Subject Three — was pacing around menacingly.

What was his name? It was so much easier to just think of him as a test subject and deny his humanity. Then it came to him with a rush of shame — Rowan Lightowler.

'You have to help her Jon. Look at her skin,' said Alice.

Jon slipped on a pair of gloves and approached the table. But Rowan blocked his path.

'This man is a monster. You cannot let him touch her.'

Mrs Arkwright looked at Daise lying on the metallic bench. 'We have no choice. Daise needs help and this is the only man who can help,' she said. Rowan's body was shaking with rage.

'You don't understand what this man is capable of,' he said. But he moved to one side to let Jon examine Daise.

'Hello, My name's Jon Greaves. People call me the Patcher. Can you tell me your name?'

Daise propped herself up on the table, 'My name's Daise and this is Rowan, Rey and Jude. Can you tell me what's happening to me?'

Jon placed a pillow underneath her head and examined her arms. Her skin was cold and pallid. Had she not been warm and talking, Jon would have thought she was her corpse. Her forearms were a strange purply green colour.

He pressed the discoloration, 'Does that hurt at all Daise?'

Daise shook her head.

'What is it Mr Patcher, is she going to be OK?', asked Jude.

There was something strange about the colour of her arms; it looked too bright to be bruising. The Patcher grabbed a hand lens from his pocket and peered at Daise's arm. He hadn't seen anything like this since his days working at Ancaster. These marks on her arms weren't bruises. They looked like patches of photosynthetic skin. This girl was transforming into a Green.

Chapter 18 – Planning

'Drink this, love', said the Patcher, offering Daise a glass of cloudy liquid.

'What is it?', barked Rowan. Daise was so startled she almost dropped the glass. She had never seen Rowan so angry and aggressive. He had always seemed so gentle and peaceful.

'It's just a mineral drink. It should help her with the transformation,' replied the Patcher.

Rowan took the glass from Daise and gave it a sniff. He pushed the drink away from his face sharply, almost spilling it. A pained expression flashed across his face.

'I remember the smell of this drink; you gave it to me after the torture.'

Everyone looked at the Patcher. His voice cracked as he tried to speak. The shadows around his eyes looked darker and Daise was sure he was on the verge of tears.

'It's true I did terrible things to this man. And I am deeply sorry.'

He wiped his eyes and took a deep breath, 'I can't change the past, but I can help this young woman. I don't know how but she seems to be transforming into a Green. The drink will help the photosynthetic machinery start working.'

'But shouldn't we be trying to stop this?' asked Mrs

The Castoffs

Arkwright.

The Patcher sighed, 'No one has been able to reverse the transformation. I worked on a research programme to find a way. We…'

Rowan interrupted, 'Don't pretend what you did was research. It was a crime against humanity.'

Nobody said anything. The weight of silence filled the room. Rowan started to rub his smooth head as if to calm thoughts boiling in his brain.

'I need some air,' he announced barging past the Patcher and out of the operating room.

It was Daise who spoke next, 'But why is this happening to me?'

The Patcher hopped onto the bench and sat next to Daise, 'I thought the ability to transform people was destroyed when the Professor disappeared but these patches on your skin are unmistakable.'

'But how is that possible? I was in Greenacres, I was shot you see,' she said pointing to her arm. 'Could they have experimented on me in the operating theatre?'

'I don't think so. The standard transformation process takes three to four weeks. You don't see patches this large until two weeks.' replied the Patcher.

'Could she have caught it from Rowan. On the posters it said he was infectious,' said Jude.

'Don't believe everything the Council tells you son. While it is theoretically possible for the transformation to be transmissible, I don't think that would be likely. I worked at the Ancaster research station with hundreds of Greens mixing with normal people and we never recorded a case of transformation by infection.'

Daise shook her head. How could she be a Green? It

just didn't make any sense. She looked at her arms; the green patches were getting bigger, extending down to her wrists. She thought back to last week. Apart from today it had been pretty uneventful.

She didn't know why. Perhaps it was the deep lines of experience etched into his face, but she trusted the Patcher. She gulped the drink and banged the empty glass down on the worktop to get everyone's attention.

'I don't know why this is happening to me but if it means I'm not dying, well, that's gotta be good news.'

'She's going to be OK then Jon?' Mrs Arkwright asked.

'Let's do a few more tests, just to be sure.'

Jon pushed himself off the bench and grabbed a beaten-up leather bag from the corner of the room. He pulled out his stethoscope and blood pressure cuff. He noted down the readings.

'I need to take a look at your wound Daise, is that OK?'

She proffered her arm to the Patcher. He carefully removed the dressing to reveal the bullet wound, which was a deep jade green colour.

'Woah, that doesn't look right Daise', blurted Jude.

The Patcher could see the fear in Daise's eyes, 'It's OK, it's just the chloroplasts in your bloodstream. They should help you heal quicker. It's all consistent with your diagnosis. Everything seems fine. You're going to notice changes in the coming days. Your appetite will diminish and your sense of taste will be disrupted. Not all green people stop eating altogether so listen to your body. If you feel hungry, eat. If you don't then don't worry about it. You're going to want to get out in the sunlight for

The Castoffs

three or four hours a day and keep yourself hydrated. I can make you up some of my mineral tonic which should help with the transition.'

Daise listened intently to the Patcher as he explained the changes ahead of her. It sounded like a video on puberty that she'd watched when she was a little girl. She'd only got used to the idea of becoming a woman and now she was changing into something else. Then there were the practicalities. How was she supposed to get three or four hours of sunlight a day? She was pretty certain if she walked around Casthorpe exposing her green skin to the sun, she would be delivered to the Guardians before her skin was even warm.

There was no point dwelling on her predicament. Her only hope was to help Rowan and his plan to expose the Council and free the green people of Ancaster Island. She was going to be one of them after all.

The Patcher was still talking when Rowan walked back into the room. Daise ripped off the blood pressure cuff dangling from her arm and embraced him.

'She's fine,' the Patcher announced, addressing Rowan. 'She just needs to keep her fluids up, a good night sleep and some sun on her skin.'

'I think it's time we called it a night. I'm pretty sure I've got room for four,' said Mrs Arkwright.

'Sorry to intrude Jon, but we really appreciate your help.' She turned to face Rey and Jude. 'Could you do me a favour? Unlock my place and show Rowan and Daise into the lounge. I want to have a word with Jon.'

Rey grabbed the keys and led Rowan, Jude and Daise to Mrs Arkwright's market stall home.

The Castoffs

***

Daise woke in a dimly lit, windowless bedroom. It took a moment for her eyes to adjust to her surroundings but she could see that the others had already got up. She could hear the gentle clanking of a teapot and crockery coming from behind her. Whether it was the mineral tonic the Patcher had given her or just a good night's sleep, she didn't know, but she felt great.

Springing out of bed, she walked into the kitchen. Jude and Rey were sitting around a small round table smiling in expectation as Mrs Arkwright dished up fried egg sandwiches. The eggy smell caught Daise at the back of the throat making her feel queasy.

'Morning Daise,' they all chimed in unison. Mrs Arkwright offered her an egg sandwich and a mug of warm tea. She took the mug of tea and declined the sandwich, acutely aware of the fact the transformation was changing her sense of taste. A fried egg was a rare treat she would have normally savoured.

'Where's Rowan?', she asked.

But before Mrs Arkwright could answer, Rowan's head appeared through a curtain of beads that led to the lounge.

'How are you feeling Daise', he asked.

'So much better, thanks,' she said, suddenly aware that she wasn't wearing her sling and her arm didn't hurt at all. She unwrapped the dressing that the Patcher had applied last night; the only evidence of her bullet wound was a small green circle on her arm.

'That's great news,' Rowan replied. His face was fixed in a broad friendly smile.

The Castoffs

'You seem in much better spirits too', remarked Daise.

'Ahh yes', said Rowan rather sheepishly. 'Sorry about my behaviour last night. I was quite upset. Meeting the man, you call the Patcher brought up many painful memories for me.'

He looked over at Rey and Jude, who were wiping thick globs of yolk from their faces, 'Are you ready to hear the plan?'

They all followed Rowan through the bead curtain into the lounge. On the coffee table, there were architectural plans of some sort. Daise sat down next to Rowan. Rey and Jude sat on the sofa while Mrs Arkwright perched on the edge of Daise's chair. Daise leaned into a patch of light that shone down from a skylight, enjoying the warmth on her skin.

Rey leaned forwards slapping his hands on the papers, 'What's all this about then?'

'These are plans of the Channel headquarters in Greater Grantham,' announced Mrs Arkwright.

They all hunched over the table as Mrs Arkwright took them through the plan to take over the broadcasting facilities at the Channel headquarters. 'We've been exploring the network of tunnels under Greater Grantham, trying to map out the network to what's above ground. We found a maintenance hatch that comes up in the car park of the Channel HQ.'

She pointed to one of the architectural drawings spread across the table and continued, 'most of the security is focused on the front gate.'

'But how do we get into the building?' asked Daise.

'Good question, we've got someone on the inside. Dr

McInnes's husband, Dave, is a sound engineer at the station. He's going to leave the car park entrance unlocked.'

The entrance was marked with a little red x on the plans.

'From here, a lift goes up to the eighth floor. Dave has managed to clone a security pass from a colleague who is at a Channel conference all week.'

Mrs Arkwright shuffled through the papers until she found one marked 'Eighth Level'. 'This is where it gets a bit trickier. We need to get to the broadcast centre. If we arrive at six- thirty Dave assures us that most of the employees will have gone home but the security Guardians don't begin the patrols until seven. So, there should only be a few staff who are working late and some cleaning staff.

'A friend of mine works as a cleaner at the Channel. He's managed to get a couple of Channel branded tabards so we should be able to blend in. We need one person to distract the duty manager and another one to switch the broadcast feed to play our film.'

'What's on the film?' Rey and Jude asked in unison.

Rowan removed a small ziplock bag from his pocket containing a plastic memory card, 'I've recorded some footage from Ancaster Island which shows the brutality of the regime. When people see that slavery is alive and well in Greater Grantham it will be the catalyst for the revolution and the emancipation of my people.'

'Steady on Rowan, let's not get carried away,' warned Mrs Arkwright. 'We've discussed this. The video is just one part of the plan. It will make the people question what they've been told, but it's going to take more than

The Castoffs

that to take down the Council.'

'But when they see what I've seen…' Rowan broke off. Mrs Arkwright put her hand on his shoulder.

'It will take time to wake the people. They've been focused on survival. Politics is a luxury few of them can afford when their families are hungry. We need to sow the seeds of revolution, nurture them and when the people are ready, we will take up arms against the Council.'

'But my people cannot wait.'

'They won't have to. You and I are going on the ship to liberate Ancaster.'

Daise spoke next, 'I'm in. Just tell us what you want us to do. What other choice do I have? The Patcher said I needed sunlight. I can't exactly walk around Casthorpe looking like this,' she said pointing to her arms.

The green patches had grown overnight to cover the insides of her forearms. Tendril-like projections curved around the front of her arms.

'All I know is that if I don't help change things, I will be detained or worse still I'll end up being experimented on, like Rowan.'

She looked to Rowan for reassurance but he had nothing to offer. The Council scientists would certainly want to know how Daise was transformed. They wouldn't let her carry on living in the towers with Rey and Jude. She was invested in this plan no matter how risky.

'Hold on a minute. Can I ask a question about this plan? If you and Rowan are going on a ship to Ancaster, who is going to the Channel HQ?', said Jude.

There was a pause before Mrs Arkwright said, 'We're

The Castoffs

going to need your help. Rowan can't go — it's too risky. He's too tall and would stand out. We need people who look anonymous. I've agreed to sail the ship. So, we need you three to break into the office and broadcast the truth.'

'Isn't there anyone else in the resistance who could do it?', asked Jude.

'We don't go by that name anymore. We are the Academy. We do have a network of people throughout Greater Grantham and beyond. But we need young people for this job. The cleaners at the Channel are all under 20. They don't want to risk employing people who remember the old times. Look, you need a bit of time, I get that. I've got to set up for the day. Why don't you guys talk it over.'

Mrs Arkwright grabbed a big set of keys and went outside to set up the trestle tables.

Rowan stood up and said, 'Mrs Arkwright has a little sheltered garden at the back of her property. She told me it is a good place to catch some morning sunshine. I'll leave you alone to decide.'

Rey got up next, 'I don't know what there is to talk about. I've made up my mind. I'm going to help, however I can. If you two need to talk, talk. I'll be outside helping Mrs Arkwright.'

Jude and Daise were left alone on the shabby sofa. Jude waited until Rey was out of earshot, 'We don't have to do this Daise. We hardly know this woman and she is asking us to risk our lives, for what? Even if we are successful, do you think that the people will rise up against the Council. I can't exactly see the towers defeating the might of Greater Grantham. It's all a fantasy.'

Daise reached across and held Jude's hand, 'I'm scared too, but what choice do I have? I can't go back home looking like this.'

'We could go away, make a boat and sail to the Wildwolds,' replied Jude. 'We've got the skills to survive. We're resourceful.'

Daise sighed, 'Listen to yourself Jude, we can't just sail away from our problems. It's our responsibility too. You heard Rowan, the stuff that's going on Ancaster. If we stand by and do nothing, we become part of the problem.'

'But we barely know these people. They are asking us to put our lives on the line.'

'Look Jude', she said squeezing his hand tightly, 'This is something I have to do. But I understand if you don't want to. Or can't.'

'Please Daise, come away with me. We can leave all this behind.' He sounded desperate.

For a moment Daise imagined a life away from all of this. She looked into Jude's face. Sometimes she imagined that they were more than friends. From time to time she watched him when he wasn't aware. She liked his warm brown eyes, his unusually long eyelashes and his thick brows that almost joined in the middle. Although he wasn't quite as tall as Daise, his body had broadened across the shoulders in the last year.

But the past couple of days had driven a wedge between them. She felt like they were out of sync — on different pages of a book.

If he'd asked her a week ago, she might have considered it. Anything to get away from the monotony

The Castoffs

of their lives in Casthorpe.

'What about Rey?' she asked, trying to bring Jude back down to earth.

'Rey's my best friend. He would come with us if we asked him. I'm sure of it,' replied Jude.

Daise looked down at her arms. The reality of her situation was written in the green lines extending out from the patches on her forearms. She knew what she was and she couldn't run from it. She leaned in and kissed Jude on the cheek, 'I'm sorry Jude, I can't go with you. I have to help the green people. I am one of them now.'

Jude pulled his hand away, 'Then I'm sorry Daise, I can't be involved with this suicide mission. The resistance… Academy, whatever they call themselves are just using you. I'm going back to the towers.'

And with that, Jude was gone. She followed him to the door and watched him as he walked away, waiting for him to look back, but he continued up the dusty track until he was out of sight.

Chapter 19 – Channel

'I'm sorry, we can't wait for him any longer', said Mrs Arkwright. Daise looked forlornly up at the tall grey stacks of the Casthorpe Reset and then along the road, hoping to see Jude running towards them.

'He's not coming', said Rey. His voice was flat with resignation.

Rey was right. Jude wasn't coming. She felt betrayed. Why had he left them when they needed him the most?

'We'll be alright,' added Rey but he didn't sound convincing.

Daise offered a half-smile in return. She looked up at Mrs Arkwright for reassurance but she looked worried too, staring at her watch anxiously. They had waited for Jude to return all day.

'If he didn't want to go with you to the Channel, he could have at least helped out on the stall.'

It was 4pm. Mrs Arkwright was annoyed that she'd had to pack up her stall early. 'There's kids who'll go to bed hungry tonight,' she grumbled.

'Come on then, let's give this our best shot,' said Daise.

A rolling blanket of grey cloud had tumbled in from the west, sinking Greater Grantham into a dull subdued light. A belligerent breeze drew goose bumps from

Daise's arms. It was unusually cold for a summer's day. She was glad of the long sleeves she wore to cover her green stained skin.

Mrs Arkwright led them up Casthorpe Road in the direction of Barrowby. She stopped next to the stump of an old telegraph pole and walked into some grassland. It looked like a patch of wasteland in the shadow of the towers but Daise could make out the bucked concrete of an old roadway. Small plants and shrubs had broken up the surface of the road, reclaiming this rugged patch of ground for nature. Ten metres down the road and Mrs Arkwright came to a stop. On her right lay a rough patch of concrete. It looked like the foundations of an old building. The loose bricks had been long since salvaged and a mosaic of weeds was growing out of the weathered mortar.

As they walked across the rubble-strewn scrubland, Daise could see where the interior walls would have divided the building into rooms. They continued across the foundations until, once again, Mrs Arkwright stopped.

'OK, we're here,' she announced, handing a small backpack to Rey.

Rey unbuttoned the bag and looked at the rolled-up schematics of the Channel HQ, cleaners' uniforms and security passes and some spray bottles of polish.

Mrs Arkwright turned to face Daise. 'Take care of this,' she said, placing a small memory card into Daise's hand.

'It's Rowan's film. Now let's get you on your way.'

Daise placed the memory card carefully in her pocket, tracing the outline with her finger to reassure herself that

The Castoffs

it was safe. She couldn't see anything that suggested there was an entrance to the underground tunnel until Mrs Arkwright kicked out at a small patch of rubble. There it was, a metal plate, which she pulled up to reveal a shaft just like the one they had found near the hospital.

'All you need to do is climb down, turn left and walk up the tunnel past the hospital. Go past the ladder we came down last night and continue on for another ten minutes to the next access ladder. Climb up this and you'll come out in the car park of the Channel headquarters. There should be some crates stacked up in front of the manhole to give you some cover.'

'Remind me, how do we get into the building,' asked Rey, a little unsure of himself.

'Just walk in the car park entrance at the back of the building. Remember, don't look anyone in the eye. As a cleaner from Casthorpe you will be invisible to them.

'What do you mean invisible? The tabards are bright green. Surely, they're going to see us.' said Rey incredulously.

'I don't mean you will actually disappear but you'll just blend into the background. They won't notice you if you just keep your distance and go about the business of dusting their desks. Cleaners are not real people to them.'

'Can you go through the plan one more time,' asked Daise.

Mrs Arkwright let out a sigh and explained what they needed to do, 'Take the lift to the tenth floor. This is where they broadcast from. Most of the office will be empty. Rey, you should cause a distraction. Do something dramatic. Knock a screen over or something. Be sure to make a fuss so that Daise has enough time to

The Castoffs

enter the glass-walled studio in the corner of the office. There shouldn't be anyone in there but if there is, don't worry, just do some cleaning. In the broadcast studio there will be a big silver deck on the table at the far end. The broadcast deck contains a row of memory card slots for the night time broadcasts. All you need to do is eject memory card number two and replace it with Rowan's card. When it is done, make your apologies for Rey and get out of there.'

'How long until Rowan's film is played?' asked Rey.

'According to Dave, slot two is broadcast at 6.30pm. So, you should have plenty of time to get out of there.'

'It seems so simple when you say it,' replied Rey.

Mrs Arkwright moved in close, 'That's because it is simple. You're going to be great.'

She patted them both reassuringly on the arm. 'I know it's disappointing that Jude bailed on us, but you know it's probably less risky as a two-person job. Although it would have been nice to have somebody look after my stall. Come on, let's have a group hug.'

They all embraced and for a moment Daise felt a little bit of hope flutter in her guts.

Mrs Arkwright broke off first, flicking her wrist to look at her watch, 'Look you really have to go now.' She removed her watch and strapped it onto Daise's wrist. Daise held the watch up to her face. It looked expensive. Mrs Arkwright held her hands and adjusted the bezel on the outer edge of the watch.

'Wait in the tunnel until ten past six. Most of the staff will have left by then. Good luck.' She held up the metal plate and handed Daise a torch.

Daise held the heavy stainless steel watch up to her

face. She had to adjust the angle to make out the time. It was half past five. They had forty-five minutes to make it to the Channel office.

'Come on Daise, let's go.'

They marched down the tunnels, the sound of their footsteps bouncing off the smooth concrete walls. Daise checked the time on the watch, and nervously picked up the pace. She felt an anxious ache in her arm around the bullet wound.

They followed the narrow beam of torch light until they reached the platform underneath Greenacres Hospital. Rey jumped on the platform and switched the lights on; it felt a bit less claustrophobic in this wider section of the tunnel. Daise looked at her watch again.

'We've got time for a break,' she said, reaching inside her bag for her water bottle. She took a big glug and passed it to Rey who shook his head.

'You're not going to catch anything from me, Rey,' she yelled, regretting her words as soon as they left her mouth.

Rey pushed himself off the platform and began to walk into the thick blackness of the tunnel.

'I'm sorry Rey, I didn't mean to snap. Please come back. I think it's this transformation. It's making me cranky.' She left the platform lights on and headed after Rey, holding his image in the torchlight as she ran.

By the time they reached the next exit, Rey had forgiven Daise. If anything, he was a little relieved. He had hesitated to share her water. Nobody really seemed to know why Daise was turning green. A part of him remained unconvinced that it wasn't contagious.

Daise checked the watch; it was 6pm. They waited

The Castoffs

patiently at the foot of the shaft for five minutes before they began their ascent of the steel ladder. Rey insisted on leading the way knowing that the cover at the top of the shaft might be difficult for Daise to push up with an injured arm.

At the top of the shaft, Rey looked down at Daise, 'Can you turn the torch off? I don't want to attract any attention as we push up the cover.'

He placed his hand up against the cool metal plate as they were plunged into blackness. Waiting a few seconds for his eyes to adjust, he whispered, 'Let's do this thing Daise'.

He pushed upwards. There was movement and a shard of light flashed down the shaft but it was promptly extinguished as Rey's hand slipped from the ladder. He lost his balance and his shoulder smashed into the opposite wall.

Daise instinctively looked up and was showered with dust as Rey flailed against the wall, desperately trying to stop himself from falling. With each blink, the dust and debris raked at her eyes. She fought the instinct to rub them, clinging onto the rungs of the ladder like a limpet on a rock. She braced herself, waiting for Rey to fall. But somehow he had managed to wedge himself against the wall and swing his hand out to connect with a rung of the ladder.

'I'm OK,' he gasped. Then he took a deep breath and pushed up with his head and shoulders. The steel cover scraped noisily across the concrete and rays of light shot down the shaft. Rey managed to climb out with the manhole cover still propped up on his back. He remained on all fours as Daise followed and helped him replace the cover over the shaft.

Squatting behind a stack of wooden crates, they took in their surroundings. Ahead of them was a car park, which was next to a ten-storey glass building. Behind them was a chain-link fence topped in razor wire that surrounded the complex.

Daise pulled the map out of her bag. It was marked out in ten panels, each showing a floor of the Channel Headquarters. On the ground floor, the car park extended underneath the building to allow the senior executives to park their cars out of the glare of the sun. From their vantage point behind the packing crates, they could just make out the glass door into the building, which was marked on the map with a green arrow.

Rey rifled around in his rucksack and removed a couple of spray bottles and dusters. Next, he pulled out two bright green tabards, along with two security passes on lanyards. He handed the items to Daise, slipped on the cleaners' tabard and put the security pass lanyard around his neck. He tucked the empty rucksack in between the crates and waited for Daise to pull her fluorescent tabard over her head.

She smoothed down the tabard and patted her pocket, feeling for the outline of the card containing Rowan's broadcast. Reassured it was still there, she pointed to her wrist and whispered, 'It's time to go.'

He nodded silently in agreement and they both stood up and strode towards the building with purpose.

As they reached the door, they started to understand what Mrs Arkwright meant. It really did feel like they were invisible. Everybody just ignored them. Even the security Guardian barely looked up from his desk as they

The Castoffs

swiped their passes on the gates. They moved along the corridor slowly, keeping their heads down as Mrs Arkwright had advised until they came to a lift.

Daise pressed the up-arrow button on an illuminated panel next to the lift but it didn't seem to work. The light above the lift indicated that it was stuck on floor five.

A middle-aged man in a tailored suit barged past Rey, tutting loudly. He tapped his pass against a sensor on the wall, rolled his eyes and muttered something about Castoffs under his breath. Daise was about to confront him but Rey grabbed her hand and mouthed the words, 'Look down.'

She had forgotten Mrs Arkwright's advice. Don't make eye contact. When the lift arrived, they hung back waiting for the suited man to walk in. The lift was small, with only enough room for four people. She thought perhaps it might be better to wait for the next one but she wasn't sure their passes would summon the lift. Rey made the choice for her by following the suited man into the lift.

Daise took a gulp of air and stepped forward, jabbing the control panel for floor ten before standing back against the dimpled aluminium walls. They both stared at the floor avoiding the gaze of the man in the suit.

The lift came to a stop on floor three. Daise realised that she would have to get out of the lift to let the man out. She stepped into an office with a jungle of desks upon which sat huge silver-backed screens. She stood nervously outside the lift as the suited man took what seemed like an age to exit.

Then the lift doors began to close, slicing through the air that separated Daise from Rey. She watched helplessly

The Castoffs

as Rey began jabbing the control panel inside the lift, desperately trying to open the doors. Their eyes met; Rey reached forward but it was too late. The doors closed and Daise heard the heart sinking hum of the lift ascending to the sixth floor without her.

She turned around and scanned the office. The man in the suit was perched on the edge of a desk talking to a younger woman. There was something unsettling about the way he was looking at her. It was leering, predatory.

There must be some stairs, she thought as she shuffled along the corridor, looking quickly left and right for a door to the stairwell.

'You, cleaner… come over here.'

Daise froze. She turned slowly to face the sleazy suited man.

'Clean that up', he said, pointing to a small coffee stain on the woman's desk. Daise pulled her duster from her pocket and approached, carefully avoiding eye contact with either of them. They carried on talking, oblivious to Daise.

The suited man spoke with a tone of overbearing condescension, 'I'm a very good friend of the Chief Guardian and he says they are close to rounding up those Academy criminals. They've gone too far this time releasing a dangerous infectious criminal from Ancaster. It's tantamount to bioterrorism.'

Daise couldn't resist looking at the woman sitting at her workstation. She was no more than twenty. Her eyes were a striking blue, behind thick black acrylic glasses. She looked scared. Daise focused on cleaning the coffee stain, trying to appear invisible.

'Is the story on the hospital attack ready to run?'

The Castoffs

'Just finishing it off,' said the woman, her voice filled with tension.

Daise could tell that she just wanted to finish her work. But the suited man continued, 'The visual effects guys have done a fantastic job. It's amazing how we can recreate the stories of the eyewitnesses like we were really there.'

The woman just nodded and returned her attention to her screen. With the coffee stain cleaned up, Daise moved to the next desk and began dusting. She felt a little safer now, like she was blending back into the background.

At the end of the row of workstations, she looked up. The man in the suit was gone and the woman had placed a pair of bulky headphones over her ears. Looking around, she saw that the suited man had withdrawn into a glass-walled office in the corner of the room. Daise could hear the noise of a telephone conversation seeping out from under the door. She continued dusting down the next row of workstations until she was directly behind the young woman.

Her eyes were drawn to the screen. She watched in horror; a grotesque green human was attacking a doctor at Greenacres. The man was as tall as Rowan but he had dark rings around his eyes and jagged yellow teeth. His eyes were thin with obsidian-black pupils. This monster knocked a doctor to the ground and followed up with a kick to the head.

Her brain raced with incomprehension. This never happened. She was there with Rowan and he didn't look like that and he certainly didn't attack a doctor. She almost screamed out in protest, biting down on her cheek

The Castoffs

in anger.

The fake news story strengthened her resolve. She folded up her duster, attached her spray to her waistband and walked across the office to summon the lift.

When the doors opened, she was relieved to find it empty. Punching the button for the tenth floor, she glanced back into the office. The suited man slammed the phone down and shouted across the office. 'Hey, you in the lift. Stop!'

Daise jabbed at the button furiously as the man charged across the office towards her. She backed into the lift, unsure of what to do. He ran like a lion focused on its prey. She could do nothing but wait and hope that the doors would close before he reached her. She closed her eyes and counted down — five, four, three, two… She heard a crash, then the sensation deep within her belly of the lift going up.

She held her breath as the lift passed through the floors, hoping that it would not stop until it reached the tenth. She let out a deep breath when she arrived. But her relief was short lived; the door opened with a gentle ping and she fell to her knees at the sight of Cillian Whitmore, the Chief Guardian.

'Ah, Daisy Dawkins, we meet again.'

Chapter 20 – Regret

Rowan looked at himself in the mirror. The face that looked back from him was like a ghost from his past, before he'd agreed to be part of the trial before he'd been transformed.

Alice Arkwright had given him some foundation to cover his face. He needed to blend in. It had been many years since he'd seen a white face reflected in a mirror. If it wasn't for his green eyes, it could be his own younger face, looking back at him through time.

His mirror image unlocked the memory of the night he took a decision that ended his old life. The past was a different country, separated in time and geography. Back when the country was united before the flood changed everything.

He recalled waking up in the middle of the night. His daughter was crying. The camp for those displaced by the flood was no place for a three-week-old baby. His wife tried to get up from their inflatable bed but she winced in pain. Rowan was worried about her caesarean section wound. A pink border extended outward from the scar-like an angry snake. He hadn't talked to her about it but they both knew it was an infection.

Even in a hospital surviving a deep infected wound would be tough. The antibiotics he remembered from his

The Castoffs

childhood were now all but useless. When infections took hold there was little that could be done.

He unzipped the sleeping compartment and went to his wailing daughter lying in her pushchair, her little legs kicking at her blankets in frustration.

The distant muffled sound of an adult sobbing from a neighbouring tent and some youths shouting in the distance blended in with the cries of his daughter like a symphony of human misery.

Tensions were running high in the camp as food and clean water were becoming increasingly scarce. A desperate voice screamed out, 'Please, for the love of God, can you be quiet?'

Outside the polythene window was a sprawling village of ramshackle tents. As the floodwaters rose and engulfed the suburbs of Nottingham one by one, West Bridgford, Beeston, Colwick, Hyson Green all submerged. Rowan had lived in Sherwood, right on the edge of the flood zone. When the sandbag wall they had built on Haydn Road finally broke, filling their home with sludgy floodwaters, they had little choice but to head up the hill to the refugee camp in Woodthorpe Park.

He turned on the dim battery-powered lamp that dangled from the central dome of his family tent, picked up his daughter and paced around in tight circles trying to soothe her. She batted her head against his chest. She was hungry; they all were. Try as he might, he was unable to lull her back to sleep. It was clear that she wanted her mother. He felt completely useless as he handed his crying baby daughter to his poorly wife. Sitting cross-legged on the tent's green plastic floor, he gave in to the crushing weight of despair. Tears dripped off his face as

The Castoffs

he sobbed in silence while his wife fed their child.

He wasn't taken in by the climate change deniers. He had moved from the Lincolnshire coast to Nottingham in the middle of the country. He had stocked his spare room with food and essential supplies. He thought he was as prepared for all that nature could throw at him. But the sea levels didn't rise gradually. The sea ice melted at a pace that was beyond all the predictions. The ice sheets in Greenland and Iceland retreated in years not decades. It was the same in the Southern Hemisphere as huge chunks of ice cleaved off Antarctica into the ocean. The sea defences were obsolete as soon as they were built. All it took was a hurricane-force storm surge to redraw the map of western Europe overnight.

The East of England was devastated. London was submerged. Towns and cities on rivers were flooded, low lying land was reclaimed by the sea. In the days and weeks that followed, the banking system collapsed and the value of Rowan's savings were reduced to nothing. His home was flooded and his food stores looted.

He reached inside his pocket and unfolded a leaflet that he had been handed at the food shelter earlier that day. A picture of a kind-looking old man dressed in a white coat stared at him. The man was perched casually on the edge of a desk. His grey hair and broad smile made him seem trustworthy and approachable. Rowan read the leaflet.

Wondering how you will feed your family?
New medical research trial may have the answer.

He turned the leaflet over and examined the long list

of bullet points:

To be eligible for this trial you must be:
- *Educated to degree level*
- *No family history of Asthma*
- *No family history of mental illness…*

The list went on, reeling off ailments like hay fever, dermatitis and others. It then went on to list characteristics that you must have; white skin, blue eyes, male pattern baldness.

The more he read, the more suspect it sounded. The talk of 'white skin' troubled him deeply. Rowan had read his history books and he knew that people were capable of terrible things in the name of science. But when he had finished reading there was nothing on this list that excluded him.

All his instincts told him that there was something very wrong with the trial but, as he listened to his wife whimpering in pain as she nursed their daughter, he made his mind up. If this trial meant he could save his family, then what choice did he really have? He sat on the greasy tarpaulin and waited for first light. He left a note for his wife and made his way to the clinic advertised in the leaflet.

Of the hundreds of people that stood outside the clinic, most did not match the eligibility criteria. The screening process was thorough and by the early afternoon, Rowan was sitting in a small waiting room with nine balding, blue-eyed white men.

The transformation process itself was simple. The group was called into a hospital ward. The perimeter of

The Castoffs

the room was lined with lacquered pine chairs finished with wipe-clean vinyl cushions. The air was thick with the smell of disinfectant and despair.

Next to each chair stood a drip stand with a bag of jade green liquid. It took 30 minutes for the bag to drain into a vein in Rowan's arm. A nurse came by to take some measurements and he was discharged with a leaflet explaining what to expect over the course of the week and a number to call if he experienced any of the adverse side effects.

When he returned to Woodthorpe Park, his tent was not where he left it and he could find no trace of his family. He recalled the panic, the desperation. And then the horror of the vicious truth; his wife and child had never woken from their sleep. Fearing the beginnings of a disease, the city Council had incinerated their bodies along with all their belongings. They had destroyed everything. As Rowan was trying to process the magnitude of his loss, he was accosted by three security guards who attempted to take him into quarantine. But Rowan ran, fuelled by adrenaline and grief.

Back in Alice Arkwright's home, he felt out of breath as if reliving his escape. Tears dripped from his face as if from a leaky tap. He wiped his face with his palms, his green skin breaking through the smeared makeup.

Alice called out from the lounge, 'Do you want a cup of tea Rowan?'

Rowan patched up his face with foundation and walked into the lounge, 'That would be lovely.' he replied, making a huge effort not to sound broken.

He entered the lounge dressed in a long-sleeved grey shirt, buttoned up to the neck with a matching pair of distressed black jeans. On his feet were heavy and scuffed black work boots. His bald head was covered with a train driver's cap.

'Wow, you look, well, very different. But you need one more accessory. Try these for size,' she said, handing Rowan a pair of sunglasses to cover his green eyes.

Rowan smiled half-heartedly, trying to hide his discomfort. He felt like he was suffocating in these clothes. His skin couldn't breathe. The sunglasses sat heavily on the bridge of his nose. It was all horribly uncomfortable. He just hoped he could bear it long enough to do what needed to be done.

'How did the children seem when you left them?', asked Rowan, desperate to move the focus of the conversation away from him.

'They looked a bit down, to be honest. Jude running out on them hit them harder than I thought,' she replied.

'Have we done the right thing?'

'We always knew it was a long shot, replied Alice, handing Rowan a cup of nettle tea. 'But we need someone to distract the Guardians from the real plan. If we are going to free the prisoners at Ancaster then we need a diversion.'

Rowan felt guilty, breaking into the Channel HQ had been his idea. The original plan was to pass the recording to Dave McInnes, who was part of the Academy network. But as Alice had pointed out they needed his intelligence. The Channel was the mouthpiece of the Council and the information Dave could share was too valuable to risk him getting caught.

Alice's plan needed Daise. If successful, Rowan's film would stir up some civil disobedience; distracting the

The Castoffs

Guardians from Ancaster Island where he planned to lead a rebellion of the green people. The Chief would be furious that Daise had escaped. If they were caught breaking into the Channel headquarters, he would be sure to go there.

So even if Daise and Rey failed, they would at the very least draw the Chief Guardian away from Ancaster.

The plan made sense but he couldn't shake the feeling that he was betraying a young woman who had shown him such kindness. He sat down next to Mrs Arkwright, who had taken a seat on the sofa, and took a sip of his tea.

'Look, Rowan. What we are doing now is war; we have to think of the greater good. From what I've seen these kids are resourceful. They may well do it. Besides, there is nothing we can do about it now.'

She looked at her wrist, forgetting for a moment that she had given her watch to Daise.

'We have to focus on our plan. We have to get to Casthorpe Harbour. The Patcher has hired a boat for the crossing. So, we are all set.'

Rowan winced at the thought of spending more time with his torturer.

Mrs Arkwright leaned into Rowan, 'Look, Jon has spent many years helping the people of Casthorpe. He wants to make up for the terrible things he did. I don't expect you to forgive him but he knows the island. He has given us plans and he's confident that he can get around their security system. There is no way we are going to achieve this without Jon's help.'

It seemed perverse that a man of his nightmares could be the saviour of his people. But Rowan had reluctantly agreed to the involvement of the Patcher.

Mrs Arkwright pulled a package out of her rucksack. It was wrapped in a chamois leather cloth. She pulled back the corners to reveal a pistol. 'It's only a replica but if you wave it around with authority it should have the desired effect. Take it. I've got a real one but let's hope we don't have to use it.'

For a moment he considered challenging her as to why he only got a replica while she had a real gun. It felt like she still didn't entirely trust him.

Rowan walked out of the shack and stood in silence as Mrs Arkwright locked up. When it was secured, they headed down to Casthorpe Harbour to meet the Patcher.

They'd been walking for ten minutes when they turned off Casthorpe Road near the bottom of the steep hill. Mrs Arkwright removed her rucksack from her back and carried it at her side.

'Watch out for pickpockets; the harbour attracts some desperate types,' she warned Rowan.

Most of the new ports that had sprung up after the flood were officially sanctioned by the Council. Grantham was the major port on the mainland of the Eastern Islands. The Council largely ignored the illegal ports like Casthorpe Harbour if they got a cut of the contraband. The illegal ports suppled specialist items not sanctioned by the Council. They also allowed you to bypass the bureaucracy of the official ports.

On occasion, the Council would send in the Guardians to raid the illegal ports. But palms were greased, someone would get detained and everything would go back to normal within a week.

As they walked down the track towards the sea, the

tarmac gave way to a dusty track. The first building they came to was an old stable building that had been converted into a pub. A faded old sign flapped in the breeze advertising the Fisherman's Arms.

A small group were drinking outside the pub in a makeshift beer garden, which was nothing more than four wooden picnic benches piled on concrete slabs. Rowan looked up at the sun descending. It couldn't be much later than 6 pm and these guys were already drunk and loud.

He was feeling irritable. He recognised the symptoms from the light deprivation experiments the Patcher had put him through. He was worried that his judgment would become impaired. He needed to keep his wits about him if the plan was going to work.

A long-haired young man spilled out of the pub carrying a tray crammed with drinks. He placed them on the picnic bench to a cheer. But instead of joining his drinking buddies, he picked up a beer, walked over to the furthest bench and put the glass on the table. Rowan watched as he sat down — facing the Patcher, who was sitting on his own reading a book.

'There he is,' said Mrs Arkwright a little loudly, pointing to the Patcher. The drinkers all turned around and glared at them. Most of them didn't look old enough to drink. There was something malevolent in their gaze and Rowan was relieved when they turned away and started talking again.

Rowan and Alice walked around the patio area. She slung her backpack on the bench and sat next to the Patcher.

'Good to see you, Jon. Who's your friend?' offering

The Castoffs

her hand to the man sat opposite.

Rowan remained standing. Over the top of his shades, he looked into the eyes of their contact. He was immediately recognisable with a black tattoo of a hand inked on his left cheek.

The tattooed man owned a boat repair shop in the harbour and had just patched up a boat that wasn't due to be collected for three days. For 200 coins they could have the boat for 48 hours. The price seemed extortionate to Rowan, but it was clear from the man's tone that it was non-negotiable.

The boat had a solar-powered electric motor and the battery was fully charged. Its range was 100 miles so it should be perfect for the trip to Ancaster Island. The plan was to make the crossing in the cover of night and camp on a small island that only appeared at low tide.

At first light, they could make the short crossing to Ancaster Island. If they landed just south of Port Fulbeck, it was only a short walk to his camp. Rowan felt sure that with Mrs Arkwright's gun, his replica and some farm tools they could overpower the prison Guardians easily.

Rowan found his patience was wearing thin. He was irritated by the Patcher. His deep raspy voice felt like nails being scraped across a blackboard. He imagined pulling his replica gun from his waistband and cracking it across the back of the man's skull.

He checked himself and let the violent imagery fade. His anger was misdirected. This man wasn't responsible for the flood, he had no bearing on Rowan's desperate decision to visit the clinic. It wasn't his fault that his wife and child were lost.

The Castoffs

The Patcher removed two small bags filled with coins from his pocket, placing them on the table. The tattooed man sized up the bags in his hands and put them in a black holdall tucked under the bench.

Alice Arkwright trusted the Patcher, this tattooed man trusted him. Could he really be a changed man? He had also been kind to Daise. Struggling with this inner turmoil, he suddenly realised the tattooed man was talking to him.

'Hey big fella, do you wanna sit down? You're attracting unwanted attention.' Two Guardians were questioning the rowdy lads on the adjacent picnic bench. Rowan took the tattooed man's advice and sat down next to Alice.

A hush descended as they waited to see what happened. The boys looked fidgety, as though they were considering making a run for it.

'They're probably just looking for underage drinkers', muttered the tattooed man to no one in particular.

Rowan caught a glimpse of a gun on the first Guardian's hip; that seemed like overkill for finding underage drinkers. His heart sank as the Guardians handed out a photograph, which was passed around the table. Each boy shook their head and handed it around the bench. They must be looking for him. Would his disguise work? His forehead felt sweaty but he was too nervous to touch it for fear that he would smear his camouflage. Rowan held his breath as the final boy lingered over the photo. The boy stood up and whispered something to the Guardian before standing and pointing at their table.

The larger of the two Guardians' eyes flashed at the

photo and then across at them. Rowan stared down at his feet as the Guardians bounded across to their table. He reached around to his back and found the handle of the replica gun. But to Rowan's surprise, the Guardian said, 'Are you, Alice Arkwright of 25 Market Street, Casthorpe?'

He didn't wait for an answer and snapped a pair of handcuffs on Mrs Arkwright's wrists.

'I am detaining you under section 12 of the Prevention of Crime Act. As an alleged member of the outlawed terrorist organisation known as the Academy, you will forgo any legal representation and be...'

He didn't get to finish his sentence. Rowan pulled the replica gun from his waistband and smashed the butt into the Guardian's temple. The man crashed down into the glasses, folding like a puppet whose strings had been cut. Mrs Arkwright, the Patcher and the tattooed man were sprayed with shards of glass and the remains of the drinks. The Guardian lay unmoving on the table. Blood trickled from his ear.

Rowan felt disconnected from his actions. Taking off his sunglasses, he wiped his hand across his face, leaving two broad green stripes. The sun on his exposed skin gave him a burst of energy. He straddled the bench to face the second Guardian. And for the second time in as many days, Rowan was looking down at the barrel of a gun.

He felt the pain in his ears first as the noise of the gun firing buffeted his eardrums. The bullet hit him in the centre of his chest, chipping his sternum as it tore into his flesh. Its trajectory changed, spinning through his body, cutting a path through a lung and then into the thick muscle of his heart. He tried to take a breath but his lungs had collapsed. He thought he heard a woman scream as his legs gave way and his body hit the ground like a majestic tree felled.

Chapter 21 – Van

Daise was helped up from her knees and guided out of the lift by Gregor. He offered an awkward smile that Daise returned with a stony glare.

They had been betrayed, that much was clear. The Guardians must have known about the plan; how else could they have got here so quickly. The list of people who knew about the plan was short.

Mrs Arkwright. What possible reason would she have for trapping them? Particularly when she had risked so much to rescue Daise from Greenacres Hospital.

The Patcher. Had Mrs Arkwright shared the plan with him? He had done some terrible things in the past and had historical connections with the Council. But he helped her last night when he could have just left his door closed. That didn't make sense either.

Rowan. He knew about the plan, of course, but it was his idea. They were there to show his film after all.

Jude. Could he have betrayed them? They were friends. Sometimes she hoped they could be more than that. But he had been acting strangely ever since he'd been captured on the fence on their way back from the beach.

Was Jude working for the Guardians now? The thought stung. She stumbled but Gregor stopped her falling.

The Castoffs

Daise looked at Gregor again. Could he have known about their plan? In this moment, she had never hated anyone so much. She stood up straight and shoved him in the chest. He stumbled back a few paces.

'Daise, Daise, look…' he stuttered, but Daise didn't want to hear it. She charged at him, head down like a bull. He held onto her as she hit him under the chin with her head and they clattered to the floor. Daise's cleaning spray spilt and erupted over the carpet tiles. Gregor's hand flailed across a desk as he fell and pens sprayed across the room.

Daise pushed herself up onto her knees and pulled back her fist, ready to plant it on Gregor's face. But she hesitated. Where was this rage coming from? It wasn't Gregor who had betrayed them. She looked at him on the floor; surrounded by a puddle of cleaning fluid he looked like he'd wet himself. She could hear the nervous laughter of a small group of office workers who were leaning on the wall.

He wasn't worth it. She relaxed her fist. But before she could get to her feet she was grabbed around the waist and hoisted into the air.

'Enough!', the Chief, who had a firm hold of her, shouted and silenced the laughter.

'You've got spirit; I'll give you that,' he said to his captive 'But if you EVER strike my son again there will be consequences.'

She tried to wriggle free, kicking her legs in the air. The Chief squeezed her tightly around the middle until she was struggling to breathe. Resistance was useless; she stopped kicking and he threw her to the ground.

As she lay sprawled on the floor, she saw a man take a

step forward. She flinched, expecting a kick. But the man bent down and gently picked her up. She glanced at his identity badge. It was Dave, Dr McInnes' husband. He smiled at her and winked.

But before she could think about what he meant, the Chief grabbed her arms and bound her hands with a cable tie. The plastic dug into her wrists so she could feel her accelerated pulse tapping out a beat.

The Chief motioned to one of his subordinates, 'Take her to Ancaster detention centre.'

The Guardian prodded her in the back toward a set of double doors, down the stairs and out into the car park where a black van was waiting. The Guardian pushed her to one side, opened the doors and threw her inside. She winced as she tumbled across the van's hard metal floor. The doors slammed shut, the sound echoing around the tinny cage. It took a moment for her eyes to adjust to the darkness. She saw the shape of a figure slumped at the other end of the van, illuminated by the thin light seeping out of the driving compartment.

The figure groaned at the noise of the door. Daise shuffled across to get a closer look. It came as a huge relief to see the figure was Rey. His face was red, puffy and streaked with tears. She reached out to hold his hand.

He pushed himself up and wiped his snotty nose on his sleeve, 'Daise, is that you?'

She hooked her bound hands over his head and tried to give him a hug. They heard the tap of a hand on the van roof, followed by the hum of its electric motor.

As Daise pushed herself upright she felt a warm, wet sensation. 'You're bleeding, Rey.' She unhooked her arms and saw him wince as he touched the back of his head.

The Castoffs

With her arms bound in front of her, Daise managed to take off her cleaning tabard to fashion it into a makeshift bandage for Rey. As she folded it she remembered. Where was the memory card with Rowan's film? She patted the pockets — nothing there. Then tried her jeans. Nothing there either.

'What's wrong, Daise?'

'The film, it's gone,' she sighed. 'I guess it doesn't really matter. We've lost now.'

Daise wrapped her improvised dressing around Rey's head like a sweatband covering the wound just above his ear.

'Perhaps Jude was right, after all,' said Daise.

Rey snapped at her, 'Don't you say that Daise. At least we tried. We stood up for ourselves. Jude's the one who's let us down.'

Daise paused, 'You don't think Jude betrayed us, do you?'

She hadn't meant to say it out loud. After all Rey and Jude had been friends since they were toddlers. But the thought was eating away at her. She needed to know whether Rey was having doubts about their friend too.

A silence stretched out between them as she waited for Rey to say something. She remembered their argument in the tower. Rey had sided with Jude and left her to find Rowan on her own.

'I don't want to think it Daise.' Rey's eyes looked as if he was going to burst into tears.

His voice cracked as he spoke, 'He was angry with us for leaving him behind at the fence but I thought when he agreed to come and find you in the hospital, he was over that. Did he say anything to you at Mrs

The Castoffs

Arkwright's?'

Daise couldn't tell Rey about Jude's plan to run away with her. It would break him, 'Just that he thought it was too risky and we were bound to get caught.'

'Well, it kind of looks like he was right. But that doesn't mean he betrayed us. We're his friends Daise,' replied Rey.

Daise decided to change the subject. 'What happened to you after we got split up?' she asked.

Rey told Daise how he was cleaning desks waiting for her when the Chief Guardian came out of the lift. He carried on cleaning but Gregor turned up and recognised him straight away and before he knew it, he was cable tied to an office chair.

The Chief had asked him about Daise. He said he was alone, of course. The words had barely left his mouth when he received a stinging slap across the face. The chair shot across the floor. Gregor stuck his foot out at the chair causing it to topple. Hands bound; Rey was unable to break his fall as the back of his head smacked into the hardwood of the adjacent desk.

'They must have dragged me down the stairs and thrown me in the van as I don't remember anything after that.'

Daise was describing the fake video of Rowan attacking a doctor when she was interrupted by a loud bang. The van started to snake violently from side to side. Daise held Rey's head in her arms and pushed her feet against the nearest side van to stop them from being bounced about and bashed against the van walls. They gripped each other tightly as the driver slammed the brakes on. The van skidded and the rear wheels slid forward, leaving the van dangerously unstable. The vehicle had lost most of its momentum now but Daise held her breath as she felt it tilt up on its side. It was like a diver balanced on a springboard at the moment just before take-off.

The van flipped, screaming as the rough tarmac tore into its metallic sides. Daise's legs buckled and she and Rey hurtled forward slamming into the side of the van. The scraping noise was deafening. Daise let out a shout as her arm pressed against the searing friction-heated metal. Their bodies bounced off each other, elbows collided with faces, knees into backs, skulls into skulls.

She tried to count the rotations but each crash knocked the thoughts out of her head. When the van finally came to a stop, all she could hear was an alarm and a banging sound. It seemed to be coming from the front of the van.

Rey groaned, 'Could someone stop making that noise. I've a splitting headache.' Daise figured moaning was a good sign.

'How are you doing Rey?' she asked, shouting above the furious banging.

'I feel like I've been put through a spin cycle of a washing machine,' he replied.

She tried again, 'Does anything feel broken?'

'Nothing that wasn't already busted, how about you?' he replied.

'A bit battered, but nothing too serious. I think.'

'Shouldn't be a problem, now you have superhuman healing powers.'

Rey meant it as a joke but Daise was hurt. It was clear that she was different now. Her old life was gone. She

The Castoffs

was never going to be able to go back to their life in the tower. But maybe that was no bad thing. Either way they needed to find a way out of this van. She slid along the side to the rear of the van and started kicking at the doors.

'Come on Rey, let's get out of here.' Rey joined her. And on the count of three they slammed their heels into the door panel.

The banging outside stopped and she heard shouting, 'There's someone in there! Let's get them out.'

They heard the crunch of metal on metal, and a screeching sound as someone tried to prise the doors apart, then finally, one of the rear doors popped open and slammed onto the ground. Daise and Rey both shielded their eyes as they were dazzled by the evening sun. Daise crawled out of the door closely followed by Rey.

The streets were teeming with people. It looked like a giant had picked up the Casthorpe towers and shaken out all the inhabitants onto the streets of Barrowby.

A tall man with a scruffy ginger beard greeted them, 'Welcome to the revolution kids. We're going to take it all back today. Here let's those ties off.'

He pulled a knife from his pocket and cut Rey and Daise's free.

'Thanks mister,' said Rey and Daise in unison.

'Not a problem my young friends. That brave green fella told it like it is. If we tolerate slavery on our doorsteps and do nothing, we're as bad as the Council. Join us, we're going to storm the Guardian station' and giving a manic toothy grin as a parting gesture, he disappeared into the crowd.

The Castoffs

The crowd flowed like a river around the van as the people united in a single purpose, heading directly to the Guardian station on the Low Road.

Daise leaned against the van door and watched the people walk by. Rey sat down next to her and they gazed into the crowd, trying to take in what was happening.

'Did you hear what the beardy bloke said? Do you think they played Rowan's film?', asked Rey.

Daise was stunned. From the moment she saw the Chief, she had been resigned to defeat. Yet, she looked around and it was almost as if she had stepped into an alternate universe where their mission had gone to plan. She replayed the scuffle with Gregor in her head and a joyous revelation hit her, 'It must have been Dave, you know — Dr McInnes' husband. I must have dropped the card when I was fighting with Gregor. I remember now, he smiled at me. He must have picked it up and played it when the Guardians left. It's the only explanation.'

Daise stood up and threw her hands in the air, 'We did it Rey, we really did it.'

She helped Rey up and hugged him tightly. They had somehow, against all odds been successful.

Rey rubbed his eyes, 'Is this real Daise?'

She smiled back at him in confirmation. This was it; the revolution had begun and they had helped start it.

As the crowd passed the van, strangers asked if they needed help. There seemed to be a sense of community. They had a sense of unity and purpose as they headed toward the Barrowby Guardian station. Young and old had taken to the streets, inspired by Rowan's message. The younger faces were filled with hope and happiness. The older people looked more circumspect. They knew it wasn't over yet. The Guardians and the Council weren't going to give in because a bunch of Castoffs had taken to the streets.

Staring into the crowd, Daise spotted the familiar olive complexion, shaved head and warm brown eyes. 'Jude!' she shouted. It was definitely him. Then Rey spotted him too. 'Jude mate, over here,' He waved his hands like he was guiding in a plane to land.

Jude pushed his way forward through the throng. Rey surged into the crowd to meet him. They hugged like bears. It was Jude who spoke first.

He looked unsure of himself, 'I'm so sorry I doubted you guys. You wouldn't believe the reaction in the towers. The whole place went crazy.'

'I'm so sorry.' he repeated.

Jude's eyes filled with tears. He caught sight of Daise and the dam broke. He shielded his face from her as the sniffs turned into sobs. Rey ushered him out of the crowd, back to the cover of the van doors.

It took a while for Jude to collect himself. There were a couple of false starts where he looked to have got himself under control but when he looked over at Daise to apologise he broke down again.

Daise was struggling with conflicting emotions. She hated seeing her friend in such a state but she couldn't shake the gnawing feeling that Jude's tears were filled with regret not just for abandoning them but also for betraying them.

She had to know the truth. She was about to ask him outright when she heard a voice screaming from the front of the van.

Chapter 22 – Broadcast

Alice Arkwright couldn't take in what was happening. She was sat on a barstool in the dark back room of the Fisherman's Arms clutching a tumbler full of beet spirit. It was a rough vodka made from the peelings of root vegetables and the bartender had placed a bottle and glass in front of her before returning to the main saloon.

The plan to overthrow the Council was sunk. It was her plan. She had become chancellor of the Academy on the back of it. They had been fighting the Council for decades as a disorganised band of resistance fighters. Alice Arkwright had changed that; she had brought the factions together using the knowledge in her vast library of forbidden books. She had taught them the value of fighting with your brains rather than your fists.

Instead of disrupting the Council with random attacks on Guardian stations, she had presented a strategy. Rather than tackle them head-on, all they needed to do was take control of the food supply. And the key to that was Ancaster Island. If you controlled Ancaster, you controlled Greater Grantham and the entire Eastern Islands.

Making contact with Rowan had been the key. One of the scavengers had sold her an old delivery drone. It was busted, of course. But with care and attention she had managed to whittle replacement rotors from old bits of pine. The battery case was a mess too. But she ripped that out and replaced it with a solar-charged fuel cell.

Getting a controller to work was trickier. She had plenty of old remote control units in the Academy workshop but nothing that seemed to be tuned to the frequency of the drone. It was so frustrating when she switched on the drone; the rotors spun for a second but without a functional remote control it was useless. It had been the Patcher who finally came up with the solution. He had found an adjustable controller. It looked a little like a video gamepad but it had a button on the base that allowed you to change the frequency of the infrared signal.

It worked beautifully until she attached the small delivery capsule. With the extra weight, the drone struggled to get more than a few feet off the ground. She stripped the drone down to its basic components and found that removing a broken camera module made it light enough to fly.

Using the Patcher's schematics of the camp, they had attempted to make contact with the prisoners. Mrs Arkwright had written a note offering them support. Then, one still day, she and the Patcher had rowed her kayak out to the channel. They had taken turns with the oars but it had still taken them two hours to get within sight of Ancaster Island.

Ancaster Island wasn't strictly speaking an island; it was a mass of land protruding out into the sea, connected to the mainland by a thin causeway behind which sat the town of Ancaster. In the years since the flood, Ancaster had been swallowed up by Greater Grantham and had

The Castoffs

become the port for the new coastal city.

Access to Ancaster Island was strictly regulated. An offshore three-metre fence topped with razor wire encircled the island to ensure that the causeway was the only way on and off the island. The drone, of course, flew over with ease. They landed it in one of the maize fields a hundred yards from the beach and waited. They hadn't heard any noise coming from the fields so they assumed that the drone had not set off any alarms. But was it damaged? It was impossible to tell.

They didn't want to get too close to the island so they waited offshore, nervously wondering how long to leave it before guiding the drone home. Too short a time and no one would have time to respond to her note: too long and the drone's batteries could run down or worse still it could fall into the wrong hands.

She had left it for fifteen minutes before making the decision to fly the drone back. A note was attached.

She was so eager to read it that she almost landed the drone in the water. The note written in exquisitely neat cursive handwriting by someone signing themselves 'Rowan'. All it said was, 'Help me free the detainees. Rowan.'

Over the past few months, she had got to know Rowan through the exchange of notes. She modified the drone over time, making it much stronger so it could carry heavier items. Eventually, she managed to get it to carry a small video camera for Rowan to record his story.

Then one day the drone didn't make it back. The connection to the remote was broken. She had sat around for hours in the channel worried that she would be picked up by a Guardian patrol. When the sun began to set, she had no choice but to leave. She spent the evening testing the remote to make sure it wasn't faulty and returned the next day but, despite all her efforts, the drone was lost.

In the days and weeks that followed she had almost given up hope, assuming the worst; that Rowan had been caught filming and been executed by the Guardians. Then she heard about the green man on the beach. The Patcher had come to her and told her about the green people. She'd heard rumours, of course, but it was only then that suspicions were confirmed that Dennis Dawkins' research had moved to human trials.

She suspected the green man that had washed up on Barrowby beach was Rowan but it wasn't until Jude and Rey came to see her that all the pieces of the puzzle fell into place.

But with Rowan dead, she could see little hope of convincing the green people to rise up against the Council and accept her leadership.

Sending the children to the Channel had been a long shot. She didn't hold up much hope that they would be successful. And even if they were, without Rowan how were they going to get the green people to trust them enough to take a stand against the Guardians on Ancaster Island?

She took another swig of the beet spirit and gazed up at the blank screen perched on a flimsy bracket above the bar. She almost fell off her stool when the screen lit up and Rowan's face appeared.

It was an automated emergency broadcast. These were used for severe weather warnings, major Council announcements and the imposition of curfews. They

The Castoffs

activated all the screens in Greater Grantham and beyond. Jumping up onto the bar, she jabbed at the volume control.

'My name is Rowan, I'm 36 years old and I live on Ancaster Island. You may have noticed something a little strange about me. My skin is green.'

Rowan was sitting in a dimly lit barrack block filled with bunk beds. The bunks were stacked three high in rows little more than two feet apart. The small pool of light from the camera showed only a small section of the room but the background noise of snores suggested the block was packed.

'You may have been told that I am sick or dangerous. I can assure you that is not the case. I am in excellent health. I am just like you. I lived in Nottingham until the flood.'

'The flood took so much from so many of us. It took my house, my wife and my baby daughter. We all have our own personal tragedies but since the flood, we have not healed. The Council has taken what little we have left; our freedom, our self-respect and our dignity.'

A faint complaining voice in the background told Rowan to turn the light off. He pulled the camera to his chest and it went dark.

Against all odds, Daise and Rey must have done it: the Channel was broadcasting Rowan's film. Mrs Arkwright smiled for a moment but as she turned to call the Patcher she saw Rowan's body lying motionless on the pool table. The victory was empty. The Patcher was sat in a crumpled heap next to the pool table, exhausted from all the chest compressions. There had been too much damage. Rowan was dead.

The Castoffs

'Jon! They did it, they're broadcasting Rowan's video'. She poured the Patcher a generous measure of beet spirit. He walked up to the bar and raised his glass.

'To Rowan,' he said, tapping his glass with Mrs Arkwright.

They downed the drinks and sat in silence as the film cut to a brightly lit summer's day in a maize field.

Rowan continued his narration as they watched dark green figures harvesting corn. The work looked back-breaking as the tall green men stooped to slice the cobs from the plants and toss them into hessian sacks. The camera zoomed in on the perimeter of the field. It took a moment to focus on a tangled barbed wire fence. The camera panned across to the unmistakable black uniform of a Guardian.

'We are the detainees. We are forced to work every day. This Guardian you can see is armed with a rifle, baton and pepper spray. If we try to run, we are shot. If we don't keep up the pace of our work, we are beaten. Make no mistake, this is not a farm. This is a death camp.

'As you can see, I am not the only one with green skin. Why are we green you may ask?'

Rowan paused for a moment as if he couldn't get the words out, 'We are human guinea pigs.' The camera picked out green faces working in the field. Most of them looked younger than Rowan, some couldn't be much older than Daise and her friends.

'We are you; the detained, the missing. This is our fate.'

The video cut to a different angle. It was later in the day. The green people were lined up next to a shiny metal scale. Three armed Guardians stood at the front; their

The Castoffs

weapons trained on the farmhands. One by one, the green people hung their sacks on a hook that pulled down on a spring, which gave a reading on a dial. There were no numbers on the face, just a thick red line that marked the weight of cobs they were expected to pick in an hour.

The tension was carved on the faces of the green men and women lined up next to the scale. You could hear Rowan let out a breath of relief as each of the detainees weighed their pickings, collected a new sack from the pile next to the scale and walked away from the Guardians without incident.

The camera zoomed in on a young woman. She was lighter in colour than the others. You could tell there was something wrong by the way she approached the scale. Her body was hunched and she groaned as she removed the sack from her back and hooked it on to the scale. The needle bounced around on the dial, jumping above the red line and then falling back before finally coming to settle some way shy of the mark.

One of the Guardians walked up to examine the dial. He tapped its glass face with his index finger and shook his head.

'Oh dear, oh dear. This will not do.' His voice was cold and condescending.

Removing a pencil from behind his ear, he picked up a thick leather-bound ledger from next to the scale and jotted down a note. The Guardian nodded to a colleague who was holding a rifle. In a flash, the second Guardian flipped the rifle around and jabbed the wooden butt of the gun into her face. The camera wobbled as if in shock.

The woman fell to the floor and curled up in a ball,

The Castoffs

her arms wrapped around her head. She was bleeding from a deep gash at the bridge of her nose. The recording fell silent as if all the detainees were holding their breath.

Then the first Guardian barked, 'Next!' and his colleagues ushered another detainee to the scale. The film cut out abruptly.

Mrs Arkwright clambered back onto the bar and banged the screen hard, desperately hoping she could make Rowan reappear.

'Alice, stop!'

She looked down at the Patcher and then at her hand, which was bleeding.

'Come on, let's get out of here. If Rowan's film has been broadcast across Greater Grantham, then people are going to take to the streets. This is our opportunity,' said the Patcher.

She turned and looked at Rowan's lifeless body on the pool table. 'We can't just leave him there.'

The Patcher held her by the shoulders. 'Look Alice, he's dead. We can't do anything about that now. But we can make a stand. Let's get on that boat. We have to finish what we started.'

They walked into the main room and found the tattooed man sat talking to the barman.

'Can we still get the boat?' she asked, a renewed determination in her voice.

The tattooed man pushed the keys into Mrs Arkwright's hands and pointed out of the window toward a small wooden pier, 'It is the blue one at the end. The battery is fully charged but she'll need a few hours in the sun to charge up for the trip back.'

As they walked to the door the barman called out, 'I

have sympathy for your predicament an' all but I've got three corpses on my premises. I can't let you leave without cleaning up the mess.'

Alice Arkwright felt a rush of fury: how dare he describe Rowan as a mess? She took an aggressive lunge toward him but jumped back when he reached down, pulled a shotgun from behind the bar and aimed at her, saying: 'You don't really want to add yourself to the body count, do you?'

The tattooed man placed his hand on Alice's shoulder and addressed the barman, 'You can put the gun away Bill. I'll take care of the bodies. I'll sling the Guardians in a pit.'

He turned to Alice and continued, 'Don't worry, I'll take good care of your friend. Those Guardians would have kept shooting if he hadn't acted. We all owe him a debt. He was a brave man. He deserves a decent burial.'

Alice was silenced by a flashback: the Guardian had locked eyes with her. He had marked her for death. Her name was on the bullet and she had almost accepted her fate at that moment. But Rowan had saved her.

The sense of loss sucked the breath from her lungs and she fell to her knees. Closing her eyes, she tried to silence the chattering voices of grief in her head.

The Patcher held her until she got to her feet and together, they left the Fisherman's Arms. They walked down to the pier where a small blue motorboat was moored to a rickety wooden post.

She grabbed the Patcher's hand and boarded the boat. The Patcher started the motor and they sped off to Ancaster Island.

Chapter 23 – Road

'What is that awful noise?', asked Daise.

The screaming was coming from the front of the van. It took Daise a moment to realise that there were Guardians trapped in the cabin. She darted round to the front to investigate.

Rey looked down at Jude, who was sitting on the tarmac floor puffy-eyed. 'It's time to get yourself together mate, we need you.' He reached down and pulled Jude to his feet.

As he stood up, Jude tripped on the crowbar that the bearded man had used to open the rear van door.

'Hey Jude, pass me that bar, will you?'

Jude handed Rey the long metal bar. It felt reassuring in his hands. He slotted it into a belt loop and gave Jude a pat on the shoulder. They both followed Daise.

The road behind them was almost deserted now. The last few stragglers looked toward the van, startled by the screams, but they did not stop to help. They were drawn inexorably to the demonstration outside Barrowby Guardian station.

Symbols of the Greater Grantham Council lay battered and broken in the streets. Behind them a huge billboard poster advertising the curfew was peppered with puncture holes created by projectiles hurled by

The Castoffs

protesters. The normally ordered, pristine streets of Barrowby were strewn with empty cartons of Smart Jooce, scattered rubble and splintered chunks of wood.

Acts of defiance and protest littered the streets. The wanted posters of Rowan, ripped violently from walls, swirled in the warm summer breeze. A felled flagpole lay across the road next to a small pile of ash where the hated black and red Council flag had been torched.

In the distance, they could hear the crowd that had assembled outside the Barrowby Guardian station shouting: 'Give us back our dignity. Freedom for the detainees! Give us back our dignity. Freedom for the detainees!' It continued over and over like a nursery rhyme.

The battered van lay on its side across the junction of Chapel Lane and the High Road. The tarmac was streaked with fresh black tyre marks where the van had skidded to avoid the protesters. The High Road, which was Barrowby's main street, was lined with a mixture of rustic cottages, restaurants and luxury shops. Frightened faces peeked out from behind the curtains; wealthy residents waiting for the Council to reimpose its authority.

The windshield of the van remained intact despite a deep, jagged crack cutting across it like a streak of lightning. The side window was rolled down, making it easy to lean into the cabin.

Rey walked around the front of the van and knelt down to look through the windscreen. Two people were trapped inside. The first was the brutish Guardian who had thrown Daise in the van. He hung in his seat limply, blood dripping from a deep gash in his head. A second, smaller figure was squashed underneath him, thrashing about and screaming as he tried to push the larger man off him.

'It's Gregor,' said Rey, letting out a massive sigh.

Daise pushed herself further into the van, 'Gregor, calm down it's me. Daise.'

Gregor's head snapped up to look at Daise and his arms went up in front of his face. Daise was puzzled, and then she remembered how close she had come to punching his lights out. The memory was strange, it felt like it didn't belong to her.

She spoke slowly in a firm but calm voice, 'Gregor, are you badly hurt?'

Rey butted in, 'We haven't got time for this shit.' He started kicking at the windscreen in front of Gregor's face.

Daise could see the terror in Gregor's eyes, 'Rey, stop!'

'Why should I?'

Daise was taken aback; Rey was normally so agreeable. Calming herself with a deep breath, she said, 'We're going to need the van, Rey.'

Rey stopped, raked his fingers through his matted long hair and took a step back from the van.

Daise gestured to the boys to join her a few steps away from the van. Rey spoke first. He was calm but serious, 'What do we need the van for?'

Before she could answer, Jude added, 'What's the plan Daise?'

Daise knew Jude was right to ask; they needed a plan. They couldn't just keep careering from one dangerous situation to another.

The Castoffs

In a hushed tone, she said, 'It's like the man who freed us from the van said, this is a revolution. But we need to ask, who are the people who really need to be set free?'

Jude and Rey spoke in unison, 'The green people.'

'That's right', she smiled and continued, 'Ancaster Island is where we need to be. Rowan and Mrs Arkwright should be there by now. It's all working like she said. All the available Guardians will be dispatched to Barrowby Guardian station to deal with the siege. But things are only going to change if the detention camps are closed and the prisoners are freed. It's too far to walk but if we can just get this van back on the road, we can drive to Ancaster and help them.'

'But what are we going to do with him' asked Rey, pointing at the van where Gregor was wailing about blood dripping in his eyes.

'Don't you see? He's going to help us.' Daise said with a grin.

Rey scratched the back of his neck and frowned. 'Gregor? Have you lost your mind?'

'Think about it Rey,' said Daise, 'Driving through the Ancaster security checkpoint with Gregor is the perfect cover. He's the Chief's son. And they'll be expecting some detainees.'

Rey folded his arms, 'But he's a weasel. He'll turn on us the moment he gets a chance. Have you forgotten that he shot you?'

Jude added, 'Come on Rey, hear her out.'

Rey blurted, 'Really, Jude. Why should we listen to you? For all we know you were the one that called the Guardians on us.'

The Castoffs

It was out there now. The accusation. It lingered in the air like the stench of rotting meat.

Daise stood between them, placing her hands on their shoulders, 'Please, we can't fight among ourselves.'

'It wasn't me,' said Jude forlornly.

All of a sudden, they realised Gregor had stopped complaining. He was laughing.

He had managed to get out of his seat belt and was clambering up over the body of the Guardian, his head poking out of the window.

Rey ran up to him, 'What are you laughing at?'

'You lot,' said Gregor. 'You think you are all so clever, don't you, but you haven't got a clue. You think you can just rock up to Ancaster and no one will know who you are. They can track you wherever you go. You're tagged.'

The three friends stared at the small square implants in their wrists. The realisation was a hammer blow. How could they have been so stupid?

Of course, thought Daise; the tags they used to access their tower. That's how the Council found them at the Channel. They had been tracking their tags.

Daise lost her temper first. She grabbed Gregor under the arms and yanked him out of the cabin, dropping him roughly on the road. He wrapped his arms around his head, waiting for kicks and punches to come raining down.

But Daise was focused on removing the tag from her wrist. She leaned back into the van and bashed the side of her fist against the glove compartment. A green plastic box emblazoned with a white cross spilled out. She caught it before it fell, her reflexes heightened by adrenaline.

The Castoffs

Gregor pulled himself to his feet and wandered round the back of the van, where he sat on the smashed rear door. Daise ignored him and crossed the road to sit on a small stone wall, carefully examining the first aid kit. She pulled out two sterile packs; one containing a scalpel and the other, a pair of tweezers.

'These should do the trick,' she announced, trying her best to sound confident. In all honesty, she wasn't sure she could do this.

As she peeled off the scalpel's paper wrapper, her hands began to shake. Rey and Jude sat next to her.

Gregor called across the road, 'Give it to me Daisy. I can do this. I was taught basic surgical techniques in cadet training. Removing tracker chips is simple if you know the right technique. If you mess it up you could cut the radial artery. You could bleed out.'

Daise was not reassured by Gregor. Rey interrupted, 'Seriously Daise, we're not planning to let this knobhead loose on us with a blade.'

'Well, do you know how to remove a tracker chip?', Gregor spat back.

But Rey didn't answer, he just grabbed the scalpel from Daise's hand and before anyone could do anything, started making a small incision into his wrist.

Daise held her breath and stared at Rey's wrist. She could see the dense network of veins and arteries carrying blood to and from his arm. A thin rivulet of blood ran down Rey's arm but judging by the gentle flow, he had not cut anything vital.

'Right now, pass me those tweezers.'

Daise did as he asked, peeling the backing off and exchanging them for the scalpel.

The Castoffs

Wincing, Rey plucked the tag from his wrist like a splinter from his foot. It lay in a pool of blood on the ground for a moment until Rey swung at it with the steel baton he had taken from the Guardian.

'What do you reckon, not bad for a first go?' said Rey, holding his bleeding wrist up in the air.

'Wow Rey. I never had you pegged as a surgeon, that's some awesome hidden talent you've got right there,' Daise replied, handing Rey a plaster.

'Do you want to help me with mine?'

Rey repeated the operation on Daise and then Jude, and then took great pleasure in smashing the tracking sensors into the tarmac.

'I don't suppose you've got a tag?' Daise asked Gregor, who was slouched against the van, watching.

'Certainly not, tags are more a Castoff accessory, as far as I understand.'

'There you go again with that mouth of yours Gregor. It's like you want me to give you a smack in the chops,' warned Rey.

'He's not worth it Rey' said Jude.

Daise started to close the first aid kit, when a thought occurred to her. Were they going to take Gregor's word for it that he wasn't tagged?

'Come here a minute Gregor.'

She grabbed his wrist and gave it a rub with her fingers. Nothing. She tried the other one. Again nothing. But there was something about the way Gregor wouldn't look her in the eye that made her suspicious.

'Show me your ankles!' she barked at Gregor.

'But I told you…'

Rey and Jude closed rank, 'Do as she says, Gregor.'

The Castoffs

Gregor sat back down on the van door and removed his Guardian-issue boots and socks, 'See! No tag.'

But Daise got a sense that he was bluffing.

She grabbed his foot and began to feel his ankles.

'What's this then?' she asked, rubbing a small piece of plastic beneath the surface of his skin.

'You lying piece of shit,' said Rey. 'Come on, give me the scalpel. I'll sort him out. His dad will be tracking him for sure.'

At this point, Gregor shrieked.

'No! Keep him away from me,' he pleaded as Rey rummaged through the first aid bag to retrieve the scalpel.

'Hold him down Jude', asked Rey. Jude struggled to pin down Gregor's writhing arms and legs at the same time.

'You can't do this to me. I don't want to be infected!'

Daise stepped forward and spoke to Gregor softly, 'Look Gregor, we don't want to hurt you. But if you don't sit still, Rey could cut an artery. As you said, you could bleed out.'

Gregor continued to thrash around. And then he shouted, 'Get your filthy Greep hands off me.'

'Greep', that must have been one of the things Rowan had been talking about when he said he had been called worse than a Green. Gregor used it with all the spite and venom of a racist slur. Daise was suddenly very conscious of them all looking at her. She pulled down her sleeves, embarrassed to see that the green patches had begun to spread across her hands.

Jude lifted his hands off Gregor and asked, 'What the hell are you on about?'

The Castoffs

Gregor scampered to the back of the van like a wounded animal. He spoke from the shadows.

'Can't you see she's been infected? She's caught the green virus. And you, you'll be next. He didn't even try to clean the blade.'

Jude was taken aback. 'But it's not infectious.'

Gregor laughed nervously, 'Is that what that Academy terrorist Arkwright has been telling you? She's just using you. She doesn't care if you are infected. Why do you think the Greenbacks are quarantined on Ancaster? If they get out, we'll all end up infected.'

'But the Patcher said infection was impossible,' said Daise, trying to convince herself more than anyone.

Gregor laughed again. 'The Patcher, that old quack. You know he was arrested for doing rogue experiments on people? Trying to turn them green. You guys think you are heroes but you're just puppets being manipulated by the Academy. Can't you see what's really going on? That Greep you are protecting has infected Daise and he's intent on breaking the others out of quarantine. If that happens, the human race is screwed — we'll all end up like her.'

He edged out of the shadows at the back of the van and pointed at Daise in disgust, 'That's what your Greep friend really wants. And thanks to your little trip to the Channel, he's that bit closer to his goal. The extinction of the human race.'

Daise wanted to hit him. But his words were sewing doubt seeds deep within her brain. How much did they really know about Mrs Arkwright? And the Patcher certainly had a shady past but had he lied to her about becoming infected? Surely not. He had seemed genuinely puzzled by her condition.

As for Rowan, he was so sincere. But would his freedom and the freedom of the green people come at a huge cost to the rest of humanity? Nothing seemed quite as certain.

'Come on Daise, you're not falling for this stuff,' urged Rey. 'He's just making it up to stop us from removing his tracker. They could send a patrol to pick him up any minute.'

Jude interjected, 'I'm with you Daise, whatever you decide.'

He paused; she knew there was a 'but' coming.

'But, are you sure driving straight in the lion's den is such a good idea?'

'Can you all just shut up for a moment? I need to think.'

Daise felt she hadn't had a moment to process events since Mrs Arkwright had packed them off to the Channel.

Rey was right; if they didn't get the tracker out of Gregor they risked being caught by the Guardians. She knew she couldn't go back to the towers. She was green now and she needed to know what that meant. If she was infectious like Gregor said, or was part of some experiment, she wanted answers. Surely the Green people on Ancaster Island would know more.

She decided. 'Rey, hand me that crowbar.'

Rey unhooked the bar from his belt loop and handed it over without hesitation. Gregor tucked himself into a ball at the back of the van.

'Look in the first aid kit for anything else that's sharp,' said Daise.

Rey pulled out a small pair of scissors. 'Will these do?'

The Castoffs

'That's great Rey.' she replied.

She got on her hands and knees and approached 'I'm giving you a simple choice. The scissors or the bar. Either you remove your tag with these scissors, or I knock you out with the crowbar and leave you at the side of the road.'

Daise fixed her eyes on Gregor, trying to appear as strong and decisive as possible. But inside she knew she wouldn't have been able to knock him out. How hard would she have to hit him? What if she broke his skull?

But her bluff worked. Gregor leaned forward and snatched the paper packet containing the scissors.

'I need some light,' he said. His voice barely a whisper.

'Come on then, get out of the van!', hollered Rey.

Gregor did as he was told, he crawled out of the van and sat on the broken van door.

Daise, Rey and Jude watched him closely as he peeled back the wrapper on the scissors and began scoring a line on his ankle. His hands were shaking.

'Careful now, all it would take is one little slip and you could bleed out or end up walking with a limp for the rest of your life,' said Rey with glee.

Gregor glared at Rey. But he said nothing. He just continued to scratch the scissors across his ankle, never pressing quite hard enough to break the skin.

'Oh, this is ridiculous, give me the crowbar Daise. I'll sort this out,' said Rey.

'No!' Daise barked at Rey, her fierce tone making them both jump. 'No' she repeated more calmly, 'Give him time.'

They stood in silence watching Gregor as if he was a

wild animal.

He was out of options; finally, he made a small cut with the scissors and pulled the tag out of his ankle. Blood was beginning to pool around his foot. He was bleeding pretty heavily. Daise threw him a sterile bandage and gave the crowbar back to Rey, who wasted no time beating Gregor's tag into dust.

She could see Gregor was even worried that the bandage was an infection risk; he brushed the packaging up against his black shirt before opening it up and wrapping it around his ankle.

'Right, let's get this van on the road,' said Daise.

Chapter 24 – Bridge

'Daise, I don't want to criticise your plan. But I don't see how we're going to get this van going. What are we going to do, just flip it over?', said Jude.

Daise smiled, 'We won't know until we try.'

'OK then, let's give it a go.' said Rey, pushing himself up against the roof of the van. He let out a grunt but the van remained welded to the ground.

'Come on guys, some help would be appreciated,' he cajoled.

'Hold on a minute, Rey. Strength isn't all about muscles. Let's use this first,' said Daise, pointing to her temple.

'What your head?' smirked Rey. 'I don't think a flying headbutt is going to do the trick.'

Daise, Rey and Jude burst out laughing. Gregor remained slouched moodily against the van.

It felt good to be together, laughing like old times.

Daise picked up the crowbar and walked off round the front of the van. Smiling, she began prising the bonnet open.

The metal clasp opened with a satisfying pop. She wasted no time in removing the screws that held the van's giant battery pack in place, lining them up on the edge of the pavement. She twisted the butterfly clip that

The Castoffs

held the battery pack in place and, thunk, it fell on the road.

She called over to the boys, 'Give me a hand Rey. And Jude, can you keep an eye on Gregor?'

Rey walked over, flexed his muscles like a bodybuilder and gave the battery a shove. It moved a couple of centimetres,

'Bloody hell, this is heavy.' he exclaimed.

Daise laughed, 'Err, yeah that's why I wanted some help.'

They both grabbed the handles on either side of the battery and lifted it clear of the van.

'OK, I suppose we'd better get that Guardian out of the van too; he's adding at least another ninety kilos.'

'Here, Gregor you come and help too.'

It took ten minutes of huffing, puffing, grabbing, pulling and grunting but they managed to get the guard out of the van. They dragged him across the road and propped him up against the wall.

Rey removed a baton, can of pepper spray and a small revolver from the Guardian's belt. 'These could come in handy.'

Daise looked at the gun and felt a twinge in her arm as she recalled the pain of being shot.

'Give me the gun, Rey!'. Her voice was uncompromising.

Rey did as he was told and handed the gun to Daise. She pushed the barrel of the revolver and bullets dropped out, tinkling like a wind chime as they hit the tarmac.

'I've seen the damage these can do in the wrong hands', she announced, before dropping the gun down a drain grate at the edge of the road.

The Castoffs

The Guardian was a tall middle-aged bald man. He was bleeding from a gash in his forehead but he'd be okay, Daise thought. She could see his chest rise and fall steadily.

'Right, Gregor take your shirt off. We can't leave him here dressed in his uniform like that; he'll be lynched.'

Gregor did as he was told. Left in just his grubby bloodstained white T-shirt, the Guardian looked more like an old drunk who had passed out in the sun. Rey kicked off tattered trainers held together with tape and put on the Guardians black walking boots.

'Now he looks like one of us', said Rey doing a little tap dance in his new shoes.

'Now Jude, put the black shirt on,' Daise ordered.

'Why would I want to put that on? It's all sweaty and bloodstained? And I could be attacked for wearing it,' he said.

Daise responded, 'I'm going to need you to drive this van. And the only way we are going to get it across the checkpoint at Ancaster is if they think you are a Guardian. So please Jude, just put the shirt on.'

Jude did not argue. He pulled the shirt over his head, his nose wrinkling at the smell.

Daise remained focused, 'Thanks, now we're going to need some rope to get this van back on its wheels'.

She thought of the climbing rope she had made to rescue Rowan, wondering if it was still fluttering in the breeze.

'What about that?', said Jude pointing to the broken flag pole. Before she could answer, he ran up the road to the post office. The flagpole lay across the road but its rope was still attached to the pulley designed to raise the

The Castoffs

flag. He kicked the pile of ashes that looked to be the remains of the flag, untangled the rope from the splintered flagpole and ran back to the van.

Though the van was on its side, it was propped up slightly by a mangled wing mirror. Daise got to work threading the rope through a small gap and over the roof of the van and, glad of her knowledge of knots, used a bow line to create a fixed loop. Then she and the boys lined up along the rope like they were taking part in a tug of war.

Daise, clearly now the strongest of them, wrapped the end of the rope around her waist. Gregor, of course, didn't take part. He complained that his ankle was hurting too much.

Daise, Jude and Rey planted their feet firmly on the tarmac and pulled with all their combined strength. The metal groaned. Daise began to edge back and with each tiny movement, the van lifted up. Beads of sweat blistered on their brows as they pulled together for what seemed like forever. Inch by blistering inch they hauled the battered van up until Daise felt it had reached its tipping point.

'Come on guys, one last pull should do it,' she said, 'PULL!'

The van crashed backed down on its wheels, bouncing on its suspension. They dropped the rope and let out a cheer. Daise and Rey replaced the battery and closed the bonnet.

They watched in silence as Jude climbed into the cabin and slotted the key into the ignition. A small leather fob swung from it like a pendulum. He put his hand on it and paused for a moment before turning it clockwise.

The Castoffs

The key clicked and the electric engine hummed to life.

'Come on, you beauty!' shouted Rey. He dashed around the side of the van to congratulate Jude. But their celebrations were cut short as the bald Guardian reached into the cabin of the van and ripped the key from the ignition.

'Where do you think you're going with my van, you thieving little Castoffs?'

Rey stepped forward and fired pepper spray at him. The Guardian dropped the key and clutched his face.

'Ahh, my face, my face,' he wailed.

Daise pushed out at the Guardian; her palms landed hard in his chest and caught him off guard. He stumbled back a few paces and toppled onto the pavement.

The Guardian screamed obscenities at them and they did not hang about for him to recover. Daise scooped the keys up from the floor and thrust them at Jude, 'Do you really think you can drive this thing?'

'I'll give it a go,' he replied, grinning.

Daise ran to the back of the van and barked at Gregor, 'Get in the back with me.'

She softened her tone as she turned to Rey, 'Do you want to join Jude, up front? And throw me that crowbar, would you.'

Rey did as he was told and threw the metal bar to Daise. He was glad not to be bouncing around in the back of the van again.

Daise followed Gregor into the back of the van and slotted the crowbar through the handles, wedging the broken door shut. Then she banged on the cabin partition with the palm of her hand.

Leaving the Guardian clawing at his face on the side

The Castoffs

of the road, Jude drove off.

The journey to Ancaster got scary as they cut through Grantham centre. Just as they had seen in Barrowby, people from the Resets had taken to the streets in large groups and were rounding on all official buildings.

Daise felt the van accelerate. She and Gregor grabbed the door handles as the ride became rough. A bang rang out like a steel drum as rocks started raining down on the van. Gripping the door handle in fear now, Daise looked through a gap in the door to see a mass of angry faces running after them. Their hate-filled shouts faded as the van picked up speed.

There was a sharp left turn, and then they were rolling along the smooth highway of the High Dike Road. When they were safely out of town, Jude pulled the van into a siding. He and Rey got out to talk to Daise, banging on the van until she slid the crowbar out of the handles to open the rear doors.

'Are you OK Daise? It got a bit hairy back there. I thought the windscreen was going to come in,' said Jude, smiling from ear to ear.

Daise responded, also with a smile, 'Nice driving by the way.'

'You should have seen him Daise,' said Rey. 'When we turned into the old town, I thought we were screwed. There was this mob marching toward the Guildhall. They took one look at the van and they came running toward us chucking rocks. I swear one of them actually had a pitchfork. Jude was as calm as you like on the accelerator, I thought we were going to smash into them but he pulled this left-hander from nowhere. It was magnificent!'

Jude blushed. Daise knew he was proud to have his

The Castoffs

contributions recognised.

The sun had set and the clear sky was fading fast. Looking into the distance, Daise could see the lights flashing off the tall towers of the suspension bridge that connected the mainland to the first of the Eastern Islands archipelago. In the half-light of dusk, she could still make out the fence-bound coastline of Ancaster Island.

The Ancaster Suspension Bridge was completed a year ago, constructed using cables salvaged from the old Humber Bridge, which was destroyed in the great flood. The new bridge was the culmination of the first phase of the Eastern Islands Connection project — a plan to connect the island remains of the old county of Lincolnshire.

The island was of vital strategic importance as the farmland was the most productive in the region. Furthermore, Ancaster Island hosted three airfields at Cranwell, Waddington and Scampton. The former air force bases had been of huge importance in the civil war that saw the breakup of the United Kingdom.

They all knew that getting on to Ancaster Island was going to be much harder than their drive around town.

'Have you thought about how we are going to get through the checkpoint, Daise?' asked Jude.

Daise had not really given the plan much thought beyond getting the van on the road. They were in a Guardian van and Jude and Rey were in Guardian uniforms but she knew that wasn't going to be enough to get them through the checkpoint. It should just get them close before any suspicions were aroused. She had originally thought she could persuade Gregor to help get them through the checkpoint but that didn't seem realistic anymore. Even if she did convince him to help there was no way Rey and Jude would just sit in the back, trusting Gregor to drive them through. No, they would have to take the direct approach.

'We wait until it's dark and we drive this van as fast as we can through the checkpoint. Are you in?'

Neither of the boys hesitated; they replied in unison, 'Yeah.'

They let Gregor out. He sat on the floor leaning up against the van, his face stretched into a snarl. Daise stood next to him gripping the crowbar tightly.

As they waited for the light to fade, the friends stood at different corners of the van, watching in silence as the sky turned to black.

Chapter 25 – Drone

The Patcher and Mrs Arkwright dragged their boat up the thin strip of beach just south of Port Fulbeck and secured it to a large rock with a thick piece of rope.

The cool disc of a full moon bathed the island in an eerie half-light. Crouching behind a dune with the Patcher, Mrs Arkwright, got a pair of binoculars from her backpack.

She scanned the horizon from the sail ships in the harbour to the Smart Jooce processing plant and the grain stores in the industrial zone.

Startled by the roar of groaning metal she focused again on the grain store: flames danced around the base of the first silo. A plume of smoke hung in the air like a storm cloud.

Before the flood, Fulbeck had been a sleepy inland Lincolnshire village. Now it was an ugly industrial port exporting food supplies through the Eastern Islands and beyond. And it was home to a hulking ten-storey Smart Jooce factory.

A mass of people marched to the harbour; Mrs Arkwright zoomed out to get a measure of the crowd. It looked like at least a thousand people, some held fiery torches aloft. They moved as one, united in their purpose.

The Castoffs

The crowd marched in the direction of a sailing ship that was being loaded with huge, stacked palettes of Smart Jooce.

As Mrs Arkwright watched, the Port Fulbeck Guardians deserted their posts. Some ran to other sail ships; some jumped off the pier into the black waters of the Trent channel.

She turned to the Patcher and smiled. 'It looks like they have it all in hand. Rowan's film has woken them up. They're not going to take it anymore. Look at them. It's incredible, the uprising is happening, it's just like I imagined. They're driving the Guardians off the island.'

She handed him the binoculars, sat back and started to cry with joy. The Patcher wrapped his arm around her shoulders and smiled a broad grin for the first time in many years.

'There's a revolution in the air. Ain't no going back from this,' he confirmed.

They sat in silence, awed by the history unfolding in front of them. Then Mrs Arkwright heard a weird whirring, buzzing sort of sound. 'What's that?' she exclaimed.

They looked up, scanning the sky for the source of the sound. The Patcher saw it first: a drone. But nothing like the glorified toy they had used to contact Rowan. This was a high-tech military machine. Eight legs projected from a central black body, with a heavy-duty rotor mounted at the end of each. At the front, a bulbous glass protrusion housed a camera. A series of three spiked antennae ran along its back. It was like a giant robotic one-eyed flying spider.

The Patcher pointed up, dumbstruck, as the spider

drone sliced through the -night sky. The underbelly of the craft flew overhead and a ball-shaped payload attached to a metal claw came into view. Mrs Arkwright grabbed her gun but by the time she took aim, the drone was out of range.

Swapping her gun for the binoculars, she followed the drone's path as it homed in on the unsuspecting crowd.

A flash of searing white light was followed by a gut-shaking explosion. Then came a slap of warm air. The final breath of the deadly payload. Mrs Arkwright and the Patcher felt it more than a kilometre away.

There was a moment of silence before the screaming began. Without a word, Mrs Arkwright and the Patcher climbed the dune and ran into the eye of the storm.

***

'What the hell was that?', asked Rey.

Gregor sprang up. 'That's the sound of defeat. The Council will not stand for...',

But he never got to finish his sentence as Jude whipped a fist across his face. It cracked as it connected and Gregor crumpled to the floor.

'Wow, that's quite a punch you're packing their champ,' chirped Rey.

Daise shouted, 'For crying out loud. Jude, why did you have to go and do that? Is that really your contribution? Really helpful'.

Rey bit back, 'Look Daise, I know your world has been turned upside down but what is the deal with this kid? He's been a thorn in our side since he nicked our stuff on the beach.'

Daise stepped toward Jude, put her hands on her hips and sighed.

'Don't you understand? We have to be better than them or what's the point? What are we fighting for if we are just going to behave as badly as they do? Don't you think I'm angry? Look at me!'

She tugged at her neckline revealing an advancing spur of green skin. 'These changes are freaking me out. I would have throttled Gregor on the floor of the Channel office if his dad hadn't peeled me off him. I've never hit anyone in my life but the rage that came over me… And I don't know my own strength anymore.'

She let out a deep breath, 'OK, let's throw him in the back of the van.'

'Come on, Jude you get his legs,' said Rey, grabbing Gregor's arms.

Rey and Jude began to swing Gregor like a sack of potatoes 'On three… One, two…'

'Be gentle, would you,' interrupted Daise.

'Three!', Gregor landed with a soft thud.

'Come on, we might as well all drive up-front now,' said Daise. 'Let's do it. The guards are all going to be focused on that explosion now.'

As they approached the bridge a sign announced.

**ANCASTER ISLAND SECURITY ALERT:
CLOSED UNTIL FURTHER NOTICE**

Daise ducked as they passed a layby where an eight-carriage road train was parked up, waiting for the island to reopen.

Jude ignored the speed limit as they approached the

bridge. It was an impressive sight. Two large towers held the thick metal cables supporting the structure. The bridge was vast; spanning the 2km channel covering the flooded village of Ancaster after which the island was named. At the centre of the bridge, there was a panoramic view of the moonlit island and, in the distance, fire flickered close to the western shore.

The bridge ended at a checkpoint. The four-lane bridge narrowed to two lanes allowing vehicles on and off the island. All that stood in their way was a road barrier; a lever arm emblazoned with an illuminated octagonal stop sign.

Jude jabbed at the dashboard to extinguish the lights.

'Good thinking Jude. We don't want to advertise our arrival,' said Daise.

The battered van began to rattle as it gathered speed down the leeward slope of the bridge.

'You guys get down', said Jude, his fingernails digging into the fabric of the steering wheel, his foot flat to the floor. Daise and Rey undid their seat belts and squeezed themselves into the footwell.

Daise looked up at Jude. His thick-set eyebrows were locked in concentration. Perhaps she had been a little bit hard on him. He had certainly got the hang of driving this van. It felt good to have both of her friends back.

As he looked down the side of the bridge, Jude knew that he had to make his driving count. His friends were depending on him.

There were three hundred metres away from the barrier now and no Guardians had appeared. Perhaps they had abandoned their posts.

Two hundred metres; the van began to shake violently

The Castoffs

but Jude kept his foot to the floor.

One hundred metres; a Guardian appeared from a hut next to the barrier. An alarm sounded.

Fifty metres; Jude slid down his seat, barely able to peek above the dashboard. A shot rang out and wind whistled through the bullet hole. Jude straightened the wheel and did his best to keep steering straight but a rhythmic thud, thud, thud indicated he was hitting the markers on the outer edge of the road. Five more bullets cracked through the screen and then a pause. Jude took this to mean the Guardian was reloading. flicked his lights on full beam and sat up. He just had time to avoid the barrier support post and smashed through the barrier arm.

The guard was reloading. Shots thudded into the back of the van, ringing out like a steel drum.

Jude gripped the steering wheel tightly and accelerated around a sweeping curved section of the road that took them out of the firing line. It was only then he sat up properly in his seat.

'You can get up now, we made it,' said Jude.

Daise and Rey scrambled out of the footwell.

'Wow, Jude! That was awesome,' said Rey.

'It's not that tricky really. There's only one pedal and a steering wheel. Just a big version of that cart we raced down Casthorpe hill last summer.'

'Except this van has brakes.'

They all laughed as they recalled the annual tower cart race. In their efforts to make it go as fast as possible they had decided that brakes would make the cart too heavy.

Jude had not only won the race but had managed to stop the cart without hurting himself by skillfully steering off into a bank of sand.

Laughing felt good. For a moment it felt like they were just off on one of their scavenging adventures.

It was five miles to Port Fulbeck and the roads were eerily quiet. They didn't pass a single vehicle. Daise figured the island was on lockdown. All the Guardians would have been dispatched to Barrowby or sent to deal with the disturbance in Port Fulbeck.

'Take the next left', shouted Rey.

'Shit! A bit of warning would be nice,' Jude shouted back as he broke sharply, just in time to take a left hand turn into Port Fulbeck.

A door clanged in the back.

'It's Gregor, the silly arse has only gone and jumped out of the van.' said Jude. He stopped and leaned out of the window to see a figure running into a maize field.

He turned to Daise, 'Do you want us to go after him?'

'No, it's probably for the best, I mean I doubt he was going to be any help after you punched him out.'

Jude gave a surprised shrug, 'Sure thing,' he said and they drove off toward whatever was unfolding in Port Fulbeck.

The moonlight cast a ghostly hue over the town. Mrs Arkwright was sitting on a bench breathing hard. Her lungs were raw from running. She had to stop. She could hear the Patcher running through the maize field behind her. Out in the open, she could see the destruction caused by the spider drone.

Hundreds of green people were running away from the docks. She heard the smack of bodies on maize as they crashed into the field, desperately running in any direction away from the carnage at the docks.

The Castoffs

The Patcher burst out of the maize field and collapsed on the bench wheezing like a pit pony.

Mrs Arkwright gave him a moment to collect himself. She was worried that he might be having a heart attack. His onyx face was dripping with sweat and he spoke in spurts between deep lungfuls of air.

'My god… What have they done?'

Mrs Arkwright knew he didn't expect an answer but one came all the same, in the screams of the victims. It was pandemonium. As they walked toward the docks, they began to see victims of the blast, not just those fleeing in panic.

A green man was propped against a tree, his face blackened and his left arm barbecued. Mrs Arkwright fumbled with her first aid kit, looking for something that might help. Then the Patcher took control. He lay the man on the grass and tilted his head back to check his airway.

He pointed his torch beam into the man's mouth and sighed. 'We can't do anything for him, Alice. His lungs are shot — he must have inhaled the heat of the blast.'

They walked until they were in sight of the dock. The spider drone had dropped its payload at the water's edge. She could see a crater surrounded by a ring of bodies. Bitter explosives mixed with the nauseating smell of burning flesh.

As they got closer to the blast zone, the injuries got worse. It was a massacre; at least a hundred bodies lay scattered.

They stopped at the edge of the scorched ground at the edge of the crater. Small fires crackled around them as wooden buildings were consumed.

The Castoffs

Beyond the crash site, a group of around fifty people were rattling the gates of the Smart Jooce factory and throwing stones and lumps of wood at five uniformed Guardians.

It looked like the last stand of the green people.

A banging noise stopped Mrs Arkwright and the Patcher. A black van bearing the Greater Grantham Guardian logo was surrounded by green people.

'This could get messy,' said Mrs Arkwright, running toward the van. The Patcher grumbled to himself before running to catch her up.

Chapter 26 – Cricket

The van was surrounded by green people. Daise was reminded of the fear she felt when they had first dragged Rowan out of the sea. She wanted to shout that they were here to help. But they were in a Guardian van and Jude and Rey were wearing black shirts. This was it. They were going to be killed by the very people they were trying to save.

Daise grabbed Jude's lapels and ripped his shirt off. Buttons flew off, clattering on the dashboard like rain. Rey followed suit tearing his black shirt off like it was on fire.

'How could I have been so stupid?' howled Daise, 'We should have parked up on the edge of town.'

They ducked into the footwell looking up at the crowd of green people like lab rats in a cage awaiting their fate. The banging stopped. Daise stole a glance out of the side window. They were surrounded. She caught the eyes of an angry looking green woman brandishing a plank of wood like a cricket bat.

Glass rained down on them as the cracked windscreen finally gave in. With the windscreen gone, the noise of the crowd was cranked up.

Daise reached out and grasped Jude's hand, desperate not to feel alone. Could this really be the end? After all,

The Castoffs

they had been through, were they going to die cowering in the footwell of a van?

The crack of gunshot stunned the green people into silence. Daise was unsure. Was this a rescue? She heard a familiar voice cry out, 'Back away from the van.'

It was Mrs Arkwright. Perhaps they might live through this after all.

All three of them hopped out of the footwell like rabbits from a burrow.

Daise cried out in joy as she saw Mrs A and the Patcher cut a path through the crowd.

Mrs Arkwright, with a pistol in her hand, was speaking to the woman with the cricket bat. She was a little shorter than the men and wore a loose-fitting singlet. Her head, like all the green people was hairless, her thin lips hung in a fixed frown.

Daise could see black tracks up her arms and small darker green patches on his skin that looked like bruises.

Mrs Arkwright glanced across at Daise and her friends with a reassuring smile and put the pistol in her pocket.

Addressing the green woman with an outstretched hand she said, 'I'm Alice Arkwright and this is Jon Greaves. What's your name?'

The green woman seemed confused by the question but lowered her bat as she answered, 'My name's Iris.'

'Well, these young people are on your side,' said Mrs Arkwright releasing her hand.

Daise felt the tension fade and made straight for Mrs Arkwright. As she threw her arms around her, Rey and Jude joined in a group hug.

'I'm so proud of you all. You have helped change history.'

The Castoffs

The Patcher stood to one side, an awkward smile on his face. He wasn't known for public displays of affection.

Daise broke off and looked around, 'Where's Rowan?'

Iris stepped forward, 'You know Rowan?' he asked.

'The man who made the film,' she added.

'Yes, these are the brave young people who got his film broadcast on the Channel.' said Mrs Arkwright proudly.

'But they drive a Guardian's van,' she replied.

Daise repeated, 'Where's Rowan?'

Mrs Arkwright didn't answer. She let Iris fill the silence.

'We saw Rowan's film. It triggered the uprising. We thought we were free. That we had them on the run. The black-shirted slavers ran. But then they dropped the bomb.'

Iris continued, 'Do you know Rowan? I worked with him on the farm before I was moved to work in Port Fulbeck. Is he here?'

Mrs Arkwright tried to speak, but her mouth flapped in the warm evening breeze.

The Patcher's deep voice crackled like an old record, 'I'm sorry. He didn't make it.'

The words slapped Daise. Her brain flipped. A jumble of images clattered around her head; Rowan waking up on the beach; Rowan's strong arms holding her after she was shot; Rowan's deep green eyes.

The news spread like an aftershock, disbelief spreading across the faces of the green people. Daise watched as the whispered words extinguished hope.

'I don't understand. How…?' she cried out. But the

The Castoffs

question dissolved in her mouth. It suddenly seemed so pointless. The cost of it all was too high. On the streets of Barrowby, they had won but looking around at the crushing sorrow in the faces of the crowd it looked like defeat.

She sat on the kerb, exhausted. Rey and Jude sat on either side, holding her hands. They were joined by Mrs Arkwright and the Patcher. Then the man with the bat and his companions joined them too. The sounds of the fire and the pained cries of the injured became sharper as, one by one, the crowd sat down.

Daise watched as it spread like a wave radiating out from her. She squeezed the hands holding hers, feeling connected to the crowd.

It felt like hope.

Her grief would have to wait; they had to refocus. If Rowan's life wasn't going to be in vain, they needed to secure the island for the green people.

As the crowd sat, Daise got a view of the destruction. the bomb had fallen on the crowd walking up the high street towards the docks. The only evidence of the terraced houses that lined the street was a carpet of fractured red bricks. The main fire was burning around a dark black crater.

Next to them stood the towering steel gates of the Smart Jooce factory. The ground floor was blacked out with steel shutters. The glass fronted panes of the upper floors were shattered but intact.

The building was surrounded by thick six metre concrete walls topped with jagged metal spikes. A large sign on the gate was illuminated by the flickering fire: Smart Jooce Processing Plant and Distribution Centre.

The Castoffs

Security by GGG.

Jude turned to Daise, 'I'm sorry. It's my fault. I never should have told.'

Daise dropped his hand, 'What did you do Jude, what did you do!'

Jude said, 'When they caught me on the fence, they took me to my father.'

'But you're an orphan', Rey interrupted, 'like me.'

'That's what I thought, but my dad was detained. They let me speak to him.' said Jude.

'Are you sure it was him?' asked Rey.

'Yes, he knew everything about me. My birthday, the birthmark on my lower back. The name of our dog. I mean absolutely everything.'

'But that stuff could have been on your file.'

'You don't understand Rey, I spoke to him. It was my dad. He was alive. I have a family.

'But we're your family,' said Rey quietly. He turned away from his friend.

Jude paused, gnawing on his lip.

Daise stood up, 'So you did betray us at the Channel, and you lied about it. Jude, how could you do that to us? You knew we were headed into a trap, and you just let us.'

'No, I would never have put you in harm's way,' Jude cried out. 'I couldn't go with you because I had to check in with my handler.'

'Oh my god Jude, listen to yourself. Your handler? I don't even know who you are' said Daise.

'But I never said anything about the Channel. I would never do that to you. Gregor told us they can track identchips. They just told me to give them information about Rowan and in exchange they said they would release my dad. They told me Rowan was dangerous. That he carried a disease. I didn't believe them at first but then when you started turning green Daise… It started to make sense.'

'What did you tell them?' said Daise.

Jude looked sound. All eyes were on him; Rey, Daise, Mrs A and the Patcher and all the green people.

'I told them that Mrs Arkwright and the Patcher were trying to rent a boat in Casthorpe Harbour. I had to tell them something,' he blurted out.

'You stupid, stupid boy!', said Mrs Arkwright. 'You sent the Guardians that killed him.'

She put her hands to her head and began to weep.

Iris stepped forward and plucked the pistol from Mrs Arkwright's pocket. Short for a green person, she still towered above the children.

Facing Jude, she said 'So, this boy is responsible for the death of comrade Rowan?', like a judge holding court.

He paused. No one said a word.

Iris looked at the gun and then the cricket bat as if deciding on his weapon of choice. He tucked the gun into her waistband and slowly lifted the bat in an arc until its roughly tapered hilt rested on her shoulder, poised to deliver retribution.

Jude looked up at Iris, his would-be executioner. He slumped forward onto his knees. His head bowed.

Daise jumped between the Jude and the bat.

'Step aside. We need justice. Someone must pay for what's been taken,' said Iris.

Daise rolled up her sleeves to reveal her green arms. She wanted Iris to see that she was like her. 'This isn't right. Rowan was my friend; he was a man of peace. He wouldn't want this.'

'Jude's made a mistake. He's been selfish and cowardly but if you do this, what makes you any better than the men that dropped the bombs?'

Iris ground her teeth and snapped at Daise, 'I don't care for your moralising. You think you know what it's like being green because you've been transformed. You know nothing. Do you wake up every morning hoping you will get through the day without getting a beating? Do your friends disappear with no explanation? You watch Rowan's film and you think you get to decide what justice looks like? You don't. Stand aside.'

Daise stood firm. Glaring in defiance. She looked out at the crowd of people, sitting down in silent respect for their fallen. Then she saw a solitary figure walking with purpose in their direction.

Rey stood up next to her. 'I'm angry with him too but it's like Daise says, we have to be better than these bastards that think it's OK to drop bombs on protesters. Or what are we really fighting for? Beating kids to death in the street. Is that who you want to be.'

Iris sighed and nodded to her companions. They grabbed Daise and Rey and moved them aside like they were bales of hay.

Mrs Arkwright and the Patcher stepped into the space vacated by Daise and Rey. They too made their plea for leniency but Iris would not compromise.

'All I can promise is that I'll be quick. You might want to look away now.'

Daise couldn't look away. Once again, Iris swung the bat back. Jude flinched, wrapping his arms around his head.

Then Daise saw the approaching figure break into a run, like a tiger focused on its prey. It was a tall green man clad in a black leather jacket and jeans. He barrelled into the back of Jude's would-be executioner, knocking her to the ground.

'Enough!' he said, taking the gun from Iris' waistband. His voice was loud, assertive but calm. He scanned the crowd with the gun as if to reinforce his authority. He watched as the startled expressions of his friends turned into joyful recognition.

'Rowan', they cried in unison.

Mrs Arkwright ran to him and locked him in a tight embrace.

'It's you, it's really you! But how? We saw you die.'

Rowan explained what had happened after the Patcher had abandoned his resuscitation attempts on the pool table at the Fisherman's Arms.

'Of course!' said the Patcher, giving himself a slap in the face, 'You went into photosynthetic dormancy!'

'In English please?' added Mrs Arkwright, finally releasing Rowan from her embrace.

'We know that wound healing is quicker in the transformed,' said the Patcher. 'Daise, your gunshot wound has completely healed in just a few days that's all well documented. Chloroplasts in the bloodstream speed up the clotting process, which allow wounds to heal more quickly with less scarring.'

'Yes, yes Jon but it doesn't explain how he came back from the dead. He had no pulse; his heart had stopped. He was dead.'

Rowan looked like he was about to speak. But the

The Castoffs

Patcher continued like an excited schoolboy.

'I thought that too. I remember some research on mice that showed it was possible to keep them in stasis. Normally when your heart stops you can't pump oxygenated blood around your body. Cells that are starved of oxygen die. Chloroplasts are amazing biological machines. They can make oxygen in the tissues even when blood has stopped circulating. In mice, at least, this low-level metabolic activity can stave off cell death, keeping them alive for up to an hour.'

'You might not believe me after the terrible things I've done. But I did everything I could to save you. We lay you on the pool table under bright lights. I did compressions for an hour but there was nothing, no sign at all that you could come back.' The Patcher's tired old eyes filled with tears.

He turned to face Rowan, 'I tried so hard to bring you back. I really did.'

'It's OK. I am here now,' said Rowan. 'That is all that matters. I have no doubt that I have you to thank for that. I think it is time that we put the past behind us. I forgive you.'

The Patcher stood still. A single tear dropped from his left eye.

Mrs Arkwright spoke. 'I still don't understand.'

Rowan broke off from the Patcher's embrace, 'Well, your tattooed friend got a bit of a shock when I came around in the grave he had dug for me. I think the impact of the first spadeful of dirt he dropped on my chest kickstarted my heart. The pain was excruciating and I let out one heck of a scream. My heart felt like it was on fire, but my chloroplasts must have plugged the hole the bullet had torn through my chest.

'It took me quite some time to calm your tattooed friend. After he had emptied his hip flask of beet spirit, he explained that you had headed to Ancaster in a boat. I convinced him to lend me his jacket and a boat and here I am. I arrived just in time to see the explosion. I was doing my best to help the injured when everyone began to sit down. I saw you all standing in the distance and thought I would investigate. And just in time by the look of things.'

Rowan turned to face Iris who, without her bat, was looking decidedly less confident.

'I know you. We worked together on the Cranwell maize farm. As I recall I topped up your harvest when you were a fresh detainee.'

Iris said nothing, just shuffled back into the crowd.

Rowan bent down, picked up the cricket bat and hurled it over the factory gates. It smacked off the unforgiving walls of the Smart Jooce factory.

'Right then. Let's see if we can clear this island of Guardians for good. I suggest we start with the factory.'

Rowan walked up to the front gates of the factory. The guardian's booth was deserted. He gave the gates a gentle push with his shoulder but they held firm.

'Why don't you just shoot it open?' said Iris.

'Because I don't want the bullet to ricochet into innocent bystanders.' replies Rowan curtly.

'And besides, I think a bit of brute force should do the trick.'

Daise smiled, comforted by Rowan's confidence as he pushed the gate open. She followed them through the gates with Rey, Mrs Arkwright and the Patcher at her

The Castoffs

side. Looking back she saw Jude hesitate on the other side of the gates. Behind him stood Iris.

'Come on Jude, you're with us,' shouted Daise.

Jude walked towards her. Some of the green people started to follow too but Iris remained still, staring at them. Daise grabbed Jude's arm and propelled him forward roughly, keen to create distance from Iris' menacing glare.

A rhythmic whirring sound pierced the night air. Daise looked up and caught a glance of moonlight skipping off rotas blades. As they came closer it became clear that there were at least three machines circling the factory.

Not more drones, she thought; scared to say it out loud for fear of making it real.

Panic spread through the crowd as people ran for cover. Some darted into the maize fields. Other up the main road out of town.

But these weren't drones; these were manned paramotors — personal flying machines that consisted of a single turbine mounted on a backpack twinned with a parasail.

They weaved through the air like sidewinder snakes, the buzzing growing louder and louder as they flew toward the flat-topped factory roof.

Daise watched as the Chief Guardian manoeuvred the paramotor in a sweeping circle above the courtyard of the Smart Jooce factory. The turbine looked fragile; a glorified fan encased in a chicken wire cage. The Patcher hurled a rock toward the Chief but he was quick to react, swooping upwards to land on the roof of the Smart Jooce factory.

The Castoffs

An amplified authoritarian voice cut through the night like that of a god, 'This is your first and final warning. Return to your barracks. Or we will bring in the drones. I repeat; return to your barracks or you will be destroyed.'

Chapter 27 – Factory

Daise watched Rowan as he bounded in long, graceful strides toward the main entrance of the Smart Jooce factory. For a man who had died earlier that day, he ran with a surprising speed and purpose. His black leather jacket framed him in a different light. She had always considered him brave but that aura of calmness was gone, replaced by a fierce energy. It was magnetic. She couldn't help but follow him across the car park.

A huge, illuminated sign stood at the factory entrance; it was the logo that appeared on all the Smart Jooce cartons. 'Jooce' was in jagged green letters, with two green smiley faced berries in place of the Os.

Daise remembered sitting in the tower canteen with Rey as he sucked on a carton of juice. She smiled to remember his catch phrase for Smart Jooce.

'Hey, Mrs Arkwright, do you have a pen?'

She took a thick black marker from her jacket with a smile.

'Will this do?'

'That's perfect,' Daise took the pen and walked up to the sign.

'What are you doing?', asked Rey.

Daise said nothing. She removed the pen cap and scrawled across the sign in capital letters. 'IT TASTES

LIKE SHIT BUT YOU CAN LIVE OFF IT.'

She started to laugh, a nervous chuckle, and Rey, reading her words, joined in.

But the smile fell from her face, 'You know what Rey?'

She paused, surveying the collapsed buildings and the bodies lying in the street on the other side of the fence. 'I'm not sure you can live off it. Whatever that stuff is, the cost is too high.'

Daise gave the pen back to Mrs Arkwright and they all stood silently, staring at the steel shutter that covered the main entrance. Rowan shook the shutter. Rey kicked the padlocks with his Guardian-issue boots.

It was an anti-climax. Daise wanted to storm the factory. She wanted justice for Rowan and the green people. She was one of them, after all.

'Have you got anything in that magic rucksack of yours that will help us get in there?' asked the Patcher.

Mrs Arkwright swung it off her shoulder and started to rummage around.

Jude jostled past Daise, running off toward the gates. 'Where's he going?' asked Rey.

'I dunno, I feel like I don't really know him anymore.'

They both shrugged and watched Jude dash out across the car park back, through the gate to the beat-up van. Much of the crowd had dispersed, fearful of another drone strike. Only the dead and dying remained in Port Fulbeck, along with a few brave souls trying to tend to the injured.

Jude pulled the van door open and grabbed the crowbar from the footwell. Running back to the group, he was blinded by the light of the Smart Jooce factory.

Someone had connected the power.

Each floor was lit up bright yellow. You could make out each individual pane of glass like a pixel bounded by a thin grey border. Like a prisoner in a spotlight, Jude shielded his eyes and continued running.

Rowan spoke to Jude as if he bore no grudge, 'Good thinking! That will do nicely. Although I would appreciate it if someone else could do the honours.'

He unzipped the leather jacket to reveal a translucent green bullet hole, 'I should probably not over exert myself.'

Daise couldn't help but stare with a strange mix of wonder and of horror; the rules of what a human body could endure were being redefined. A translucent piece of skin had formed across the entry wound like a small window through which you could see the pulse of his heart. He looked strong yet fragile. It reminded her of the feeling she had when they first met on Barrowby beach.

Jude took a deep breath and prised the shutter open, popping each lock with ease. He tried pulling the shutter from the centre but it was too heavy.

'I need help here,' he cried. The friends spaced themselves along the shutter. Waiting for Jude to give a signal.

'Ok, now let's lift it up, on three. One... two... three!'

The shutter rolled up to reveal a revolving glass door. Rowan pushed on the revolving door, 'It's locked' he exclaimed. Jude swung the crowbar at the glass and the door collapsed.

Once again Rowan took the lead. They all followed him into a huge white reception, with a deserted desk to their left. As they walked toward it they heard the crackle

The Castoffs

of a PA system.

'You are trespassing on private property. This facility is protected by Greater Grantham Guardians. If you do not vacate the premises immediately you will be met by lethal force. This is your first and final warning.'

Rowan continued forward but the Patcher and group of green people stood on the threshold as if stopped by an invisible forcefield.

Daise stood in the middle of the white stone floor with Jude, Rey, and Mrs Arkwright. It seemed as if this was going to be down to them. Rowan looked back at the green people by the door. Daise expected him to confront them, but he just smiled.

The Patcher spoke first, 'I'm a doctor, or at least I was. I think I can be of more help out here. There are plenty of injured people that need help.'

He paused to look at the people at his side. They nodded in acknowledgement.

'I think we can set up a field hospital and save some lives. I need to help them. I have debt to pay.'

Rowan walked over to the Patcher, his feet crunching on the broken glass. He offered his hand. The Patcher grasped it, cupping his other hand over the front of Rowan's.

'As far as I am concerned, you have repaid your debt. You saved my life and are helping us now. The past is another country,' said Rowan.

'Bu… but the things I've done.' the Patcher said, his deep voice cracked as he spoke.

Rowan hugged the Patcher, 'Let it go. I forgive you.'

Daise felt a tear running down her face. But there was no time to dwell on her emotions. Whatever was going

The Castoffs

on in the Smart Jooce factory, the Guardians were willing to make it their last stand. They had bombed Port Fulbeck and sent in the Chief to secure the building. As much as she wanted to help those injured in the attack, she needed answers.

Rowan turned to the green people standing at the entrance, 'Thank you my friends for all your courage and support. I think my friend Jon is right. It is time to help the fallen. Please help him. For my own part I beg your forgiveness, I need to find out why the Guardians are so determined to keep us from the factory. I think there are people inside that need our help too.'

Mrs Arkwright ran over to the Patcher and hugged him, 'Stay safe, Jon. And thank you, you old grump.' She ran a finger affectionately across his bristly cheek to pull his frown into a smile.

Daise, Rey and Jude walked up to him.

'Thanks for all your help, I'm so glad you opened your door to help me. I don't know what I'd have done without your tonic,' said Daise.

The Patcher gave her a hug and ruffled Rey's mop of unruly hair. But when he spoke, he addressed Jude, 'Don't let one mistake define you son. If Rowan can forgive me for the things I've done, then your friends can too. Just make sure you learn from your mistakes.

'But before I go, there's something you need to know. That man you met. He wasn't your dad. He was an actor. It is a standard procedure the committee use to recruit informants. You weren't the first kid to be manipulated by the hope of a fresh start and you won't be the last.'

Jude's legs buckled but Daise and Rey grabbed him before he fell. They spoke together, 'We are your family,

The Castoffs

Jude. Now, let's see this thing through.'

They waved goodbye to the Patcher and his new companions and followed Rowan. He had already disappeared behind the reception counter, returning with a security card.

The reception had an atrium that stretched up five storeys to the roof of the building. Daise gazed upwards and felt dizzy; the vast open space seemed like a trick of the light. It was so at odds with the tiny breadbin sleeping pods in the towers, she felt like it was mocking her. There was something strange about the building. It reminded her of Greenacres Hospital. The same disinfectant smell hung in her nostrils.

While the reception area was white, the glass wall was black and impenetrable. She guessed the factory itself was housed beyond this. A single broad staircase led up to a huge set of double doors a storey up in the glass wall.

'Rowan, what's your plan? asked Mrs Arkwright.

'I've got a bad feeling about this place. There are stories of green people coming here to work but I've never met anyone who's made it out. You know I am a peaceful man but we need to be prepared. What weapons do you have?'

Mrs Arkwright showed Rowan her gun. Jude waved the crowbar above his head.

'What about you guys?' Daise and Rey shrugged.

'OK, make sure you stay behind us. I'm not sure how many Guardians will be holed up in here. I think a lot of them made for the port when they heard we had taken to the streets.'

'This place, it's not an ordinary factory, is it?' said Daise.

The Castoffs

Rowan put his arm on her shoulder, 'No Daise, I don't think it is.'

'What about the Chief?', added Rey.

'If that was his voice on the PA system, they'll be in the comms room on the fifth floor.' Rowan pointed to a plan of the building he had found behind the reception desk.

'Come on then, let's see what's behind those doors. Daise, get behind me. Rey and Jude, you stay with Mrs Arkwright.'

They followed Rowan up the stairs in a line. He swiped the security card across the sensor pad on the wall. There was a beep quickly followed by a click. The door slid open to reveal a vast factory floor.

The factory floor was an orchestra of noise; from the rhythmic hum of the pumps, the rumble of the conveyor belt and the clanking of the carton packing and stacking machine. All the sounds ricocheted of the metallic surface of the storage tanks.

Rowan and Daise stepped through onto a metal grate and the door clamped shut behind them. Mrs Arkwright, Jude and Rey were locked out.

They heard muffled banging on the other side of the door. Rowan swiped his security card on the sensor; it beeped but the door remained firmly closed.

They heard shouts from the other side of the door but the voices were too muffled to distinguish words against the cacophonous, clanking roar of the factory floor. The bangs of fists changed to the frustrated thuds of the crowbar, but the door remained resolutely shut.

Daise peeked out from behind Rowan and scanned the metal walkway for any sign of guards but the place

The Castoffs

looked deserted. They walked up to the metal rail and looked down at the cavernous expanse of the factory. She couldn't see the threat but she knew it was there nevertheless. It was hard to imagine that the Guardians would just abandon this heavily fortified factory.

She felt like they had just stepped into a trap. What sort of access card let you into a room but didn't let you out? Had it been left deliberately for them to find?

She had seen the Chief's paramotor land on the roof. He must be here; hiding in the shadows ready to pounce. The thought of his cruel face made her shudder.

They were standing on a steel grate platform that ran, about a metre wide, around the edge of the factory. At the edge of the platform there was a chain-link barrier topped with a smooth metal rail to prevent you from falling onto the machinery below.

The factory floor was sunk three storeys down into the basement. Shiny copper tanks stood in rows like vast tombstones. Leaning further over the rail, she could see a network of conveyor belts that were used to package the Smart Jooce into cartons. Even with the chaos on the streets of Port Fulbeck, the facility continued to run.

She had never been inside a factory before but this seemed, well, what she'd expect. It was only when she looked up the sides of the building that she could see that something strange was going on.

Standing with her back to the factory floor, she could see that the building was more like a prison. Each floor was full of steel doors spaced two meters apart. The surface of each door was perfectly smooth except for a small shutter in which hid a letterbox shaped window. There must be hundreds of these doors.

Narrow copper pipes ran out of each room connecting like a spider's web to tanks on the factory floor.

Daise ran along the steel grate walkway to the first room. Rowan followed her. She paused for a moment, her hand on the shutter.

'What is this place, Rowan?'

Her question remained unanswered as Rowan slid the shutter open and they were blinded momentarily by a bright light.

Chapter 28 – Cell

It took a moment for her eyes to adjust to the brightly lit cell. They were looking into a small square white box. It reminded Daise of the hospital room in Greenacres. The back wall was a single pane of thick glass. Mounted to the floor was an exercise bike; a young woman was cycling at a steady pace. Her hands and feet were bound to the machine.

Just above head height was a giant bottle of water, like a supersized version of the kind you might find attached to a hamster's cage. The young woman was dressed in nothing but a pair of shorts and a crop top. Her skin was a deep emerald colour, much darker than Daise had ever seen Rowan's. Her forearms were wrapped in bandages. At first glance Daise thought there were green wires attached to each arm but on looking closer she could see that they were plastic tubes connected to a copper pipe. She realised it was one of the pipes that ran from the cells into the large tanks on the factory floor.

The young women looked at them. Daise could see they were a similar age; maybe the woman on the bike was a bit older. She was the first green girl Daise had ever seen and, for the briefest moment, she felt a little bit less lonely. But any joy she felt was quickly extinguished by the sight of the most desperate face she had ever seen.

The Castoffs

The girl's eyes were a dark muddy green, the whites streaked with green blood vessels. She lips quivered as she mouthed two words; 'Help me'.

'This is how they make Smart Jooce; from our blood', said Rowan. The anguish in his voice was unbearable.

Daise staggered backwards into the metal rail and sank to her knees. Rowan's words were horrifying. Smart Jooce was made from the blood of people just like her.

There must be at least 1,000 people imprisoned here. She had been drinking this stuff ever since she had been sent to the towers.

It was too much to bear. She fell to her knees and vomited. The liquid dripped through the metal grate to the factory floor below.

She felt frozen in that moment. She wasn't ready to go on with this knowledge.

'Daise, take a breath, you have to breathe', said Rowan.

Rowan sat down against the fence and held Daise as she finally took in a deep breath. 'It OK Daise, you're going to be OK.'

'But it's not OK is it? This is some sort of human-powered solar power plant. They give the green people light and that tonic - like that drink the Patcher gave me.'

She paused for a moment to take another deep breath and continued, 'And they harvest their blood and feed it to us Castoffs.'

Rowan nodded, 'There is such a cruel efficiency about it. The exercise bikes are used to generate the electricity to power the lights which keep them photosynthesising so their blood will be full of sugar.'

'Why didn't you tell us?', she whispered to Rowan.

The Castoffs

'I didn't know. I heard they were taking the youngest detainees to Port Fulbeck. We stopped seeing anyone under 20 on the farms. There was talk of experiments and hard labour but no one had pieced the truth together because no one ever escaped.'

'We have to get these people out of here,' said Daise.

Rowan nodded, 'Let's work out how to get these doors open.'

Daise began rubbing the rough breeze block wall, searching for a mechanism that might unlock the door. Rowan ran his fingers round the steel door but there was nothing. The door itself had no handle or keyhole. The hinges were hidden and a lip ran around the edge of the door hiding the frame. It looked impenetrable.

'They must open electronically,' said Daise. She ran back to the entrance. Scraping sounds continued from the other side of the door — Mrs Arkwright, Jude and Rey were still trying to get in.

As she stared at the walls running along the entrance corridor, she spotted a square of timber embedded in the wall.

'I think I've found something,' she shouted to Rowan.

Rowan raced up and banged on the panel. It sounded encouragingly hollow. He hammered harder with the fleshy side of his fists. The sound echoed around the cavernous factory like a mighty drum beat.

As his fists rained down on the wall the wood began to splinter. Daise helped him work the wood free, revealing a panel of small ball-headed metal switches.

'These must control the locking mechanisms on the cells', cried Daise.

They both stared at the switches for a moment.

Rowan nodded and Daise tentatively flicked the first one. The double doors swung open and Mrs Arkwright fell forward, sprawling across the floor. The crowbar flew out of her hands and clattered across the steel grating before dropping over the edge of the platform and striking a copper storage tank. The clang rang out like a bell.

Daise and Rowan helped her up. Closer to the door, Daise could see down to the reception area; Rey and Jude were pulling a struggling Gregor up the stairs, gripping tightly to his arms as he thrashed about.

A minute later, they were reunited next to the control panel. The boys dragged Gregor to his feet, each of them holding an arm tightly. Gregor had a face like Medusa sucking a wasp but he had pretty much stopped struggling.

'Look who we found?', said Rey.

'He was caught trying to steal the van and a couple of green guys dragged him into the reception. They figured we'd know what to do with him.'

Gregor looked defeated. He had cuts all over his hands. His black jeans were ripped and his white vest was covered with mud stains.

'I guess we're going to see this out together,' said Daise.

'This is the boy that shot you on the beach, isn't it?' said Rowan, looking Gregor up and down. 'The one that knocked me out and left me for dead. Your powers of forgiveness are admirable Daise.'

'No, you don't understand Rowan. I don't forgive him, but he might be a good bargaining chip. He's the Chief's son.'

A deep voice boomed out of the shadows, 'Ah all

friends together, how nice.'

Excited by their reunion, the friends had failed to notice the stealthy approach of a figure along the landing. It was the Chief.

He grabbed Daise around the waist and pressed the tip of a blade up against her pale green neck.

Daise was terrified. The skin on her neck felt paper-thin against the cold metal blade. With each breath she felt the blade push into her. She fought the urge to scream out. Losing control would not help.

From the corner of her eye, she saw Damon and Tommo run up the landing. It looked like Gregor's meathead cadet companions had been promoted to Guardians, judging by their GGG badges. Of course, there had been three paramotors so there would be three Guardians. They had been so focussed on the horror of the factory they had let their guard down.

'OK, put your weapons on the floor and kick them my way,' barked the Chief.

'Unless you want to see this poor girl bleed out on a cold metal floor.'

Mrs Arkwright looked to Rowan. He shrugged and she removed the gun from her waistband and placed it on the floor.

The Chief beckoned to Tommo, 'Look after that gun Tommo. We don't want anyone getting shot by accident.'

He let out a little laugh and continued. 'So, you were planning a jailbreak, were you? Well, that's not going to happen. I WILL have order returned to the facility.'

Rey rushed forward but Rowan blocked him. 'Leave her alone you bastard', he spat at the Chief.

The Chief let out a hollow laugh. 'Very wise my green

friend. I don't really want to hurt these children. After all, I could make much better use of them.'

He pushed the knife gently into Daise's neck. A small drop of green blood formed at the tip of the blade.

'It looks like she's ready to check in.'

He stepped forward and ruffled Rey's mop of hair, 'I would have thought you would have learned something from our last meeting boy. Resisting doesn't really work out for you, does it?'

Rey's face seemed to boil with rage but Rowan gripped him tightly around the shoulders.

The Chief gave a deep self-satisfied chuckle and said to Rowan, 'You don't see how pathetic this is do you? Look at your team. You have an old woman and three children. One who looks like he's been joyriding in a tumble dryer and this one,' he said pointing at Jude, 'I think you'll find that he's working for us.'

The Chief beckoned Jude to join him. But he remained at Rey's side.

'Oh, switching sides now? Well, thanks for the tip-off at the Channel, oh and this knife is proving to be useful.'

The Chief took the knife from Daise's neck for a moment, waving it at Jude. Jude saw the locking mechanism and his own initials scratched into the handle.

He wanted to disappear but the Chief continued talking, 'The deal's off kid. I'm afraid your dad's dead. He has been for years. It never fails to amaze me just how gullible you Castoff kids are. You're so desperate to be part of a family you'll accept an actor who has spent half an hour with your file as your dad. Personally, I don't get what the big deal is with family. I mean, look at my boy. Being a father; it's just one big disappointment after another.'

The Chief clapped his hands together, 'Now, here's what's going to happen. You are going to give me my son. Or the Greep is going to bleed out.'

Jude and Rey looked defeated. They looked up at Rowan who simply nodded. They released their grip on Gregor and he walked over to his father and his friends.

'OK, Gregor, make yourself useful. Hold this Greep for a moment. You can do that can't you?' said the Chief.

He passed Jude's knife to his son while keeping a firm grip on Daise. 'I know you've got the better of my boy before. But don't be getting ideas. Any funny business from you and … Damon, Tommo, you know what to do.'

The Chief's voice trailed off as he pulled his gun from its holster and spun it around in his hand, showing off like a street performer. He strutted over to the control panel, flicked a switch and the door on the first cell opened with a popping sound.

'Right, Gregor, follow me and bring her with you.'

The Chief walked over to the cell and opened the door, keeping his gun trained on Rowan. Gregor folded Jude's knife and stuck it in his pocket. He grabbed Daise by the wrist, dragging her toward the open cell.

Daise considered resisting but she couldn't really see the point. At least she no longer had a knife pressed up against her neck.

A shaft of light shone out of the cell as if it was a portal to a better place. But the reality couldn't be further from the truth.

'I can take the grubby little Greep from here', said the Chief, grabbing Daise in a headlock. He turned to his son, 'Now you go on and release the one inside. It's time Daisy Dawkins realised that she's nothing more than a degraded sub-human.'

'But dad, I don't want to touch one of them. What if I get infected?' said Gregor.

'Don't worry about that son. That's not how it works,' the Chief replied.

Gregor looked confused but did as his dad asked and walked into the cell. He had to shield his eyes from the dazzling bright lights at first.

He turned back to look at his dad. His expression had changed from submission to shock.

'Jessie?', Gregor's voice was thin and croaky. He hit a red button on the centre of a panel on the exercise bike but the wheel continued to turn.

'Jessie', he repeated, a little louder. 'You can stop now.' And a beat later, confused he added, 'Dad said you'd gone to be a maid for the council leader. I didn't know…'

Eventually she stopped pedalling and when she came to a stop Gregor started to undo the buckles that bound her to the bike.

He unwrapped the bandages on her left arm. He could see the outline of a needle pushed under her skin that was draining blood from her body. He pulled it from her arm and a trickle of green blood dripped on to the pristine white tiled floor. He did the same with her other arm and when she was finally free from her bindings, she slumped forward on the handlebars.

Gregor spoke to her softly, 'Come on Jessie, let's get you out of here. I'm so sorry, I never meant for you to get into trouble.'

The Castoffs

Daise couldn't tell whether there was genuine compassion in his voice or just guilt.

He helped Jessie off the bike and supported her with one arm. She was unsteady on her feet. 'Let me sit for a moment,' she gasped, still out of breath from cycling.

Gregor propped her up against the wall outside the cell and confronted his father.

'You said, she'd got another job.'

'What of it?' the Chief snapped impatiently.

'But what have you done to her — she's been infected. She's green.'

Daise could help herself, even though she knew antagonising the Chief was a bad idea.

'Don't you get what's happening here, Gregor? This is where they send us. If we think for ourselves or ask questions, we get detained. They turn us green and demonise us. There is no infection; that's just propaganda designed to keep you scared. Perhaps it's time you started thinking for yourself. You were in the room — you saw what was happening. They were draining her blood to make Smart Jooce. Look around...'

Gregor looked up at the web of pipes that radiated from the cells to the copper tanks on the factory floor.

The Chief interrupted with a laugh that vibrated through Daise's skull, 'Nice try Daisy, what do you think is going to happen now? Do you think my son will grow a spine and save you?'

He tightened his grip on her neck and continued laughing. Daise looked at Gregor: he was shaking with rage.

There was a chance she could turn this round. It was time to muster every ounce of strength she had left. She bit down on her tongue until it bled. The earthy tang of Smart Jooce filled her mouth. With a surge of pain, adrenaline and raw anger she swung the point of her elbow into the Chief's ribs.

He let out a grunt and loosened his grip on her neck just enough for her to wriggle away. Her freedom would have been short lived if Gregor hadn't taken that moment to attack his father.

Running at his dad, head down like a cannonball, Gregor hit him square in the chest. Already off-balance from the jab to his side, the Chief toppled backwards toward the iron railing. His gun clattered across the iron grate as he fell. Damon was first to react, grabbing the weapon and aiming it at Mrs Arkwright.

Tommo waved his gun at Rowan and shouted, 'None of you move or we'll start shooting.'

The Chief was a tall man and the highest rail caught the top of his leg. He waved his arms around, desperately trying to grab anything that could stop him from plunging to the factory floor.

There was a slapping noise. Daise felt a sting on her arm and then a wrenching tug as if her arm was being pulled from its socket. The Chief had spun over the barrier. His grip on Daise's wrist was the only thing keeping him from crashing to his death.

His weight dragged her toward the edge. She came to an abrupt stop as her rib cage smashed into the barrier. Instinctively she anchored herself against the metal to stop herself being pulled over the edge.

Daise felt her arm stretching as the Chief's entire weight pulled down on her. He was flailing around, his right arm desperately trying to connect with something solid. Daise screamed as she felt her shoulder pop.

The pain from her dislocated shoulder was searing. Her arm hung useless and floppy like a piece of meat. Her vision blurred. As she blinked, she saw a black curtain start to close over her field of vision. Wobbling on the edge of consciousness, her body began to lift up.

'This is the end. The Chief is going to pull me over the barrier. I'm going to die.'

But she heard the slap of flesh on metal and the pressure on her arm dissipated. The Chief had managed to grab the barrier. Her arm was no longer holding his full weight.

She turned her head to face him. He was grinning at her, like a lion about to devour its prey. He flexed his right arm and pulled himself up so he was able to lodge his feet on the edge of the metal platform.

Held at gunpoint — Rowan, Mrs Arkwright, Rey and Jude could only watch on in horror as the Chief stood up on the other side of the barrier and grabbed Daise under chin, lifting her off the ground.

Gregor, sprang back to his feet and jumped at his dad.

The Chief let go of Daise and held one arm out to fend off his son while gripping the barrier with his other arm. This time the Chief was not caught by surprise and easily batted his son to the floor.

Daise clambered away from the Chief, watching helplessly as he lifted a leg over the top of the barrier. Gregor struck like a mouse trap. He removed the knife from his pocket, pulled the blade out and locked it in place. And for the third time he ran at his father, plunging the blade into his chest. He held the black hilt and looked up into the father's eyes, waiting for some

The Castoffs

admonishment, but the Chief just let out a cough and fell backwards in silence.

Daise held her breath until she heard the thud of the body hitting the concrete factory floor.

Rowan and Mrs Arkwright rushed at Tommo and Damon, who had lowered their guns in shock, staring at Gregor, who had fallen to his knees still clutching the knife.

Stripped of the guns and their leader, Damon and Tommo ran.

Daise, Rey, Jude, Mrs Arkwright and Rowan all approached the metal barrier. The Chief's body lay splayed out on the shiny concrete floor. A dark pool of blood radiated out from his head. It was over; the Chief was dead.

Chapter 29 – Truth

The azure sky was immense as Daise looked out across the Trent Sea. She pushed her feet into the powdery sand as she walked barefoot along the beach. The rays of the morning sun danced on her skin, filling her body with warmth and sustenance. Jude and Rey walked either side of her. For the first time in weeks, she felt safe.

They had spent the night releasing prisoners from the cells in the Smart Jooce factory. It had taken hours to empty the prison. Daise, Jude and Rey had each taken a floor and released each prisoner cell by cell. Some of the prisoners were full of exuberant thanks, hugging them and cheering with joy. The majority were silent, so unused to speaking they tried to croak their thanks. Many of these were now on the beach, with a warm cup of tea in their hands. Some seem to have recovered a little and were talking to each other.

But not all the prisoners wanted to leave. Some clung desperately to their bikes even when their bindings were untied and the needles removed. Daise had spent 30 minutes with one prisoner until she was left with no option but to focus on helping those who could still be helped.

They returned to the cells in the early hours of the

morning and with the help of some of the released prisoners managed to coax many of the traumatised inmates out of the building.

A small number remained and had to be forcibly removed. Daise and the boys stood back as they were dragged out. Some were kicking, spitting and punching, unable to cope with the change in their circumstances. The guttural grunting and wailing was heartbreaking.

The beach was a hub of activity. The Patcher had been true to his word and was putting his medical skills to good use. With the help of his new friends, he had set up a makeshift field hospital on the beach to treat those injured by the drone strike.

The survivors had managed to salvage some first aid kits, knocking door to door on the undamaged houses. Many of the residents had barricaded themselves in their homes, fearful that the green people would turn on them. Curtains twitched but slowly they unlocked their doors and brought out blankets and bandages. Soon the transformed and untransformed were working side by side. The local pharmacy opened up and the owner offered all his stocks of painkillers, dressings and saline to those down on the beach.

The wounded were triaged into three categories: the seriously injured, the walking wounded and those who were physically unhurt but emotionally traumatised. The Patcher had been working all night. For the most part he had been extracting shrapnel, sewing up wounds and treating burns. He had to focus on those who stood the best chance of surviving.

Further up the beach behind the dunes lay ordered lines of the fallen. The Patcher had been careful not to call them dead. He laid them out in the sun, hoping that they, like Rowan, would be able to heal themselves.

Mrs Arkwright had set up a stall dispensing tea on a small patch of tarmac next to the beach. She had built it from an old door and a couple of battered chairs dispersed by the explosion. On her way out of the Smart Jooce building she found a metal urn in a staff kitchen. She had rustled through the cupboards and the discovery of tea and a stack of paper cups had given her a purpose.

She waved her arms as she spotted Daise, Rey and Jude walking up the beach.

'Daise!', she yelled.

They ran up the beach to greet her. Mrs Arkwright pushed a hot cup of tea into their hands.

'Mrs A, it's going to be alright, isn't it?' asked Daise. She needed reassurance after a night of human tragedy. They all did.

Mrs Arkwright looked around. The town was bustling with activity. Green people were clearing the streets. Sifting through the piles of rubble, they were stacking the bricks into neat piles. Others were extinguishing fires. They had even begun filling in the crater in the centre of the road.

'I really think it is Daise, I really do. Even Gregor and his black shirted friends have been cooperative. They helped us get into the Port Fulbeck Guardian station. The Guardians look to have abandoned the whole island.

'What about the mainland? Do we know what happened in Barrowby?'

Mrs Arkwright smiled; 'Rowan got through to Barrowby Guardian station on the radio and spoke to Dave McInnes. He'd taken charge there when the crowds descended on the Guardian station and they all surrendered. Well, all but the Chief, Damon and Tommo. They managed to escape in the paramotors parked in a shelter on the roof.

'What about the Council? Are they still in power?'

'It's less clear what's going on in Grantham. There was a drone strike there too. But we've heard reports that the people on the streets torched the Council building.'

Daise shuddered at the thought of more death and destruction.

'Have we made things better?' asked Rey.

Mrs Arkwright came out from behind the stall and gave Rey a hug. Daise threw her arms around both of them. Jude held back.

'Come on Jude, let's leave our mistakes in the past. We've all made them. We're family, remember.' said Daise.

The sun danced off Jude's teeth as he buried his smiling face into the mass of bodies.

Daise closed her eyes and focused on the soundscape; the crackling fires and screams of last night were gone, replaced by the sound of the waves lapping on the shore, the thud and crack of the clear-up operation, and chatter of people going about their business. She could almost feel the place healing.

The familiar voice of Rowan interrupted them. Daise spotted him first and was about to ask him to join the hug. But his forehead was furrowed with deep lines.

'What's wrong?' She asked.

Rowan pulled an unconvincing smile that looked more like a grimace, 'I need to talk to you Daise. On your own.'

The Castoffs

Jude and Rey released her. She looked up at Rowan but there was nothing reassuring in his eyes. He started walking up to a small patch of grass next to the beach. She waved at her friends and followed him.

When they were out of earshot of the others Rowan started to talk, 'I've spent the morning searching the Port Fulbeck Guardian station. In the basement there were rows and rows of filing cabinets full of paper records for everyone who has ever lived on the island. I found this.'

He held out a dark green file and pressed it into Daise's hands. On the cover of the file was a white sticker across which read a name, 'Professor Dennis Dawkins (staff)', and a photo of her father. She looked at his untidy mop of hair and his thick black plastic rimmed glasses. He was just as she remembered him.

'It's your father's file from when he worked here,' said Rowan.

'My father worked here?' Daise shuddered to think that her father was connected to the horrific human suffering taking place on Ancaster Island.

'And there's more Daise. We found a file for your mother.'

Daise felt her stomach turn. Her mother had died giving birth to her. How could she have ended up on Ancaster Island?

Rowan passed her another file. She read the printed script. 'Jenny Dawkins (prisoner)'. She stared at the photo of her mother. Her jaw agape.

She was green.

Tears dripped from her face as comprehension settled. Rowan put his arm around her, 'It's a lot to take in. Daise. Take your time. Read the files on your own.

The Castoffs

Come and find me on the beach after. I'll try and answer any questions you might have.'

Daise watched him walk away. The branches of fallen oak afforded her some privacy from the busy town. She gripped the thick files tightly, unable to open them, fearful of the information inside. The answers she had been looking for were hidden in these files. The truth about her parents. She stared into the green eyes of her mother. She had no memories of her, only stories her dad had told her and the photos he had displayed around the house. But she wasn't green in any of them. She wanted to open her mother's file first but she wasn't ready.

Instead, she thumbed her father's file. It began with an extensive CV documenting his academic successes. He had transformed mice to be photosynthetic while working at the University of Nottingham. Then he had moved to the private sector to start human trials. Her father had created the green people. His CV was missing a couple of years around the time of the flood and the war that followed but he had moved to Ancaster Island to set up the Institute of Transhumanology.

The thought of her father setting up this place was almost too much to bear. She remembered him dropping her off at the gates of Barrowby School on his way to work. He had worked here for seven years. Was he ultimately responsible for all this suffering? She felt guilty by association.

She dropped his file on the floor unable to reconcile the memories of her gentle, loving father with the architect of the Ancaster labour camps and the horrors of the Smart Jooce factory.

Her mother's file was much thinner. On the first page

The Castoffs

was a patient record. It held basic information. Details about her mother she had never known. Her birthday, her height and then in capital letters running across the middle of the form she read, her date of transformation. It was six months before she was born. It took a moment to process what that meant.

It suddenly made sense why she was changing. She hadn't been transformed in Greenacres; she had been transformed 13 years ago, inside her mother. She looked back down at her mother's medical records. It was signed by Dr Jon Greaves. The name was familiar. She rubbed her forehead trying to bring a thought to the surface. Then it came to her, the Patcher. Mrs Arkwright always called him Jon. He said he worked on Ancaster Island. It must be him.

She tucked the files under her arm and ran toward the beach. She sprinted; the sand soft underfoot warmed her feet. The sun on the backs of her legs propelled her forward. She slowed down as she approached a group of wounded green people. She asked if they had seen the Patcher. They pointed up the beach beyond the dunes in unison like soldiers saluting.

A sandy path cut through the dunes winding upwards into the tufts of marram grass that bound the sand together tightly. The crest of the dunes was thick and lush, the spiky grass dancing in the morning breeze. Daise took a moment to catch her breath as she looked out at the sandy bowl that stretched out in front of her. She could see the Patcher in the distance, the only figure standing.

Bodies were arranged in a grid-like open air morgue. There were at least a hundred green people. They were all stripped to their underwear, laid on their backs, tilted on the edge of the bowl and facing the sun. Silence hung in the air like cotton wool, she walked toward the Patcher, slowly and respectfully. Trying not to look at the broken bodies. The Patcher seemed locked in his own thoughts. As Daise approached he sank to his knees over the body of a tall green woman.

Daise cleared her throat to announce her arrival. The Patcher looked startled as he flicked his head toward her. She was struck by how old he looked. His salt and pepper beard was unkempt. Deep lines radiated out from his eyes, like tears had eroded his face.

She used his real name for the first time, 'Jon', her voice sounded weird in the sandy makeshift morgue.

'I need you to tell me about my parents. You knew them both didn't you?'

He nodded and pushed himself up from the sand, letting out a gentle groan advertising his age.

'I've not been entirely honest with you Daise...'

He paused, but she remained silent waiting for him to continue. He walked to the edge of the makeshift mortuary and sat on a bank of sand. Daise followed and sat beside him.

'If I could take it back. I would.' He paused again and the confession came flooding out.

'I met your dad 20 years ago. He was a genius. He was only twenty-five when he revolutionised the solar cell industry. When he decided to change fields and look at enhancing humans, he approached me. I was a dermatologist at Nottingham University. I'd been doing some work on skin cells to make them more resistant to ultraviolet light. I'd hoped it would mean the end of skin

The Castoffs

cancer. But we had problems with our trials in mice. I was about to lose my funding when your dad convinced me to join his bold new project transforming animals with chloroplasts. We had just started human trials when the flood came. We had transformed 15 men and 15 women when we had to abandon the lab and move to Ancaster.

'I knew your mum too, she was beautiful. But her pregnancy was tough. She had terrible sickness, she lost weight. I did what I could but the hospitals were overwhelmed. Your dad had a terrible choice. He feared losing both of you so he transformed her. It would have been OK but when the Council took over, things changed pretty quickly. He tried to protect her but when they brought in the Citizenship Act, all the green people were rounded up. Our research facility became a prison camp. But your father wouldn't stand for it. He got your mum out; he put her on a boat out to the Wildwolds.'

Daise was suddenly excited. Her mum had escaped. She could be alive, living in the Wildwolds, an island in the Trent Sea, remnants of the Lincolnshire wolds. But she was getting impatient.

'Jon, what did you do?'

'I liked your dad, we were friends. But I was jealous. He had a beautiful wife and a beautiful daughter and the man was a genius. I lost my wife and son in the flood. It all seemed so unfair. Your father didn't see eye to eye with the Council. He had a strong sense of right and wrong. He was angry with the way they were treating the green people. He felt responsible for them, like he was their father.'

She felt like he was stalling. She didn't understand why

her dad hadn't taken her and followed his wife to the Wildwolds.

'Come on Jon, what did you do?', her voice was clipped.

He rubbed his forehead sheepishly and continued.

'When he helped your mum escape. I saw an opportunity to take control. I did something terrible. I reported him to the Guardians. They didn't arrest him or imprison him. It was worse; they demoted him. He stayed working in the lab but I was in charge. I was part of the inner circle. I was invited to the best parties. I'm ashamed to say, I did terrible things. I am the architect of this place, not your father.

'But why didn't he take me and escape with my mum?' asked Daise.

The Patcher couldn't look her in the eye, 'I told him that the boat sank and your mother was dead. I am so sorry.'

Daise had no time for his self-pity. 'So, what happened to my dad?' she asked.

'He stayed working here but he refused to share the formula for the transformation. His original vision was to help people through the famine. He thought the transformation would make our lives easier. But the Council had a very different vision.

'But when my attempts to recreate the transformation process failed the Council lost patience with him. They threatened you. He wouldn't stand for that. He arranged for you to be given a new identity and you were moved to the Casthorpe Reset. When he didn't turn up for work one morning, an arrest warrant was issued. I never saw him again. I like to think he got a boat and found your

The Castoffs

mum in the Wildwolds.'

Daise began to smile at the thought of her parents being reunited. For all the terrible things the Patcher had done, he had given her hope; she could be reunited with her family. All her anger faded like breath on the wind. She hugged him.

Chapter 30 – Forgiveness

In the weeks that followed, Rowan became the de facto mayor of Ancaster Island. All the green people had been freed. He'd been pleased that many of the civilian population had decided to stay. They had preferred to take a chance with his brand of benevolent leadership. It was better than the chaos that reigned on the mainland; factional fighting had broken out as the Council regrouped with the support of many Guardians to fight the new provisional government.

Of the forty people laid out in the Patcher's makeshift morgue, eleven had made a full recovery, a further seven were left with life-changing injuries. The remainder had died and were buried. The Patcher wrote up his notes meticulously and gave them to Rowan.

'We need to build up our knowledge so you can get decent health care. Take these notes. They summarise my findings from all the work we did treating the injured. We can't make the same assumptions we do for the untransformed.'

Rowan smiled; the Patcher was looking to redeem himself. He asked him to become the community's doctor. It was the penance the Patcher was looking for.

The Patcher took a trip back to Casthorpe with Daise, Rey and Jude to collect Bertie. When they walked in, the old dog lay still on the battered leather armchair. Daise thought the Doberman was dead but he gave a grumpy little growl as they approached. All was forgiven when the Patcher gave his belly a little rub.

They bundled a selection of drugs, potions and remedies along with his surgical instruments and a small suitcase of clothes and personal effects into the van. He dropped off the keys and a note for his assistant at the towers. Daise, Rey and Jude went to collect their belongings but couldn't get past the identscanners into Tower Five without their tags.

On their return to Ancaster Island, Daise had wanted to get the first boat to the Wildwolds but Mrs Arkwright had cautioned her that she needed to plan for the trip. The currents around the sunken Lincolnshire towns would make the voyage perilous. They needed a strong seaworthy ship to venture that far out in the Trent Sea and they needed provisions and camping gear.

Rowan introduced Daise to a friend of his who was a skilled boat builder. He agreed to take Daise and Rey on as apprentices, teaching them the skills they needed to transform the small motorboat Mrs Arkwright and the Patcher had used to get to Ancaster Island into a boat that could make it out to the Wildwolds. Daise was desperate to find her parents but enjoyed the routine of boat building after the chaos of the past few weeks.

Jude had been keen to leave Port Fulbeck. Daise and Rey had forgiven him but he knew something was broken that could never be fixed. Despite their kind words, he felt they would never entirely trust him again. He had made some poor choices. He should have stayed loyal to the family he had rather than craving a fictionalised

The Castoffs

version of a happy family. But he had met Jessie; the girl they had rescued from the factory. She had barely been able to speak when they set her free. But he had helped her. He was torn between accompanying Daise and Rey to the Wildwolds and staying in Port Fulbeck with Jessie.

It was the Patcher who inspired him to stay in Port Fulbeck.

He had made some poor choices too, way worse than Jude. But he had changed. The people of Port Fulbeck knew about his past but they were judging him on his actions rather than his past. Jude felt like if he stayed, he too could become a better person.

Rey and Daise tried to convince him to come with them. But they had become much closer as they worked on building the boat.

Jude had become the Patcher's new apprentice. He enjoyed learning about all the medicines and found he had a talent for listening. The Patcher called it 'talking therapy' but Jude found that Jessie and the other greens who were struggling to come to terms with what had been done to them felt better after talking to him.

Mrs Arkwright didn't stay in Ancaster long; she wanted to be sure that the Council was gone. It was the Academy's time to come out from the shadows. With the help of her extended network, she formed an interim Council.

Her first challenge was keeping order; looting had been rife as the Guardians left. She took Gregor, Damon and Tommo back to Greater Grantham and, with all their parents gone, she looked after them. And put them to good use cleaning up the damage caused by the riots.

Three months after the drone strike, the boat was

The Castoffs

ready. Daise woke up in the small house overlooking the harbour. It had been vacated by one of the prison Guardians who had run off during the uprising.

The house was modest but it felt huge to Daise. She had suspended a white sheet from the ceiling on four ropes to create the illusion of sleeping in a small, enclosed space. When she first moved in, she had laid in bed at night unable to sleep, staring up at the ceiling. It made her feel like she was falling. The sheet made her feel like she was back in her breadbin in the tower.

Today was her last day in Port Fulbeck. She got out of bed and drew the curtains. The view was spectacular. The morning sunshine twinkled on the crest of the waves as they rolled into the harbour.

She had packed everything the night before. The residents of Port Fulbeck had generously donated a tent, sleeping bags and stove. She had bought some tinned sardines from the local shop with some of the wages the boatmaker had given her. When she was ready, she picked up her backpack and knocked on the house next door where Rey was staying.

Rey had the bulk of their luggage stacked on a trolley. Daise threw her backpack on top of the stack and Rey wheeled it out of the door.

There was a reception party waiting to see them off. It seemed like most of Port Fulbeck was there. The harbour master's cottage was adorned with bunting and some of the crowd held placards emblazoned with their names.

Jude was the first to greet them. He was carrying a small sackcloth bag out of which stuck a roll of paper.

'What's in the bag', asked Rey.

'Never you mind', replied Jude playfully.

The Castoffs

He took the handle of the trolley from Rey, leaving him and Daise free to shake the hands of the people in the crowd. They felt like celebrities. Their bravery at getting Rowan's film broadcast was a story told and retold many times.

The heartfelt outpouring of kindness was overwhelming. Port Fulbeck had become more of a home to them in the last few months than Casthorpe had ever done. By the time they reached the pier and saw the familiar faces of Mrs Arkwright, the Patcher, Jessie and Rowan, their faces were already streaked with tears.

Mrs Arkwright was looking smart; her hair was cut into a business-like bob and her clothes were less fussy. The brightly coloured coats, hats and layers had been replaced by a serious grey business suit; she was interim leader of the new Greater Grantham Administration after all. She would have looked like a completely different woman were it not for the warm smile plastered across her face. She embraced them both and pressed a bag of coins into each of their hands. Rey opened the drawstring of the bag and gasped; he had never seen so many coins in his life.

Rowan stepped forward next.

'I want to thank you both for all you have done for us.'

He had to stop for a moment as the crowd burst into applause. When the clapping died down, he continued.

'You risked so much for people you hadn't met and are an inspiration to us all. You deserve a rest but I know how much finding your parents means to you, Daise. I would like to go with you but I have so much to do to build this community, which is, of course, your home too.'

Rowan gave Daise a hand-held electronic device. Daise had seen devices like this on the dump. They were communication devices but the networks that carried the signals had been destroyed in the flood and they were useless.

'This is a Personal Location Beacon. If you get into trouble set this off and we will find you. I hope that you find your parents. Remember you and your families will always be welcome here.'

Daise embraced Rowan and the crowd cheered.

Daise and Rey hugged their friends in turn and walked up to the pier. But Rey stopped, 'Hold on a minute, where's Jude?'

They scanned the crowd but he wasn't there. Rey looked panic stricken. He began to chew on his lips, 'I can't go without saying goodbye. He's my oldest friend.' His eyes started to pool with tears.

There was a hush as the crowd started to shuffle around looking for Jude.

There was a cry and Jude head popped above the deck of the boat. He had loaded all their things aboard. Rey ran along the pier, the banging on the wooden slats ringing out like a drum solo.

'I thought you'd gone', said Rey wiping the tears and snot from his face.

'Don't be daft mate, I just had to add one last thing to the boat. It needed a name.'

Jude stood to one side and he smiled as the read the letters freshly painted on the side of the boat

It read, 'The Castoffs.'

'It just seemed apt somehow. Reclaim the insult and

all that. Oh, and I wanted to give you this. He pulled his knife out of his pocket and placed it in his friends' hand.

'Now, look after it. We've been through a lot together.'

Rey held out his hands and accepted the knife, 'Thanks Jude. I know how much this means to you. If this knife could talk, the stories it could tell eh?'

'How about you show it some more stories?', said Jude

Rey nodded solemnly.

'Are you sure you won't come; it won't be the same without you.'

Daise bundled into them, throwing her arms around their shoulders.

'Come on Jude, it's not too late.'

'But I'm working for the Patcher now. I made a commitment.'

'I've spoken to him,' interrupted Daise, 'He'll keep your apprenticeship open. Besides, we might need you new skills on our trip.'

'What about Jessie? I've been helping her.'

'Look!', Rey pushed him around.

Jessie was standing next to Mrs Arkwright and the Patcher, waving cheerfully. As Jude looked at her, she blew him a kiss.

'She's doing great Jude. Rowan's given her a job in his office. She'll be fine.'

'But, I haven't got any of my stuff.'

'That's not exactly true. I took the liberty of packing you a bag' said Rey grabbing a rucksack off the pile stacked on the deck of the Castoffs.

Rey and Daise stepped onto the boat and looked up at

The Castoffs

Jude.

'Do you remember the first time we went sand sledging and I was scared?' asked Daise.

'Yes' replied Jude.

'What did you say to me?'

'I said fear is the price you pay for new experiences.'

And with that Jude untied the rope that bound the boat to the pier and jumped onto the deck of the Castoffs.

About the Author

GJ Fletcher has ghost written articles for The Guardian, The Times and the Telegraph. They have also published research in the Journal Experimental Botany.

Acknowledgements

I would like to thank everybody who read my manuscript and gave me feedback, including Sophie Fletcher, Marjory Fletcher, Jenny Buckwell, Franca Tranza, and Ava Morrell.

A special thanks to Rebecca Thomas for her patience and attention to detail in editing my manuscript. Any mistakes that remain will have been added by me during last minute tweaks.

My deepest thanks to George Mann for his invaluable insights into the craft of writing fiction. His enthusiasm, encouragement and support were very much appreciated.

Finally, I would also like to thank Finlay and Rosie, my brilliant children who contributed ideas, gave me unfiltered feedback and made writing this book such a worthwhile pursuit.

Printed in Great Britain
by Amazon